'All right, Anna. What the hell is going on?'

Rose blinked. Anna? Who was Anna? More to the point, who was this man, and why did he look as though he wanted to kill her?

In her dreams this man, or the one who looked so much like him, was always smiling— sometimes widely, revealing strong white teeth, or with his full lips curved into a lopsided grin. Upon awakening from these night visits, Rose was always filled with a languid warmth, prompting her to keep her eyes closed for a few moments so she could hold on to the image of his face, the eyes that teased her and the lips she wanted to kiss.

None of those half-awake feelings warmed her now. She felt as if she were trapped in a nightmare, cold, terrified, desperate to escape—and yet utterly incapable of moving…

Dear Reader,

Welcome to Silhouette Sensation, where you can find all the best romantic suspense novels.

A YEAR OF LOVING DANGEROUSLY continues with the exotic *Someone To Watch Over Her* from Margaret Watson, who will be handing the baton over to Linda Turner next month for the next book in this set of 12 linked stories.

36 HOURS provides us with a Valentine holiday visit to Grand Springs in *My Secret Valentine* by Marilyn Pappano; Marilyn's always a wonderfully emotional writer and this secret baby book does not disappoint. And there's more excitement when Merline Lovelace returns with another of her sexy Henderson brothers in *Twice in a Lifetime,* and he becomes the prime suspect in the heroine's investigation!

Newcomers Cheryl Biggs and Elane Osborn both make outstanding contributions to the line-up with a military hero to die for in *Hart's Last Stand* and an intriguing mistaken identity plot in *Which Twin?*

Terese Ramin returns with a rather unusual story, *An Unexpected Addition*, with lots of kids and a wonderful, gorgeous dad who's really doing his best, which is just as well as he's about to become a dad all over again!

Enjoy!

The Editors

Which Twin?

ELANE OSBORN

*Silhouette, Silhouette Sensation and Colophon are
registered trademarks of Harlequin Books S.A., used under licence.*

*First published in Great Britain 2002
Silhouette Books, Eton House, 18-24 Paradise Road,
Richmond, Surrey TW9 1SR*

© Elane Osborn 2001

ISBN 0 373 27137 9

18-0202

*Printed and bound in Spain
by Litografía Rosés S.A., Barcelona*

ELANE OSBORN

is a daydream believer whose active imagination tends to intrude on her life at the most inopportune moments. Her penchant for slipping into 'alternative reality' severely hampered her work life, leading to a gamut of jobs that includes, but is not limited to, airline reservation agent, waitress, salesgirl and seamstress in the wardrobe department of a casino showroom. In writing, she has discovered a career that not only does not punish flights of fancy, it demands them. Drawing on her daydreams, she has published three historical romance novels and is now using the experiences she has collected in her many varied jobs in the 'real world' to fuel contemporary stories that blend romance and suspense.

Chapter 1

This was it—the place of her dreams. Or her nightmares. She was never sure which.

Rose Delancey drew in a breath of cool, sea-scented air as she peered through the black wrought-iron gate at the three-story gray stone house. A gust of cold air whooshed past her hair, blowing back her dark wavy bangs.

She shook off a sudden chill.

There was no doubt in her mind that this particular house, with its eight-foot brick wall and spear-topped gate, had haunted her dreams for as long as she could remember.

Another chill, one that had nothing to do with the weather, slithered through Rose. There was no point asking herself why gazing upon this scene in the light of day was so important to her. She'd done enough soul-searching before starting out on her quest. Now that she was in this exclusive neighborhood south of San Francisco, staring at the cobblestone driveway leading to three double garage doors made of oak, the question was *how* she would manage to gain access to the rear of the house and the place from which she could see the vista of her dreams.

The wind rose again to rattle the leaves of a large olive tree growing at the left corner of the garage, drawing Rose's attention to a set of iron steps behind some low-hanging branches. Her heart began to race. Those stairs most likely led to a deck off the second story of the house. All she had to do was walk up them, and she would reach the spot from her dreams.

Of course, she reminded herself with a wry twist of her lips, that would be *after* she found some way through or over the black iron gate that barricaded the driveway.

As she frowned at the unfriendly looking spikes running along the top bar, her moment of elation faded. An impatient sigh bloomed in her chest before escaping past her lips. If this were a dream, the gate would magically open right now, allowing her to glide across the driveway and up the stairs. But this was *not* a dream. This was a windy, about-to-rain, end-of-January morning in real life, where nothing magical was likely to happen.

Or was it?

To Rose's right, somewhere in the wall, a motor hummed to life. The gate in front of her began to move. Rose barely breathed as the space opened. Then, as calmly as if she were an expected visitor, she stepped onto the driveway and started toward the stairs.

When the garage door closest to the stairway started to rise, it just seemed part of the unreal atmosphere that had impelled Rose down the driveway. Then it struck her that the garage door and the gate were probably activated by a remote-control device, both of which had undoubtedly been activated to admit an approaching vehicle. A vehicle, her thoughts warned, that very likely contained someone who would stop a trespasser, thus bringing her quest to an immediate halt, just short of her goal.

Unless, of course, she was up the staircase, hidden by the canopy of leaves, before the vehicle turned into the driveway.

Rose broke into a half run. Once she started up the steps, her black flats struck a staccato, metallic beat. She slowed her racing feet as she neared the intricate wrought-iron gate at the top of the stairway, a gate that clicked open easily, admitting her to an expansive veranda, tiled in a brown herringbone pattern.

Tingling with anticipation, Rose gazed past the flowers spilling from the low, brick planter at the edge of the veranda some twenty feet away. She could now see the view from her dreams.

Almost.

The angle didn't quite match the image that had so often appeared to her. She wasn't standing quite high enough for one thing, and the red-tiled roof she'd gazed over in her dreams was nowhere in sight.

Turning to her right, Rose spied at the far end of the patio a circular staircase leading to a wooden deck above her. Without a second thought she crossed in front of a wide bank of French doors.

A slight drizzle moistened the iron stairs as Rose began to climb again, her footsteps ringing with an odd double echo. She ignored this, focusing on the metal gate at the top of the stairs. It opened easily onto a deck made of wide wooden planks, inviting Rose to step forward.

On her right the red-tiled roof of the house next door came into view as Rose walked slowly to the iron fence at the edge of the balcony. Drawing a slow breath, she placed her hands on the top rail. Cold metal chilled her palms as she gazed at the Golden Gate Bridge, stretching rusty-orange over gray-green water.

The view from her dreams. Finally.

Sometimes in her dreams the bridge gleamed in the brilliant sun. Other times it was a scallop of tiny lights against the black sky. Today gray clouds enshrouded the tops of the bridge's two towers. Below her the ocean crashed onto a narrow beach at the bottom of a sheer cliff, and tiny drops of rain accompanied the wind and set her long, beaded earrings dancing against her neck.

Rose's chest expanded with her sense of achievement, only to deflate a second later as the questions began. Why would she dream of this particular view over and over? And why had it seemed so vital that she find this spot so soon after her mother's death, that she stand here in real life? It wouldn't change anything. It certainly wouldn't bring her mother back, nor would it fill that odd, empty, lost place in her soul. It wouldn't—

"Do you think you're fooling anyone, sneaking up the back way?" a deep voice demanded.

Rose jumped, then swiveled around. Just inside the gate stood a man wearing a brown leather jacket, a crisp white shirt and faded jeans. Approximately six feet tall with broad shoulders, he had a square face and short brown hair, tattered by the gusting wind. She noted rough-edged features that indicated he was in his mid to late thirties. His eyes were narrowed beneath his furrowed brow, preventing Rose from seeing their color, but she knew they would prove to be a muted blend of green and brown. For, just like the bridge, this man had repeatedly appeared in her dreams.

As the familiar-yet-strange man began to approach, Rose fought a wave of dizziness, and her mind struggled for a foothold in reality. Was any of this—the house on the cliff, the bridge in the distance, the oddly familiar stranger—real? Had she actually gotten out of bed this morning and taken that cab ride to this spot above the sea? Or was it possible that she was still lying on that hard hotel room mattress, sound asleep, lost in yet another dream?

Or nightmare?

This must be real, she decided as the man grasped her upper arms. Never, in any of her dreams, had she felt her flesh being pressed beneath his strong grip, nor had she experienced the dream stranger's warmth as he drew her toward him.

Looking into his penetrating eyes, she saw they were indeed a warm mixture of brown and green, though perhaps darkened a shade by some emotion she couldn't discern. Anger, perhaps? Rose opened her mouth to apologize for having trespassed, but the man spoke first, his deep voice harsh with impatience.

"All right, Anna. What the *hell* is going on?"

Rose blinked. Anna? Who was Anna? More to the point, who was this man, and why did he look as though he wanted to kill her?

In her dreams this man, or the one who looked so much like him, was always smiling—sometimes widely, revealing strong white teeth, or with his full lips twisted into a lopsided grin. Upon awakening from these nighttime visits, Rose was always filled with a languid warmth, prompting her to keep her eyes closed for a few moments so she could hold on to the image of his face, the eyes that teased her and the lips she wanted to kiss.

None of those half-awake feelings warmed her now. She felt as if she were trapped in a nightmare—cold, terrified, desperate to escape and yet utterly incapable of moving other than to pull her gaze from the thin, tight line of this stranger's mouth to the combination of fury and worry in his eyes.

It was the fury that kept Logan Maguire momentarily silent as the wind whipped dark tendrils around Anna Benedict's pale face, emphasizing the blank, dazed expression clouding her dark-blue eyes.

Clenching his jaw, he drew in a steadying breath. "What's going on here, Anna?" he demanded. "You left two messages on my machine saying you were in trouble, that you needed to see me. The next thing I know, there's a message from your father, worried sick because you're missing."

When Anna only blinked at him, Logan went on, "It's been a long three days, and the flight back from France was no picnic. Do you have any idea what it was like, retrieving those messages from the phone aboard the plane, waiting anxiously for the flight to end?"

Upon landing he'd rushed to his car, then swerved through streets clogged with morning commuters, *San Francisco* traffic, to the Benedict house. All the while he'd cursed himself for allowing Robert Benedict to bow to his daughter's refusal of a bodyguard six months ago, when the man had decided to run for the U.S. Senate seat once held by Robert's father, Charles.

"So," Logan went on. "I drive like a bat out of hell to get here, hit the remote to open the front gate as I turn onto Sea Cliff Drive, only to see you step calmly through the opening and head for the outside stairs."

As Logan had raced up the steps, he'd realized that he'd been worrying about her needlessly. And now, slightly out of breath, bone tired from his long flight and completely out of patience, Logan gripped Anna's arms more tightly.

"Well, what was it that sent you off this time?" he asked. "Another excursion to 'find yourself'?"

As Logan waited for Anna to reply, he became aware that the soft drizzle had become a steady rain. He watched her half-dazed expression turn to one of utter confusion. She shook her head as if to clear it, and damp curls fell forward to brush her eyebrows and cling to her cheeks. When she started to brush the short tendrils back, Logan grabbed her hand.

"When you said in your first message that you were in trouble," he said with far more control than he felt, "please don't tell me you were referring to the fact that you suddenly decided to cut your hair."

Logan rarely spoke so sharply to Anna. He knew that what might seem like vanity to others was Anna's desperate attempt to maintain the image her mother was so obsessed with. More than once Anna had threatened to chop off her long hair, only to have Elise convince her that the change would spoil the "classic lines" created when Anna's slightly wild hair was pulled back tightly.

Releasing her hand, Logan reached toward the damp tangle of curls. His fingers brushed her cheek before they combed through the thick waves at her temples, then encountered the beginning of her familiar waist-length braid.

"Okay," he said through clenched teeth. "You cut bangs.

Elise will probably hate them, but it is *your* hair. If she really flips, you can use gel or something to slick…them…''

Logan's words trailed off as he became aware that a strange tingling heat had begun to grow in the palm of the hand cupping Anna's head. The fingers still gripping her slim arm had developed a similar sensation, which was now racing up through his chest, then down his legs, grounding him to the planks beneath his feet like some capricious electrical current.

Anna's upturned face registered wonderment blended with confusion. The confusion seemed to be contagious, for Logan suddenly found himself shifting his attention from her shadowed eyes to her lips—noting how full they were, how softly they curved, how the raindrops falling onto their parted surface shimmered in pale pink dots. And for the first time since Logan Maguire had seen Anna Elise Benedict a little over twenty-seven years ago, he found himself wanting to kiss those lips, to pull her slim body into his arms—not as the older brother he'd always considered himself, but as a lover.

Few things frightened Logan. Not taking the curves of Highway 1 at top speed in his '65 Mustang convertible, nor negotiating a deal that could make or lose millions of dollars for the family he owed so much to. But this—this sudden change in the way he'd always felt about Anna—scared him silly.

Instantly he untangled his fingers from her damp hair and released her. As he took a step back, he forced his attention to Anna's eyes once again and saw that her confusion had been replaced by a look of terror. Logan's eyebrows moved together in a tight frown. Never had Anna looked at him this way before—as if she were afraid of being attacked. True, he could never remember being quite as angry with her before, but his role of ''big brother'' had necessitated a certain amount of discipline, to which Anna normally reacted with stubborn silence. Perhaps she'd felt the same strange tingle of attraction he'd experienced and was just as stunned by it. If this were the case, he decided, the two of them would simply talk it out, then laugh over it and return to treating each other as brother and sister.

But not out here, he realized as the falling raindrops suddenly grew fat and sharp as the wind rushed in from the sea.

Logan shouted against the roar of the sudden downpour, "Let's get out of this before we're completely drenched."

He turned toward the sliding glass door that led to Anna's room. Her hesitant footsteps on the deck told him that she followed, but as he reached for the door handle, he realized that those footsteps sounded more rapid and increasingly distant.

Logan looked up just in time to see Anna disappear down the circular staircase. Immediately he gave chase, twisting down the now-slick steps, blinking away the rain to watch Anna through the openings in the ironwork beneath his feet, scowling more deeply each time his wide shoulders rammed the center post, refusing to slow in deference to the narrow curve.

By the time he neared the bottom, Logan had almost caught up with her. He missed grabbing Anna's hand by mere inches as she released the railing and headed toward the second set of stairs at the far end of the veranda. However, he knew he had her now, knew she would need to slow down in order to keep from slipping on the expensive tiles that Charles Benedict had installed forty years ago only to discover that they became dangerously slick in the fog and the rain.

Anna, like Logan and her brother Chas, had been indoctrinated from the time she could walk never to run on the veranda, especially when it was wet. Logan prepared to slow his rushing feet as he reached the bottom step. Anna, however, hadn't paused for a second. Across the now-shiny tiles she ran, and when she started into the sharp turn that would take her to the second stairway, her feet flew out from beneath her. She landed flat on her back, then slid to a sudden stop against the brick planter.

In moments Logan was at her side, down on one knee bending over her and asking, "Are you hurt?"

Her dark eyes stared up at him as she gave her head an uncertain shake. Her mouth opened and formed the word no, but not a sound passed her lips. At that point her eyes widened, filling with sheer terror as she fought to breathe. When she tried to sit up, Logan placed his hands on her shoulders.

"Lie back. You've had the wind knocked out of you. You have to relax."

Relax? Rose wanted to scream. A weight was pressing on her chest, threatening to squeeze the very life out of her, and this man wanted her to relax? Panic stiffened every muscle and she again fought to struggle into an upright position.

"Take it easy," his deep voice soothed as strong hands restrained her attempts to rise. His touch felt terrifyingly like the pressure around her chest. With a vehement shake of her head she battled both.

"Don't!" His voice was harsh again; he was digging his fingers into her shoulders. A second later he said more softly, "You have to stop fighting and let your lungs take over. It will happen. Trust me. Just listen to me."

Believing she had no choice, given the man's greater strength, she gazed into his eyes as he continued to utter re-assuring words. Her world began to turn black as she sank against the cold, wet tiles and tried not to fight the painful constriction in her chest.

A second later her ribs expanded and cold air rushed into her aching lungs. Along with a mouthful of rain.

Immediately Rose began to choke. This time the man helped her to a seated position, slipping strong arms around her, holding her as violent coughs racked her body. By the time the coughing fit eased, Rose realized she was too weak to attempt another escape. She would be forced to explain how and why she'd come to trespass on his private balcony.

Just as she was getting ready to do that, however, the man suddenly slipped an arm beneath her knees, cradled her to his chest and stood. Her abused lungs barely managed to draw a startled gasp before he began striding along the balcony. Rose shook her head and squirmed as she tried to form a verbal protest.

"Oh, no you don't, Anna." The man's arms tightened around her as his harsh voice rose above the rattle of the rain. "I'm not going to put you down and give you the chance to pull God-knows-what new stunt. Not till we're inside where it's dry and I get a damned good explanation for what you've been up to."

Rose was fully prepared to explain *her* actions, but she wasn't about to take the heat for what someone named Anna might have done. Aware that they were moving past the French doors she'd noticed earlier, she opened her mouth to tell him that he was making a mistake.

"Look," she started, but before she could say another word, one of the doors opened.

The man stopped, and Rose turned. Framed in the doorway was a blond woman dressed in a champagne-colored jacket over a matching skirt. She was maybe a shade over five feet tall, and from the lines marking her delicate, perfectly made-up features Rose guessed she was somewhere in her late forties or early fifties.

The woman's fingers tightened around a small ivory purse as she frowned and spoke sharply. "Logan, what are you—"

She broke off as her dark-brown eyes met Rose's. Lifting a slender hand to cover her mouth, the woman blinked and breathed a stunned-sounding, "Anna?"

Again the Anna business. Rose shook her head, but the man named Logan was already replying.

"Yes, Elise. She slipped on the tiles and took a fall. I need to get her inside and see if she's broken anything."

As the man carried Rose through the doorway, the woman backed into the cream-and-beige room, her wide brown eyes gazing in surprise before narrowing slightly.

"Anna," she said. "You know how dangerous those tiles are. I must have told you a hundred times that—" The woman broke off. Her eyes narrowed further as she went on, "Where have you been, young lady? What have you done to your hair?

And *where* did you get those clothes? Not to mention those vulgar earrings?''

Rose frowned. *Young lady?* No one had addressed her in such a patronizing, belittling tone since her junior year in high school. And as to the comment about her earrings, she touched the long tangle of beads strung in hues of blue and purple that her mother had given her this past Christmas, then opened her mouth to protest the term *vulgar*. But before she could say a thing, again she heard, ''Anna?''

This time the word was barely a whisper, filled with unmistakable relief. Rose turned. A tall man with gray hair that nearly matched his light-charcoal suit stood on the threshold between the bedroom and the hallway behind him. He appeared to have paused in the act of tugging loose his red silk tie to stare across the room at Rose.

The man holding Rose was quick to reply. ''Yes, Robert. Anna took a fall, and I want to lay her down on the bed and see if anything is broken.''

He'd barely taken one step forward before Rose gave a protesting wiggle and managed to blurt out, ''That's not necessary. I'm fine, just let me—''

''Logan,'' the blond woman interjected, stepping toward them. ''I really think it would be better if you took your sister up to *her* bed.''

Rose followed the woman's gaze to the water dripping from her thoroughly soaked purple skirt and turquoise sweater, then over to the large bed draped in a pristine ivory coverlet.

The arms holding her tightened convulsively. A second later she was being whisked past the bed, then the man named Robert. The action took place so quickly that Rose found herself halfway down a cream carpeted hallway before it occurred to her to twist violently in an attempt to escape this Logan person's hold.

''Put me down,'' she demanded.

When he ignored her, instead turning and mounting a set of stairs, Rose tried again. ''Look, I'm sorry about sneaking up to the balcony. That was wrong of me, but—''

Rose stopped speaking as she realized that Logan had reached the top of the stairs and turned down another hall without even looking at her. When he came to a stop in front of a closed door, Rose demanded, "Have you heard *one word* I've said?"

The man ignored her as he stretched out the arm supporting her legs, grasped the doorknob and twisted it several times. When the door didn't open, he finally looked at her, his eyes narrowed with undisguised fury.

"All right, Anna. Dig your key out of that dammed suitcase you call a purse."

Rose shook her head helplessly. This was her fault, she supposed. The first time he'd called her Anna, she should have pointed out his mistake. And she shouldn't have run, shouldn't have acted so irrationally.

"Please listen to me," she said in a low, level tone. "I've been trying to explain that you are mistaking me for someone else. I don't have a key to this room, because I don't belong here. So just…put me down and allow me to leave."

"What do you mean, you don't…" he began.

"Hey, kiddo," another voice broke in. Rose turned to see the gray-haired man approach, followed by the blond woman. "Give me your purse," the man went on, "and I'll fish that key out."

When he reached toward the bag's shoulder strap, Rose twisted away. "No!" she yelled. "What's wrong with you people? Why won't you listen to me? I've been trying to tell you that I don't know you. I don't know…"

She paused, frowning as she realized that both these people's faces were vaguely familiar. She gave her head an impatient shake and finished, "I don't know *any* of you."

The gray-haired man frowned, the woman gasped, and the stranger named Logan sighed. "Anna, give your father that damned key."

Before Rose could tell him she didn't *have* a father, the woman stepped forward and snapped open her ivory purse. "When Anna insisted on getting a key made for her room, I suspected she'd eventually lose it, so I had the locksmith make one up for my key ring. Here, I'll get us in.''

As Logan backed off to allow access to the lock, Rose once more demanded to be put down and began kicking for emphasis. Aware that her actions had broken his grip, Rose tried to twist out of his arms, but as the door clicked open those arms tightened again and he carried her into the room. She opened her mouth once again to attempt to make these people, especially the one holding her so firmly, understand that some mistake was being made. But once she caught sight of her new surroundings, all she could do was stare.

The carpet was the color of amethyst, the walls a pale shade of lilac. The bed she found herself being carried toward was covered in pale aqua—the exact color scheme of her room back in Seattle. Well, perhaps not *exact*. The tones she'd used were several shades darker, but, still, Rose found the similarity startlingly uncanny.

Even more uncanny was the neatly folded quilt at the foot of the bed, composed of yellow and pink flowers appliquéd onto alternating squares of turquoise and purple. It matched perfectly the one lying across the foot of her own bed—the exact same colors, faded slightly from repeated washings.

She knew her quilt was one of a kind, made by her mother the year she was born. Yet this one was...

''Just like mine,'' she whispered.

''It *is* your room, Anna,'' Rose heard Logan say, as he placed her on the bed.

Rose looked up. The man remained bent over her, frowning deeply, but the concern in his hazel eyes lent a certain softness to his scowl.

''I'm going to get Dr. Alcott,'' the blond woman said abruptly. She glanced at Logan. ''Aunt Grace somehow learned that Anna was missing and became so upset that we had to call the doctor in.''

She dropped a disapproving frown on Rose, then turned to leave the room. A second later the woman's voice echoed from the hall.

"Robert, Martina says that Chas is on the telephone. He needs to speak to you about tonight's speech."

The man glanced at the door, down at Rose and finally to Logan. "I should only be gone a moment. Keep an eye on your sister, won't you?"

Rose saw one corner of Logan's mouth lift in a ghost of a smile as he watched the older man leave. Taking advantage of her captor's momentary distraction, she rolled off the opposite side of the bed and onto her feet, then made a mad dash for the still-open door. But before she even made it around the edge of the bed, Logan was blocking her escape with his body. When she raised her hands to push him out of the way, he grabbed her wrists and demanded, "Blast it, Anna, what the hell is *wrong* with you?"

Rose looked up as she tried to pull her wrists free. She winced as the large hands tightened around them, then shook her head.

"Haven't you been listening to me at *all?*" she asked. "I do...not...know...you. I'm not someone named Anna. My name is *Rose.* I know I shouldn't have come onto your grounds. I certainly shouldn't have been up on your balcony, but—"

Rose stopped speaking. She had to. The man in front of her had begun to laugh.

Chapter 2

The laughter had started as a soft chuckle, but it quickly built in strength and volume until it was nearly deafening. As he continued to chortle, his grip on Rose's wrists relaxed slightly, though not enough for her to break free.

Rose knew this because she jerked her hands down, hard, in an attempt to escape. At this point he stopped laughing, and although he tightened his grip, a slight smile tilted one corner of his mouth as his eyes once more locked on to hers.

"Good grief," he said with a shake of his head. "Not *that* again."

Rose stared at the crooked smile she'd seen so often in her dreams, then looked up to the amused eyes. Behind the gently teasing glint she saw a mix of anger and concern. Her response was a mutinous frown. Who was this man to stand there laughing at her, judging her? For that matter, who were *any* of these people? What was this place? Just what sort of nightmare had she stumbled into?

She gave an uneasy glance to the room. It was nearly three times larger than the one she occupied in Seattle. The bed was a queen, where hers was only a twin. These walls were nearly blank, while hers were filled with pictures and memorabilia. But the color scheme and placement of the furniture was eerily similar, even without the inexplicable presence of the turquoise-and-purple quilt that matched hers so precisely.

Then there was the matter of the blond woman and gray-haired man. They'd looked familiar, also, in a misty, half-remembered way. Was it possible that they had appeared in her dreams, as well?

A shiver raised gooseflesh on Rose's arms. It was as if she'd fallen through Alice's rabbit hole into a world filled with oddly familiar sights, like this room and the view of the bridge outside. And the man holding her wrists.

Rose looked at him and found that the remains of his smile had been replaced by another frown. "What do you mean by 'not that again'?" she asked.

His green-brown eyes seemed to assess her before they narrowed. "Come on, Anna," he replied. "You know. *Rose*— the imaginary friend you made up when you were little? And that business about missing a part of yourself."

The floor beneath her feet began to roll from side to side like the bridge of a ship in a wind-tossed sea. All her life Rose had felt an odd sense of loneliness, as if she were somehow incomplete. Somewhere around the age of six, when she'd asked her mother about this, the woman had reminded Rose that she'd been born prematurely. Perhaps, her mother suggested, in Rose's hurry to arrive on earth she had somehow inadvertently left some part of herself back in heaven.

At the time, Rose had accepted this explanation. After all, she'd rarely been alone. Early on she and her mother had lived in an artist commune in Oregon, where she'd been surrounded by other caring adults and their children. After she and her mother moved to Seattle, there had been classrooms full of children to interact with, along with after-school music teachers and the customers who visited her mother's shop. During her brief marriage, she'd been surrounded by people. And for the past two years she'd been in the constant company of her mother, always conscious of the inoperable tumor, dictating that Rose's time with Kathleen Delancey would all too soon come to an end. So, she could hardly claim to have been lonely in the conventional sense. Yet whenever she looked inside herself, she'd felt as if a part of herself was missing, some odd hole in the fabric of her existence.

And now this man was suggesting that someone else felt this way. Someone, moreover, who apparently looked enough like Rose to make everyone she came in contact with think that she *was* this person. Someone who'd once had an imaginary friend named Rose.

This was all nuts. It was no wonder that her head was spinning, her ears ringing and her legs suddenly wobbly. If it weren't for the tight grip this Logan maintained on her wrists, she was certain her legs would give way, leaving her to collapse on the floor at his feet.

She couldn't let that happen. She couldn't give in to the whirling eddy that threatened to drag her into unconsciousness. She had to stay alert, on her feet, and somehow find her way out of this nightmarish place. Drawing a deep breath, Rose forced herself to meet the man's dark eyes and speak as calmly as possible.

"I know this must sound crazy, but I am who I say I am. Let me go, and I'll prove it to you."

The man—Logan, she reminded herself—seemed to search her face for a moment before releasing her wrists. Rose continued to stare into his eyes a moment longer, oddly reluctant to look away. Finally she took two steps back, pulled her gaze from his as she slipped her large purse from her shoulder. She reached in and fished out her turquoise leather wallet. Drawing her driver's license from its plastic sleeve, she handed it to the man. Shivering within her damp sweater, she watched as he studied it.

"Well, I know you use false IDs to avoid the attention that comes with the Benedict name," he said at last. One corner of his mouth lifted in that half smile of his as his eyes met hers. "But why choose Seattle? Was there a sale on fake Washington State licenses?"

His smile became a mocking grin as he handed the document back, hardening Rose's frustration into anger.

"For your information, that license is *real*. And it says I'm legal to drive in the State of Washington because *that* is where I live."

"Right. And what about the wallet? This was my Christmas present to you a little over a month ago."

Again Rose felt the floor begin to shift beneath her feet. The turquoise wallet had been a day-after-Christmas-sale purchase at Nordstrom's. It was something she hadn't really needed, but upon seeing it, she'd felt she *had* to have it—as if it was somehow meant to be hers.

The fact that this Anna possessed the exact same wallet sent another wave of shivers dancing down her spine. Rose straightened that part of her anatomy. This was no time to get giddy over coincidences, she told herself. Such a reaction would only make it more difficult to convince this stranger of her identity.

Not that it mattered if he believed her or not. *She* knew who she was. What was more, in spite of all the unanswered questions tumbling through her mind regarding this look-alike of hers, she now only wanted to get out of this house, to escape from these people and the vague unsettling sense that she'd seen them before.

"Look, Logan whoever-you-are." Rose spoke softly as she shoved her driver's license back in place and dropped her wallet into her purse. Pushing her damp bangs out of her eyes, she glared up at him as she went on, "I'm through trying to reason with you. I *am* Rose Delancey, just as my license states, and I refuse to be kept in this *madhouse* one moment longer."

She pivoted toward the door, but before she could take one step, strong fingers gripped her elbow and spun her back around. The man's lips twisted scornfully as he asked, "If you aren't Anna, then how do you know my name is Logan?"

"It's what that woman called you."

His eyes narrowed. "That *woman* is your mother."

"No. My mother is…dead."

Immediately Rose clamped her jaw shut, trapping the sob that wanted to follow. She wasn't going to cry. Not now. Not after she'd promised her mother.

It was just that this was the first time she'd actually said the word *dead* out loud, with all its echoes of finality. The small group that had gathered for her mother's funeral had all known what had happened, so there had been no reason for Rose to explain a thing. The end had been expected, after all, and Rose had heard several people murmur that the suddenness of it had been something of a blessing. Rose knew, of course, that they'd meant that her mother was now beyond pain, not that it was a blessing that Kathleen Delancey was gone, leaving her daughter truly alone.

And feeling, suddenly, crazy.

Swallowing hard, Rose stared at the lapel of the man's leather jacket. She should have stayed in the apartment above her mother's gift shop, should have gone through all her mother's papers as the lawyer had suggested, then gradually come to terms with her loss. She never should have followed her crazy visions without first putting her life in order and getting her emotions in hand.

"Rose?"

The soft inquiry brought Rose's head up and hope into her heart. "You called me Rose," she said as another damp chill shuddered through her. "Does that mean you believe what I've been—?"

The shake of Logan's head left the rest of Rose's question unasked.

"I tried Anna," he replied. "When you didn't look up, I decided to give Rose a try." He paused a moment, frowning into her eyes as if weighing a decision before he went on. "Look, Anna. You're wet, cold and probably tired. We can talk after you take a warm shower and get into some dry—"

Now it was Rose's turn to shake her head, interrupting him to insist, "For the last time, I am *not* Anna. I don't live in this house, have never even *been* in this house, or in this…room.''

Rose shuddered as her gaze slid from his to the hauntingly familiar decor.

''Then why are you here?''

Rose closed her eyes as a sense of hopelessness engulfed her at the thought of telling this obviously cynical man about her recurring dreams of the view from the balcony outside this particular room.

When she felt Logan's hand gently grasp her upper arms, she realized he must have seen her shoulders slump. Her knees seemed to bend of their own accord. Once she was sitting on the edge of the bed, she opened her eyes. Aware of the man seated next to her, she stared at the bridge through the sliding glass door, realizing that her explanation would sound insane.

''Dreams,'' she said anyway. ''I have repeatedly dreamed of this particular view of that bridge. I came here to find if this view existed in reality. I needed…''

As her voice trailed off, Logan couldn't miss the despair shimmering in her dark eyes. The expression on her face was so damned sincere that he was half tempted to believe that this truly might not be Anna Benedict. But he knew Anna's vivid imagination all too well for that. Like Alice In Wonderland, she was fully capable of imagining ''six impossible things before breakfast'' and believing each of them completely.

Logan had always suspected that this characteristic was a reaction to her family's expectations. Keeping an eye on Anna had been a duty he had gladly fulfilled ever since the day that Robert and Elise Benedict brought their new daughter home. The tiny infant's cry had elicited a fierce sense of protectiveness in his ten-year-old soul that had never waned no matter how she'd tried his patience over the years.

Not, he reminded himself with a twitch of his lips, that he was a paragon of patience, but he understood the introverted young woman's battle to find her place in a family of over-achievers. In the past six months, though, he'd been so busy overseeing Benedict family legal concerns that he hadn't spent much time with Anna.

It occurred to him now, as he studied the combination of confusion and fear on Anna's too-pale face, that her brief disappearance might have been in response to the numerous social and political functions she'd been required to attend. But whatever the cause, it was obvious that *something* had made Anna snap. Something serious enough, it seemed, to cause her to fantasize that her mother was no longer alive.

Logan recoiled from the thought. Fifty-three-year-old Elise was a dynamo of organization, capable of simultaneously setting up a charity bazaar, overseeing the arts foundation her husband had established for local schools, and designing the interior of a homeless shelter. The fact that Elise managed all this without losing an ounce of composure, getting a spot of dirt on her tasteful haute couture outfit or allowing one lock of hair to escape her meticulously arranged hairstyle might intimidate any daughter.

But to imagine her mother *dead?*

"Look. You *have* to believe me."

Anna's words pulled Logan's attention to her pleading eyes. "I don't belong here," she went on. "I want to leave this house, now."

The desperation in her voice made Logan look at her long and hard. Anna's face seemed thinner and very pale, considering her fondness for the California sun. Her indigo eyes appeared more deep set, yet larger and more luminous.

Luminous? Logan blinked. Where the hell had *that* word come from. Never, in all the years he'd known Anna, had he paid much attention to her eyes. Well once, when she was twelve and insisted that her blue eyes, combined with the fact that both her parents had brown, proved that she'd been adopted. The explanation had been simple enough, of course. Elise and Robert each had one blue-eyed parent, supplying the recessive gene that Anna, but not her brother, Chas, had inherited.

Logan's sudden poetic attention to the young woman's features was far less easy to explain. Even more confusing was his sudden awareness of the gentle curves that formed the body so close to his. As his flesh began to warm, his muscles tensed. He'd known Anna all her life, and never before had he reacted to her with this…this—

He shook away the half-formed thought. Anna was his *sister,* dammit. Okay—she was Chas's sister, but as an unofficial Benedict that was how he'd always viewed her. Yet, insane as it was, he found himself mesmerized by the hopeless expression in those dark eyes of hers, fascinated by the curve of her lips, felt his head bending inexorably toward hers.

It was at that moment, without any warning, that Anna stood. Logan got to his feet as well, instinctively grasping her upper arms again, the strange moment of temptation forgotten in his concern about Anna's mental state.

"I can't let you leave," he said. "Not the way you're acting. I'm sure your moth—that Elise will be along with the doctor any minute. Then—"

"Then what?" she demanded. Concern tightened the straight black eyebrows beneath her new bangs. "This doctor will give me a *sedative?* Something to ease my poor befuddled mind? Absolutely not."

Again she pulled away from him, this time with so much force that Logan was jerked forward. Rather than risk hurting her arms more than his bruising grip must already be doing, he let gravity draw her backward, onto the bed. Following her down, he pinned her there with his body.

This didn't end the struggle, however. Instead of lying still, Anna continued to twist and squirm as her arms flailed in an attempt to hit him. Logan slid his hands down each arm, until he again captured her wrists. Although her upper body was now relatively still, the area below her waist continued to shift wildly. When she began to buck, Logan decided he'd had enough.

"Knock it off."

He purposely spoke in the low growl he used when dealing with a roomful of arguing lawyers and clients. It apparently worked on half-crazed women, too, for Anna not only stopped moving, she went completely limp.

Slowly Logan raised his head and looked down. Her eyes were closed, her features soft and without expression. Pushing himself into a sitting position, he grabbed the obviously unconscious Anna's left wrist. As he searched for a pulse, Elise Benedict's voice echoed down the hall.

"Yes, Doctor. Anna is claiming she doesn't know any of us. She seems disoriented and unusually excitable. I think she needs something to calm her nerves—to keep her from doing damage to herself."

Logan managed to scramble to his feet at the side of the bed seconds before Elise entered the room. She was followed by a tall, thin man with white hair and black-framed glasses. The dark eyes behind those spectacles glanced at Logan before focusing on the inert young woman in the bed.

"I think she fainted," Logan said.

Dr. Alcott bent down to place two fingers on the side of Anna's neck. After a second he straightened. "Good strong pulse," he said, then once more looked at Logan, his dark eyes narrowed. "Elise tells me that Anna fell and hit her head. Is this true?"

Logan nodded. "Yes. She lost her footing on the veranda, and her feet flew out from under her. Her back took the brunt of the fall, but her head apparently hit the tile surface, too. She appeared to be a bit dazed when I reached her."

Something of an understatement, Logan thought as Robert Benedict reentered the room. The man was under a great deal of pressure, between serving in California's legislature and battling to win the primary that would, hopefully, propel his political career into the national arena. The last thing he needed to hear was that his daughter had been acting strangely even before she hit her head.

"Dr. Alcott," Robert said as the man opened his bag and removed a stethoscope. "Do you think that blow to Anna's head could have caused her to act as if she'd suddenly found herself in a house of strangers?"

Alcott glanced up with a frown. "Is that what's been going on?"

"I'm afraid so," Elise replied with a sigh. "Of course you know how she was before...before I called you the other day. But at least *then* she seemed to know us. Now—" the woman paused to bite her lip as she gazed at her daughter "—amnesia." She shook her head. "Oh, Anna."

Logan tensed at the almost undetectable note of disapproval in Elise's soft voice. The tone had the power to cut like a lash, in spite of, or perhaps because of, the charming smile that accompanied the words. He knew this because that tone had been directed toward him more than once after the death of his parents placed him in the Benedicts' care.

And in their debt.

No, he reminded himself. In Robert's debt. It had been Robert who had recognized a ten-year-old orphan's fear of being sent to live with strangers. It was Robert to whom he owed his loyalty, along with whatever help he could offer now.

Logan turned to the man and said quietly, "You left word that Anna was missing. What's been going on?"

He purposely didn't mention the messages that Anna had left him. In her second call, she'd begged Logan not to tell her family that she'd been trying to reach him. Until he knew more about what had been happening in his absence, he would honor that request.

Robert glanced toward his wife before replying. "Well, I mishandled a question Anna placed to me yesterday morning." Robert's hand rose to comb through his hair as he went on. "The timing couldn't have been worse. You were in France, Chas was making arrangements for the campaign, Elise was up to her earlobes in arranging tonight's fund-raiser, and I was putting the finishing touches on a speech. I'm afraid that I—"

"Robert," Elise broke in softly as she placed a graceful hand on his arm. "I refuse to allow you to feel guilty. Despite our busy schedules, we've always been there for Anna, always encouraging her, even when it became obvious that she was incapable of seeing anything through, that she would always be chasing after something new.''

There it was again, Logan thought as he gazed at Elise, the disparity between the concern wrinkling the woman's brow and the barely discernable note of exasperation beneath her sad tone. He was never sure which emotion was real. And at the moment this was beside the point.

He turned to Robert. ''What exactly was it that Anna confronted you with?''

The man seemed to hesitate. In the silence Elise replied, ''Oh, it was that silly old *not belonging* in this family nonsense. I'll never understand *what* prompted my daughter's notion that she was adopted. Probably those fairy tales Aunt Grace read to all of you, full of princes and princesses, faithful knights, changelings and evil stepparents. Such a waste of time.''

The woman sighed. ''I thought Anna had given up that silly fantasy until the other day. Good Lord, she even brought up that imaginary Rose creature again. It frightened me so that I had no recourse but to call Dr. Alcott.''

Logan glanced over to see Alcott pry Anna's right eye open and shine a flashlight into it. ''Why the doctor?'' he asked as he turned back to Elise.

The woman's lovely features tightened. ''I reminded Anna that we'd been totally up-front about the fact that she'd been conceived in a fertility clinic. I again assured her that she was the product of my egg and her father's sperm, but she just kept insisting she was not our child. Then she threatened to have someone investigate this if we didn't confirm her suspicions.''

Elise glanced at her husband. ''Considering that Stephen Dahlberg is just looking for a hint of scandal—no matter how absurd or unfounded—we had no choice, really, but to ask for Dr. Alcott's help. He suggested she be placed under close observation.''

A cold chill crept up the back of Logan's neck. ''Close observation?''

"That's right." Elise lifted her chin. "Dr. Alcott arranged to take Anna to a very private facility run by a psychiatrist friend of his, where we hoped a discreet professional might get to the root of her problems. But yesterday, when the doctor stopped at the gated entrance, Anna opened the car door, ran down the street and somehow managed to hop onto a city bus just as it pulled away."

Elise paused to once more shake her head. When she resumed speaking, the defensive tone was replaced with what sounded like heartfelt regret. "Unfortunately, this just proves how much she needs help. She's always preferred to run away rather than face her responsibilities."

Robert took a step toward the bed, then stopped. "You know," he said softly, "when Anna announced she had enrolled at UC Berkeley again, I thought she'd at last decided to take control of her life."

Silence filled the room for several moments. "I see," Logan said at last. "And when these questions came up, you simply decided to have Anna…" He paused to search for the word. Unable, and suddenly unwilling, to come up with something politically correct, he finished, "…committed?"

"There was nothing 'simple' about it." For once the steel in Elise's voice matched the hardness of her expression. "Things have been difficult enough since Victor died, what with Grace's mind slipping in and out of reality at the most inopportune times. Grace's mutterings, however, are easily explained as the onset of senility. But Anna's rantings are quite another story—perfect fodder for a scandal, which is something Robert can't afford this close to the primary."

She paused, took a deep breath, then reached out to touch Logan's arm as she went on in a softer tone, "You're doing a good job, keeping the family holdings and charities running smoothly so that Robert can concentrate on the matter at hand. Victor taught you well. But you don't have the time to watch over Grace as he did—nor to baby-sit Anna."

The honest sympathy in Elise's eyes touched Logan. His jaw clenched against the pain shooting through his chest at the mention of Victor Benedict. While Robert had been his surrogate father, Robert's uncle Victor had been Logan's mentor, schooling him in the ways of finance and the law. He missed the older man's rock-steady presence, couldn't help asking himself how Victor would have handled this situation.

"So, I hope you understand," Elise went on. "That when Robert and I consulted Dr. Alcott, we felt it best to go along with his suggestion that Anna go to a quiet place where she could...pull herself together."

It wasn't until Elise spoke these last three words that Logan once again found himself biting back words of anger. That little undertone of sarcasm was there again, whispering that Anna wasn't living up to the picture of Benedict family perfection.

"Excuse me." Dr. Alcott's voice broke the silence following Elise's last statement. "Anna's injuries seem minor—some scratches to her palms and perhaps a bruise on her hip. Her vital signs are strong, and while her pupils show no sign of head injury, a CAT scan might be in order. This can be performed at Dr. Shriver's clinic. Did you want to use the limousine, as before?"

Robert gazed at his daughter before he nodded and slowly turned to Logan. "Would you mind carrying Anna down and placing her in the back seat?"

Chapter 3

After hearing Robert ask Logan to carry her to the waiting car, Rose barely let herself breathe. Despite the instinct urging her to leap from the bed and rush from the room, she forced herself to remain inert, eyes closed, just as she had since the moment she realized it would be impossible to escape Logan's powerful grip.

Little did she think this "playing possum" trick would ever be useful when, at the age of twelve, she'd reluctantly taken the self-defense class that her mother enrolled them in. There had been no fancy moves to learn, just basic common-sense kicking and twisting and hitting, all of which she'd tried to use against Logan in her attempt to escape from his hold—and this house.

Pretending to pass out had been a last-resort move, meant to lure the attacker into complacency until an opportunity to escape arrived. It had never occurred to Rose, as she listened and gathered information, that she would be forced to remain inert while some strange doctor poked her and pried open her eyes, one by one, to examine them from behind a blinding light.

And for what? She was fairly certain that the clinic the doctor had just referred to was the nut house that this Anna person had been headed for—a place *she* had no intention of ending up. It appeared that this was just what would happen, however, if she continued to lie there.

Rose was wondering if the element of surprise would be enough to allow her to escape, should she suddenly jump up and dash past all these people, when she heard Logan reply, "As a matter of fact, I *would* mind taking her to the car."

"*Logan.*"

The scandalized protest came from the woman Rose had come to know as Elise. Logan responded evenly.

"I don't want to send Anna off to some institution if it's not necessary. From what I understand, she's been gone all night. Simple exhaustion might be the reason she passed out. I'd like to let her rest a bit and see if she won't wake up on her own, then try to find out what's behind her confusion."

"It won't do any good." It was Elise again. "I tried reasoning with her, but her rantings only escalated. My daughter needs *professional* help, not someone to hold her hand and encourage her unreasonable behavior. Or to indulge her, as her father has done."

Rose was aware of a long pause before Logan asked in a quiet, steely tone, "When have I ever *encouraged* Anna to behave in any way that would be detrimental to herself, or to the family?"

"Never." This came from the man called Robert. "While I may have occasionally been guilty of 'indulging' my daughter, you've always been a steadying influence on her. But her behavior the past few days—" he paused to sigh before finishing "—I'm really afraid her mental stability is in danger. You heard her claim that she didn't know any of us."

Another long pause followed this. Rose's heart began to race as she recalled the less-than-sane way she'd been behaving since first seeing Logan on the deck outside. She wouldn't

blame him at all for giving in to the pressure, and letting her—
or rather Anna—be locked up.

"I want an hour," Logan said suddenly. "I'd like to see if
she won't regain consciousness, then talk to her here, in surroundings that are familiar to her. *Alone.*"

Dr. Alcott's "I don't think—" blended with Elise's
"We've already agreed that—"

Robert interrupted them both. "Logan is right. I would
much prefer Anna be treated at home, if possible."

As Rose's tense muscles began to relax she heard a soft
sigh, followed by Elise's voice. "Well, I suppose that would
prevent news of this…breakdown, or whatever, from reaching
the press. But Dr. Alcott is—"

"A good man," Robert finished. "And for just that reason,
I'm going to ask him to stay around until Logan has had time
to work with Anna. You have an hour, Logan. The rest of us
will be downstairs, visiting with Aunt Grace. I know you'll
call if you need us."

Rose listened to the sound of multiple feet shuffling away,
followed by the click of the door as it closed. She heard a
single set of footsteps approach the bed.

Logan. Rose drew a slow, soft breath. She didn't know who
this Anna person was, but she did know that the woman was
lucky to have such a determined friend. And so, by extension,
was she.

But, despite this man's frequent appearances in her dreams,
Logan was a stranger. She didn't feel she could trust him to
listen to her explanation of the other set of dreams—those
involving the Golden Gate Bridge—without calling the doctor
back to cart her off to the hospital with the rubber rooms.
However, if she wanted to prevent this, she would have to put
an end to her "unconscious" charade sometime soon.

Besides, she had her own reasons for wanting to stay in this
house, in this room, for a little while longer. And that reason
was Anna Benedict. Rose had a lot of questions about the
young woman she apparently resembled so very closely. For-

tunately, the conversation she'd just overheard had suggested a way to get answers to some of these.

Elise had mentioned amnesia. How perfect. All she had to do was continue to say that she didn't know any of these people. Since amnesia was hardly a reason to lock someone up—and with Logan around to champion her, believing that she was Anna—she could stay in this room long enough to investigate this look-alike of hers. And then she could wait till the gate was open, slip down those iron stairs, walk back to the gas station with the pay phone she'd noticed when the cab turned into the area, retrieve her luggage from the hotel she'd checked into yesterday, then return to Seattle. And sanity.

With this plan in mind, Rose took a deep, loud breath as she let her eyelids flutter. When she felt the mattress dip near her head and heard a deep voice say, "Anna?" she waited a heartbeat before slowly opening her eyes.

Logan was bending over her, his hands resting on the bed, his eyes dark with concern. Rose was struck suddenly by the weak-muscled sensation that flowed through her body, the sensation that always followed her dreams of this man. This time the heat rushing through her veins engulfed her in an even stronger wave as she continued to meet his gaze.

"Anna," he said again, this time more firmly. "Are you all right?"

No, she wanted to reply, *I think I'm running a fever.*

Hardly the thing to say, of course. Not if she wanted to be left alone to search this room. Instead, she pulled her eyebrows into a slow frown as she asked, "Who...who is Anna?"

"You are," he replied.

Allowing her frown to deepen, she shook her head. "You called me that before, but it doesn't sound right. My name is—"

"Rose," he finished. "So you keep saying. And you live in Seattle?"

It was obvious that the man was trying to humor her—or rather, the woman he *thought* she was. She decided to play along.

"I..." She hesitated before nodding slowly. "Yes. I...I must be."

"Why do you say that?" Logan asked. He smiled slightly, lifting his eyebrows as he went on. "Is it because that's where your driver's license says you live?"

Oh, this was almost too easy, Rose thought as she widened her eyes and focused on his. "Well," she said at last. "Yes."

Logan moved away slowly, leaning against the back of the chair next to the bed. Rose turned her head to watch him study her. A moment later his lips curved into a smile as he asked, "How do you feel?"

Rose blinked, then shrugged. "A little stiff."

"Would you like to sit up?"

The moment Rose nodded, Logan leaned forward, placed his hands beneath her shoulders and eased her into an upright position. Rose found her heart beating wildly again. Whether it was a reaction to having lain flat for so long or the heat from this man's touch she wasn't certain. But once she was upright, she placed her hands on the aqua coverlet and scooted away, seeking refuge against the wrought-iron headboard.

This didn't place her very far from Logan, but the distance was enough to break the strange, warm current that seemed to flow between them and allow her to continue her act. Reaching for the back of her head, Rose felt the tender spot that had struck the bricks of the veranda. It took no acting ability at all to wince as she asked, "Did I pass out?"

"You did. Do you remember anything else?"

Rose hesitated, not certain how far to take this. "I remember you carrying me up here—and that I fought with you."

Logan nodded. He continued to smile but his eyes narrowed ever so slightly as he said, "That's right. But now can you tell me how you arrived here, at this house?"

Rose frowned as she gathered her thoughts. Careful, she warned herself, before starting slowly. "I...arrived in a taxi. I knew I was looking for my home...I somehow must have directed him to this neighborhood, but I don't recall doing that."

So far, so good, Rose thought as she paused. Now, all she had to do was explain how she came to think her name was Rose.

"I remember feeling foolish, suddenly realizing that I didn't know the address I was searching for. I...my mind was fuzzy, but I felt certain I was heading home. So I checked my wallet and found a driver's license with my name on it. Then I—''

"How did you know it was *your* name?"

Rose blinked as she stared at Logan. She had no idea how— then it came to her in a flash.

"There's a little mirror in the wallet," she said quickly. "I could see that my features matched the license photo. So I assumed I was Rose."

"Except the address shown is in Seattle."

Rose wasn't going to allow herself to be tripped up. Without considering why it was so important to win this battle of wits, she gave her lips a wry twist and nodded.

"I know. That puzzled me. But still, I had this sense that I was somehow looking for my *home.* And then we drove by this place, and I caught a glimpse of the bridge between this house and the one next door, and the scene was so familiar that I was sure this must be the place I was looking for. I...remember thinking that perhaps I grew up here, or that I had relatives here. Anyway, I was embarrassed by the odd looks the driver was giving me, so I told him to drop me off at the gate."

Rose ended her story with a satisfied sigh. For someone who had been reared to speak only the truth, she hadn't done a bad job of lying. Of course, other than the bit about thinking some relative might live here, most of her tale had been true. And from the looks of things, Logan seemed to be buying it. Until his eyes narrowed.

"Are you telling me you made up that story about having dreamed of the bridge?" he asked.

Damn. She'd forgotten about that.

Rose bit the inside of her lower lip hesitantly before she

shrugged. "Sort of. I do know that the view seemed familiar—the dream thing seemed the only explanation."

Logan stared at her for a moment. Slowly his scowl relaxed and the suspicion in his green-brown eyes softened into an expression of speculation and concern.

"Do you remember anything from *before* you got in the cab?"

Rose sat quietly, staring at the open vee of his white shirt, pretending to think. Instead she was struck with a memory from one of her dreams in which she'd stared at that same chest. Only in the dream there had been no shirt, just bare, muscled skin. Feeling her face grow warm, she blinked the image away and quickly shook her head.

"No. Nothing."

"Well then," he said quietly. "Will you accept the idea that you *just might* be Anna Benedict?"

Rose fought off a shudder that had nothing to do with the fact that her clothes were still slightly damp. She wanted to shake her head, insist that she was Rose Delancey, but controlled the impulse. Slowly she lifted her shoulders in a shrug.

"I'll consider it." She paused. "Perhaps it would help if you'd tell me a little about Ann—me. So far all I know is that I have a mother named Elise, a father named Robert and an aunt named Grace. Elise mentioned someone named Chas. Who is he?"

"Your older brother," Logan replied.

Rose frowned. "I thought *you* were my older brother."

"No, I'm not," Logan replied. "Not really."

Logan watched Anna's eyebrows twist into a puzzled frown, which told him just how confusing this might sound—especially to an already confused mind.

"My parents, Thomas and Brenda Maguire, worked for your grandfather," he explained. "I was ten when they died, and I didn't have any other family. Your father managed to get himself appointed my legal guardian and has always treated me like a surrogate son."

Logan saw an expression of sympathy darken Anna's eyes.

His chest tightened around the pain he'd locked away so long ago, and he frowned.

There was something deeply empathetic in that look of Anna's, almost as if she knew just how that loss had affected him. But she couldn't. By the time Anna learned about the accident that had killed his parents, the young girl had long been accustomed to thinking of him as her "bigger brother," which had been her way of distinguishing him from Chas, two years his junior.

Receiving sympathy from Anna now was something entirely new to him, and rather than try to deal with the uncomfortable emotions she evoked, he did what he did best—focused on the business at hand.

"Come with me," he said. "And let me introduce you to the family."

Logan noticed Anna offered no resistance when he took her hand to pull her to her feet, then lead her across the room to stand in front of an oak rolltop desk. The wall above was filled with framed photos. He pointed to a five-by-seven on the far right.

"There's Elise, holding you on the day you came home," he said. "Other than her hairstyle, you can see that her looks have changed little. And I think you can recognize Robert, despite the fact that his hair was nearly black back then. Just like yours is now. And the shorter blond boy on the left? That's your brother, Chas."

Logan watched Anna scrutinize each figure until a sudden frown formed and she abruptly turned to him. "And the other blond boy. Is…is that you?"

Her eyes were wide. Thinking he saw a hint of recognition in them, he nodded. "Yes. Look familiar?"

An expression very close to fear darkened her eyes before she blinked and shrugged. "Maybe…a little. I don't know."

"Well, maybe looking at some of these other photographs will stimulate your memory."

Logan directed her attention to the images that Elise had

framed in silver and placed on the wall of her daughter's room. He started with a large oval sepia-toned photograph at the top.

"That's your great-great-great grandfather, Lucas Benedict. He established the family fortune back in the 1870s when he struck a vein of silver in Virginia City, Nevada. No one can find a picture of his wife, but the men in the two pictures on either side are his sons, Jonah and Jerald. Beneath those we have Jerald's sons, Raymond and William, along with William's wife, your grandmother, Anna. Some think you bear a close resemblance to her."

He watched as Anna studied this last photo. "I don't agree."

Logan shrugged. "Well, you do both have curly hair—and there's a widow's peak beneath those new bangs of yours. The picture is rather faded, so it's hard to make out any further resemblance. Anyway, the next set of pictures are of William and Anna's two sons and their wives. That's Victor and Grace on the left. The other couple is your grandfather, Charles, and your grandmother, Louise. You wouldn't remember your grandmother, because she died before your first birthday."

"And this picture on the top of the desk?" he heard her ask softly.

Logan frowned at the photo of two dark-haired men sitting at a piano. "That's a shot of your father," he said slowly, "with his brother, your uncle Joe. You wouldn't remember Joe, either. He died…shortly before you were born."

Logan swallowed against the sudden tightness in his throat and blinked back the sudden memories of the day that Joseph Benedict died, and the two people who had perished with him.

"Oh, Anna! You're up."

Elise Benedict's voice echoed from the doorway. Logan turned as the woman stepped into the room, followed by her husband and the doctor.

"How is our patient?" Dr. Alcott asked as all three stopped in front of Anna and Logan.

When Anna said nothing, Logan replied, "She's fine, physically. At least, she hasn't complained of any major aches or pains.''

"And her mind?''

Logan turned to Elise. "I think I've convinced her that she *is* Anna Benedict. She appears to recognize some things, but her memory is far from clear.''

"Oh, dear.'' Elise sighed, then turned to the doctor. "Well then. Perhaps we should still consider sending her—''

"No!''

Logan glanced at Anna, who had broken into her mother's suggestion just moments before Logan could reject what was undoubtedly going to be another suggestion that Anna be placed in the hospital. He turned to Anna's father.

"I don't think that's necessary, Robert. *Or* particularly wise right now. I'm sure the facility that Alcott recommended is discreet, but this sort of thing has a way of leaking out. Not that I think there's any shame in a person checking in for mental help, but you know how it could look.''

Robert nodded.

"Besides,'' Logan went on, "Anna might benefit by being around familiar things and people. Don't you agree Dr. Alcott?''

The man's dark eyes narrowed a moment behind his glasses before he nodded. "Possibly. Theoretically, being exposed to familiar items speeds recovery in persons suffering from amnesia.''

Logan looked to Elise, half expecting her to show some kind of displeasure at having her plans denied. Instead the woman was treating her daughter to a speculative gaze.

"Well, perhaps that *is* best. I wasn't sure how I was going to explain Anna's absence at the campaign dinner tonight. And many of our longtime friends and associates will be there. Maybe seeing one of them in a relaxed atmosphere will prompt Anna's memory. What do you think, Dr. Alcott?''

Logan gave his head a small shake. Only Elise Benedict would consider a campaign dinner and dance a "relaxed" atmosphere. Anna certainly would not. She hated spending time in the public eye.

Before he could bring this up, however, the doctor replied, "Excellent idea."

This brought a wide smile to Elise's lips. She turned to Logan. "You'll be there, of course."

"Actually," he said, "I got very little sleep during the past three days, so I'd planned to catch up on it after I filed the paperwork from my trip to France and explained the details of your father's will."

Only the slightest tightening of the woman's jaw gave any hint of Elise's feelings about the now-deceased man who had abandoned his wife and daughter so many years ago. A second later she was smiling again.

"Oh, there will be plenty of time to discuss dreary financial matters at a later date. What's important now is that you escort Anna to this affair tonight and keep an eye on her. You know, point out the people she should know and, of course, see to it that she doesn't say the wrong thing."

Before Logan could reply, Robert spoke up. "I'm not so sure this is a good idea, Elise. Logan is obviously suffering from jet lag, and Anna looks as white as a sheet."

The woman glanced from Logan to Anna, concern wrinkling the brow over her dark brown eyes. "Yes, they do both look a bit ragged. But it's *hours* yet until they need to make an appearance. I've reserved a suite at the hotel, where you and I can change so that I can be on hand to oversee the last-minute arrangements. When I planned this months ago, I'd figured that Anna would go with us, and keep Aunt Grace company until it was time to go downstairs. But Chas and Nicole can take care of Grace. That way, Anna can stay here and rest up while Logan goes home and catches up on his sleep before dressing and returning to get her. And who knows? Perhaps after Anna takes a nap, her memory will have returned and everything will be fine."

Rose knew that neither of these things were going to happen. First, she had no memories of Anna's life *to* recall. And second, nothing was going to be fine until she escaped from this mad house.

That was going to have to wait a bit, however. No one would believe her now if she were to suddenly insist that she was Rose Delancey. Most likely they would cart her off and lock her up in the room they'd reserved for poor Anna. So, until she could get them to leave her alone she would be forced to go along with this charade.

"Anna."

Rose's heart beat two or three times before she realized she was being spoken to. Turning to the speaker, Robert Benedict, she was met by soft brown eyes full of concern as he took her hand.

"Are you up to this plan?"

Rose took a deep breath. As soon as these people cleared out of this room, she had every intention of slipping out the sliding glass door and making her way to freedom. She no longer gave a fig who this Anna person was, or why she'd had all those dreams of the view outside this window. She just wanted to get back to her own life. This might not happen, though, if she gave these people any reason to suspect that she might do anything other than what they were suggesting.

But she'd been raised not to lie, so she forced a small smile to her lips and said simply, "I'm feeling okay."

"Wonderful!" Elise leaned forward to brush a kiss across Rose's cheek before stepping back, saying, "Robert, we need to be hurrying along. Logan, you go home and rest up. Anna, are you hungry? No, well then you take a long nap. Your dress hasn't arrived yet, but I've been assured it will be here in plenty of time."

The woman started to leave, then stopped and reached out to take Rose's hand. "Anna, dear, your father needs to be seen with his family. Promise me you will be there, and on your best behavior."

Rose stared into those dark eyes. *Promise?* Kathleen Delancey had held promises sacred and taught her daughter to do the same. If she promised, she would have to follow through. And if she didn't, the slight narrowing of Elise's eyes suggested that she might end up in a nut house.

"I promise," Rose breathed.

At that, Elise released her hand. "Robert," she said. "Doctor—I think we can leave now. Logan. You, too."

Logan nodded but didn't follow the other three out of the room. When they'd disappeared into the hall, he looked at Rose and asked, "Are you going to be all right here?"

After a moment of hesitation, Rose shook her head. "No. Not at all. I thought I could do it, but I can't."

She expected him to scowl. Instead his gaze softened with understanding as he asked, "The crowd thing?"

Rose blinked. "What crowd thing?" Before he could reply, she stuck her hand out in a halting motion. "Never mind. I don't want you to explain. I want you to listen. I can't keep the promise I just made. I can't go to this dinner campaign thing and pretend to be someone I'm not. I can't—won't—live a lie. I am *not* Anna, and I will no longer pretend to be her."

Logan closed his eyes and shook his head. A jolt of anger and fear made Rose grab his upper arms, much as he had held hers so many times that day, and shake him.

"Listen," she hissed as his eyes flew open. "You have to believe me. If I am telling the truth, then Anna is out there somewhere, alone, confused and probably frightened."

"Confused," he said quietly, gazing at her pointedly. "Undoubtedly."

Rose shook her head. "*I* am not confused. I have people you can call who will confirm that I am who I say I am. The woman who owns half of my mother's shop, for instance. I'll give you the number. Call her."

"Why should I believe someone I've never met?"

Rose's frustration was building by the moment. She clenched her teeth. "All right. Then…then have me write something and compare it to something Anna has written."

"You could easily disguise your handwriting, so that won't

prove anything,'' he said slowly, his eyes narrowing. ''However, I could arrange to have your fingerprints analyzed.''

There was no mistaking the challenge in his gaze. Instead of retreating from this, Rose smiled.

''You're on.''

Chapter 4

Twenty minutes later Rose was seated in Logan's red Mustang.

"Where are we going?" she asked as Logan finished pulling off the quiet residential street and onto a busy boulevard.

He gave her a quick glance before turning his attention to the traffic ahead. "To see a friend of mine from college."

Rose blinked. Her life had been turned upside down and he wanted to *socialize?* Slowly she asked, "And we would do this because…?"

"Because he works in the police forensics lab." Again Logan glanced her way. "You *are* still willing to prove your identity, aren't you?"

"Of course."

"Well, I have the glass from Anna's bathroom, one of her perfume bottles and her brush, which should hold her fingerprints. I also have a clean glass for you to leave your prints on. My friend Dennis agreed to do a quick comparison. That is, if you're still so sure of yourself."

Logan turned narrowed eyes to Rose as the car stopped for

a red light. She stiffened beneath his suspicious glance. "I'm sure. And once I prove to you that I *am* Rose Delancey, I want you to promise—"

"One step at a time," Logan broke in.

Rose had barely managed to nod before Logan's attention was once more captured by traffic. As the car moved forward, he shifted into second gear; then into third to race down the street. As he swerved from one lane to another, passing the slower vehicles, Rose's heart leaped, then began to race.

Was this due to fear, she wondered, or excitement? The last few years had become a blur of doctors' offices, hospital rooms and the small chamber her mother retreated to after each chemo treatment. There had been ups and downs to deal with, hopes and fears, tears and laughter. So her life had hardly been uneventful. And although she and her mother had been dealing with death, together they had learned to live each day as fully as possible, to notice the way the clouds moved in, the taste and texture of each bite of food.

But since the funeral Rose had come to see how narrow her world had grown, and how empty she felt. She'd greeted this numbness with fury, seeing it as a poor way to remember the woman who had given her life, showed her how to live, encouraged her to dream and to follow those dreams, even as all of hers were fading.

Rose sighed and stared out the window at the tall buildings and the business-lunch crowds bustling along the sidewalk. Kathleen Delancey had undoubtedly been referring to life choices and career direction when she'd urged her daughter to "follow your dreams," but the woman's death had left Rose feeling too lost to address such imposing matters. So she'd followed the only dreams she could think of, those involving the Golden Gate Bridge and the laughing-eyed man who so resembled Logan Maguire.

This thought brought Rose's attention back to the man sitting next to her. The sense that she somehow knew this man warred with the knowledge that he was really a complete stranger. A stranger who thought—no, *wanted*—her to be someone else, something quite ironic, considering that two years ago she'd walked away from what she knew had looked like a fairy-tale marriage for just that reason.

"Yesss!" Logan hissed as the car braked to a sudden stop. He glanced over to smile at her puzzled look and explained, "The parking gods have smiled upon us."

Rose looked ahead to see a large silver car pull out of a parking space directly in front of them, then held her breath as Logan gunned his motor and angled into the spot practically on the heels of the departing vehicle.

After switching off the engine, he reached into the back seat for the black backpack that held the items he'd referred to earlier. He whipped a handkerchief out of the inside pocket of his leather jacket, then wrapped it around his hand as he retrieved a plain drinking glass.

"Grip this," he said. "Make sure all five fingers leave a mark. All right, now. Give it back."

Rose placed the glass in his handkerchief-wrapped hand, then watched him fold the white fabric around the item before returning it to the backpack.

"Okay." He gave her a smile. "Now we feed the meter, then go confirm that you are who you say you are. Or rather, who you aren't."

Rose fought a strange sense of nervousness as she exited the elevator on the third floor of the building Logan led her into. This was silly, she told herself as she followed him down the hall and into a green-and-stainless-steel room, where Logan introduced her to a man wearing a white lab coat over a denim shirt and tan tie.

Dennis Langtrey stood a little over five-seven. He had light, caramel-colored eyes, a round, youthful face beneath short, wavy blond hair and a smile that could only be described as angelic, which instantly put Rose at ease. Once Logan explained what he wanted, the man placed the items taken from Anna's room into one tray and the glass holding Rose's prints in another. He then brushed gray powder over them and used tape to lift the resulting smudges. All the while, Dennis chatted with Logan about "old times" at Stanford University. Occasionally he glanced at Rose, as if expecting her to comment, leaving her to assume that this man must have met Anna on several of those occasions.

"Yes, that was *some* party Robert threw for our graduation," Dennis said, then smiled as he straightened from his work. "Well, I have a pair of perfect thumbprints. Now for the fun part."

He moved over to a desk, fiddled with the computer sitting there, and a moment later he was staring at a screen displaying two gray ovals formed of tight concentric lines.

A look of total concentration creased Dennis's features as he repeatedly glanced from one print to the other. When Rose realized she was holding her breath, she slowly and determinedly released it. This was ridiculous, she told herself. Any second now, this man was going to announce that the prints did not match. She was, after all, *not* Anna Benedict.

"Wow. These are close," Dennis said on the heels of her mental declaration. Lifting his head, he looked at Logan and went on, "But, as they say, *close* only counts in horseshoes."

"Are you trying to say the prints don't match?" Logan asked.

"That's right." Dennis stood and stretched before going on. "But, damn, they are close."

"I got that. Are you *sure* they're from two different people?"

Dennis glanced at his computer screen with a frown, then looked at Logan again. "Ye-es," he said slowly.

"Is there some question?"

"No. Not about—"

"Because this is vitally important," Logan said. "I need you to be 100 percent sure on this."

"I *am* 100 percent certain," Dennis replied. "However, I have a theory I want to check out. There are some hairs on this brush. Can you get me some from the person who donated the other set of prints so I can run a DNA test?"

Logan turned to An—Rose, he reminded himself. He raised

one eyebrow inquiringly and after a moment's hesitation she nodded. Opening her purse, she drew out a small brush and handed it to Dennis.

As the man removed the few strands of hair tangled in the bristles, Logan asked, "Just what are these suspicions of yours?"

"Suspicions?" Dennis's full lips curved into a particularly cherubic smile as he returned the brush to Rose. "Let's see…I agreed to look at these fingerprints, despite the fact that you said that you couldn't tell me what all this was about. So, until I've run this test, I think it only fair that I keep my own counsel. Wouldn't you say?"

Logan met his friend's wide-eyed, innocent gaze with narrowed eyes. Games. He'd forgotten how much Dennis Langtrey loved to play guessing games. Most likely this characteristic was what enabled the brilliant mind behind that round, childlike face to focus on tiny bits of minutia day after day, trusting that eventually they would lead to the unraveling of a puzzle.

And this was definitely a puzzle worthy of Dennis's mind. Two women who were almost identical—no, who *were* identical—yet came from completely different backgrounds. And to make things even *more* interesting, the day after one of them runs off, her look-alike shows up.

Logan glanced at Rose. And what about this claim that she'd appeared on the Benedict veranda in response to some *dream?* The story sounded preposterous—like one of Anna's more outrageous fantasies. But…Dennis had just unequivocally stated that her fingerprints didn't match the ones he'd lifted from Anna's glass. They were *close,* Dennis said. An impossible suspicion grew in his mind. Maybe this test of Dennis's would confirm it. In the meantime, he needed to keep the Benedict family as normal as possible.

Aware that nothing would get Dennis to tip his hand before he was ready, he asked, "How long before you have the results?"

Dennis shrugged. "Tomorrow, probably."

"I thought DNA testing took weeks."

"It can, especially in a murder investigation when you must compare several samples and run multiple tests for accuracy. But if my guess is right in this case, I should only have to run the most basic screen. Also, I don't have any pressing cases going right now to hold me up."

It was clear that the man had no intention of giving out any more information. "All right, Dennis," he said with a sigh. "Keep your little secret for the time being. But call me as soon as you finish running your test."

"Of course," the man responded with a nod. "And then you'll explain what is going on?"

"As soon as I know the whole story."

And know it's politically safe to reveal, Logan thought as he ushered Rose out the door. As they walked to the car, he found himself recalling the speculative glint in his friend's eyes. Upon reaching the car, Logan held the passenger door open for Rose, then walked around to the driver's side, deep in thought. It was *his* job to see that the family name remained above reproach, he reminded himself. It was even more important now, with Robert running against an opponent known for gleefully slinging any mud he happened upon—or dug up.

Robert's track record in state government was above reproach, but news that his daughter might be unstable could kick up a media frenzy that would drain attention from the proposals the man wanted to communicate to the electorate. Logan drew a deep breath. So he had landed in the last place he wanted to be—a political campaign.

Schmoozing and charming was Chas's department. However, damage control was Logan's. It was up to him to straighten out this situation, and quietly.

A not-too-polite honk broke Logan out of his thoughts. Realizing that he'd put on his seat belt and placed the key in the ignition only to sit and stare out the window, he switched the engine on. Glancing in the rearview mirror, he noted with a grim smile that the car behind him slid into his spot even as he moved forward, just as he'd done over an hour earlier.

An hour in which he hadn't learned much more than the fact that the woman next to him was definitely *not* Anna.

"Now what?" she said, echoing his own thoughts.

Logan glanced at her as he stopped for the next light. "Good question. How about some food? It's after noon, and the last meal I recall was something in a plastic dish served on the airplane an hour before I landed. I don't think all too well on an empty stomach."

Rose frowned. "What's to think about? Your friend confirmed that I'm not this Anna person. End of story. The hotel I'm staying at is around here somewhere, I think. Just drop me off, then you can—"

"Which hotel?" Logan asked as the light turned green.

"The Herbert, on Powell and O'Farrell."

Logan nodded. He needed a plan, and to give himself time to come up with one, he made small talk.

"I know where that is. Small place. Rather old."

"Yes. And all I can afford."

Rose turned to stare out the window, her jaw stiff with chagrin at the ever-so-slightly defensive note she'd heard beneath her words.

It wasn't that she was ashamed of the reduced state of her finances. She didn't regret for one moment the money spent on battling her mother's illness, nor her choice to cut back her performing and teaching schedule to spend as much time as possible with Kathleen rather than taking on new students.

She was a bit embarrassed by the way she'd set off on this trip without considering the cost—driven by a need to escape Queen Anne Hill, to get away from the hustle and bustle of the well-to-do customers who patronized her mother's gift shop, to escape the sudden emptiness that filled the rooms above that had once rang with loving laughter.

"I can help you with that."

Logan's quiet words captured Rose's attention. She turned to him with a lift of her eyebrows. Before she could ask what he meant, he gave her a smile. It was a wide, warm smile.

But this time she noticed right away that it didn't reach his eyes. Immediately she stiffened suspiciously.

"You can help me with what?"

"Money?"

"And why would you do that?"

"As payment."

"Payment? For what?"

The smile widened as the car slid to a stop. "For services rendered. And hopefully for services to be rendered."

Rose frowned. "What are you talking—"

"Park your car, Mr. Maguire?"

A thin brown face appeared at the driver's side window. Anticipation glittered in the teenager's dark eyes as Logan replied, "We'll see. Give us a moment, okay?"

When the boy stepped back, Logan turned to Rose. "I have a proposition for you. It's of a rather sensitive nature, and given that I'm rather well known in the city, it's not something I'd feel comfortable discussing in a crowded restaurant. I live in the building across the street. There's a conservatory on the top floor, an area that's both public and private at the same time, so you needn't worry that I'm luring you to my lair. We can stop at the deli to pick up some sandwiches. What do you say?"

Rose wasn't sure *what* to say. She glanced around, disoriented.

Apparently, while she'd mulled over the question of her finances and the pain of her recent loss, she'd failed to notice that Logan Maguire hadn't been driving toward her hotel, as she had assumed. Instead of finding herself in the heart of downtown San Francisco, she discovered that they'd come to a stop on a street running along the southern edge of the bay.

The silver-toned Oakland Bridge soared off to her right. On her left, the building Logan had referred to stretched down the street in both directions, a peachy stucco several stories high with iron balconies and windows framed by brightly colored shutters. High-priced condos, she decided, set up to look like something in a quaint Mediterranean fishing village.

Quaint and expensive.

Tension crept into her shoulders. Once upon a time quaint and expensive had called to her like honey called a fly. And had caught her, just as surely. But, she reminded herself, she'd escaped. Now, forewarned was forearmed. She could walk into quaint and expensive with no fear of becoming entangled in its silky web. She could satisfy her still-unquenched curiosity about this Anna person, then walk away and return to her own pared-down and simple life.

Freed, hopefully, from the dreams that had so haunted her.

"All right," she replied.

"Leon." Logan turned to the boy. "Do you know how important my car is?"

The kid nodded solemnly. "You restored every piece of her yourself, and you will hurt anyone who so much as scratches her bumper."

"Right," Logan said as he got out. "I'll call the garage when I'm ready for you to bring her back, in an hour or so."

Rose watched the boy's face light up as Logan handed him the keys. By the time Logan reached her side of the car, Leon was behind the wheel, obviously ready to take off as soon as Rose got out. And sure enough, the moment her door closed the kid gunned the motor to a loud roar. He then let it ease to a purr before shooting a grin toward Logan and pulling sedately away from the curb.

Logan led her across the street, then pulled a cell phone from his jacket. As they entered the small deli located on the building's ground floor, she heard him ask about "the family home project" as she gazed at the selection of salads behind the slanted glass counter.

When the phone conversation ended, Logan stepped up to the counter to order. After the food was prepared and packaged, Rose noted Logan's composed response to what she considered an exorbitant amount of money for food and beverages that barely filled one small grocery sack, while it was all she could do to keep from choking.

She should be accustomed to people who thought little or

nothing of spending large amounts of money, she told herself. After all, her mother's shop would hardly have supported the two of them, along with her partner, Goldie Lander, for the past nineteen years, if not for customers who were willing and able to pay top dollar for the items on display.

And, she reminded herself as she followed Logan to the stainless-steel elevator, there was nothing intrinsically wrong with that heady lifestyle. She'd simply learned that the cost to maintain it was too high for her blood. No regrets, she told herself as she followed Logan into the elevator.

The area that greeted Rose when the doors opened again whispered of understated elegance. The terra cotta floor was open to the blue sky above, protected from wind and rain by large panes of glass. Here and there lacy potted palms and dwarf citrus trees screened benches or umbrella-covered tables.

Aware that Logan had been as silent as she since leaving the deli, she followed him to one of the tables, where he placed a sandwich and container of salad in front of her. He then took a small pad of paper out of his jacket pocket and began making notations on it with his right hand as he devoured the sandwich in his left.

Rose realized that this was the first chance she'd had to really study the man since those first breathless moments on the balcony, when he'd seemed a dream come true. And, if one went by looks alone, that was just how this man would appear, with his square-jawed, tanned features. The fact that he was every bit as well built as the fit of his jacket indicated had been something she'd learned as she lay pinned to Anna's bed beneath that powerful body, a memory that now brought a blush to her cheeks and heat flowing wildly through her veins.

Oh, yes, the man of her dreams, she thought as she placed a forkful of macaroni salad in her mouth. Except for the fact that Logan Maguire seemed to be every bit as controlling as the last man she'd thought of in that way. Logan was a man of power, just like Josh—a man who knew what was best for everyone and didn't hesitate to use charm, coercion or even force to get others to see things his way.

Feeling old angers rise, Rose glanced at her surroundings. She had to admit it would be easy to get used to this sort of life again. Chewing a bite of sandwich, she took in the vistas provided by the windows and the glass roof above. Without even working at it, she could easily allow herself to slip back into the world of wealth and privilege.

Except, she doubted that the price had changed since the last time she considered such a move. And her soul was no longer for sale.

Rose sighed and swallowed her last bite of the vegetable foccacia, then realized she hadn't said one word to the man who'd paid for it. *Lovely manners,* she chided herself before saying, "Great view you have here."

Her words had caught Logan with his mouth full of meatball sandwich. In reply he lifted his eyebrows and nodded.

"Yeah, it is," he said after swallowing. He glanced around slowly. "I'd almost forgotten about this place. The real estate agent walked me through this area when she showed me the condo, but this is the first chance I've had to spend any time up here."

Rose shook her head. She didn't know why his words surprised her. Her experience with Joshua Whitney should have taught her how little the very well-off *really* knew about getting the most out of life.

"Something wrong?"

Logan's question pulled Rose's gaze from the magnificent San Francisco skyline rising beyond the glass wall in front of her. When she turned to him, the corner of her eye caught a glimpse of the green water stretching out toward the east bay.

"Yeah," she said slowly. "I tend to get irritated when natural beauty is ignored."

Logan's eyes narrowed. "Ignored? By me?"

"Yep. You have this great place you can use anytime, and you don't even *take the trouble* to come up here."

"And that bothers you, because…"

"Because," Rose started, then shut her mouth. Waste of time, she told herself. She'd had this conversation before, or at least a strikingly similar one. And the last thing she needed at the moment was to have someone point out how naive and unsophisticated she was, then attempt to teach her about the "finer things in life," like caviar.

Unable to prevent the shudder brought on by the thought of those salty, slimy little eggs, she made the gesture into a shrug.

"Never mind. Look, the lunch was delicious and the view spectacular. I appreciate your sharing both of them with me, but—"

"*But,*" Logan broke in, "we have more important matters to discuss. I want you to stay at the Benedicts' house a bit longer, to pretend to be Anna. You won't have to do much. Everyone already thinks that you are—"

"No," Rose managed to break in.

Logan frowned. "Why not?"

"Why *not?*" Rose echoed. "My life is in Seattle. I have…things to do. Obligations to fulfill." *A life to put back together,* she finished silently.

Logan seemed to consider her words carefully before he leaned forward, looked deep into her eyes and asked, "You mean to tell me you're going to leave without meeting Anna? You claim that you've come all the way from Seattle to find a view that has been haunting your dreams for years, learned that it can be seen from the room belonging to a woman who looks exactly like you, and you're going to leave without *taking the trouble* to meet this person?"

Rose could hardly miss the way his tone mocked the words she'd so recently flung at him. She also thought she caught a teasing glint in his eyes, but his lips showed no hint of a smile.

"It's not the same thing," she replied. "Besides, as I said, I have a—"

"Life to get back to. Of course. You have kids?" Rose shook her head.

"A husband?"

Again Rose shook her head. Careful to keep her voice neutral, she replied, "Not any longer."

Logan lifted one eyebrow. "Bad breakup?"

"No, actually. I think we were both relieved when it ended."

With that response, Rose shifted her attention to the skyline again. That wasn't the complete truth, of course, but she didn't think this man needed to hear the entire story.

After several seconds she heard Logan ask softly, "Then what are you running away from, Rosie?"

She turned to face him quickly. "My name is *Rose*. Only my mother—" She broke off, took a deep breath then said slowly, "I'm not running away from anything. I just want to go home. Where I belong."

"I see." His expression was skeptical. "And you're not even *curious* about Anna?"

"Of course I am. However, I don't have the kind of money, or the time at my disposal to—"

"As far as money goes," Logan broke in, "I have enough at my *disposal* to make it worth your while to stick around. And I'm more than willing to do so."

Every muscle in Rose's body stiffened. The rich and powerful had one easy answer to everything. She knew better.

Getting to her feet she said, "I'm *not* interested in your money." Then she turned and headed toward the elevator.

Chapter 5

Surprised by Rose's reaction, Logan still managed to stand and reach her side in three long strides. When he placed a hand on her shoulder, she whirled toward him.

"What do you want?" she asked.

Beneath her angry scowl Logan could see fear. He found himself scowling in return as he became aware of the sudden urge to pull her into his arms, to reassure this woman as he had so often comforted Anna, with a brotherly hug.

However the tingle in the hand that gripped Rose's shoulder warned that his feelings while holding *this* woman would hardly be brotherly. This didn't make any sense, but then *none* of this made any sense—not Anna's sudden breakdown, nor the fact that she'd run away from the doctor she'd trusted to treat her and every member of the family for over ten years. And the presence of Rose Delancey, with her uncanny resemblance to the missing Anna made the least sense of all.

Logan wasn't used to things not making sense. For more years than he could count, he'd worked at perfecting the art of making things fall into place. At this moment, though, the only way he could imagine getting things to work out right was to buy some time.

And Rose Delancey was the only currency at hand.

"I'm not asking this on a whim," he said quietly. "I *need* you to pretend to be Anna a while longer."

Rose's dark blue eyes grew wary. "Why?"

"Because I need time to find her."

"Isn't that a job for the police? From what I understand, she's been missing nearly twenty-four hours now. Put them on the case."

Logan shook his head. "That would mean telling the family that you aren't Anna, that the real Anna is off somewhere, getting into God-knows-what sort of—"

"Trouble," Rose broke in. "Exactly my point. If she's as…unbalanced as her mother seems to think she is, you shouldn't be standing here talking to me. You should be notifying the authorities, getting an all-points bulletin out or putting her picture on a milk carton. Whatever it takes to get her back under proper care."

Logan considered her words before shaking his head. "First off, I'm 99 percent certain that Elise is exaggerating Anna's mental state. When I listened to the messages Anna left on my machine, she sounded urgent but hardly unbalanced."

"Then it's *normal* for Anna to insist she was adopted?"

"More or less. From the age of eight or so, Anna would periodically insist that she was a changeling, that she really didn't belong in the family. After a while it became a family joke, along with the imaginary friend Anna invented." He paused. "The Benedicts' idea of a joke, that is. It was more like a not-so-gentle chiding."

Rose noticed the way Logan's features tightened, as if he was trying to brush away an unwanted thought before he spoke again.

"Anyway, I suspect that when Anna confronted her parents with whatever new *proof* she's come up with this time, Elise reacted with her I-refuse-to-discuss-this-until-you-calm-down routine, which frustrates Anna no end. She probably became even more emotional, causing Elise to imagine a threat to Robert's campaign, then bring on the doctor and the mental health clinic. Of course, if I hadn't..."

Logan let his words trail off as he thought about the trip to France, where he'd been dispatched to deal with the winery Elise had inherited.

"If you hadn't what?" Rose asked in a tight voice.

Logan released a sigh. "If I hadn't been out of the country, I would have been here to run interference, and the entire thing would most likely have blown over. But I wasn't, and now it's my job to put things back in order."

"Your job?" Rose asked. "What *is* that, exactly?"

Logan shrugged. "Mechanic."

"Mechanic?"

Her puzzled expression made Logan smile. "Sort of. I think I mentioned that my father worked for Robert's father. Charles Benedict had a collection of classic cars and several airplanes, and it was Dad's job to keep them running smoothly. Now I do the same sort of thing. As the family lawyer, I make sure that the Benedict business investments continue to pay off without creating a conflict of interest with Robert's political career, and I take care of the legal details of the various charities the Benedicts fund."

Logan paused, released a deep breath, then stared deep into Rose's eyes before going on, "Look, you won't have to stay long. Anna's bound to call me again, and I know I'll be able to talk her into returning. I was originally due to return late tonight. Anna has no way of knowing that I caught an early flight back, so she'll probably call tomorrow. So, I would really appreciate it if you would stay and attend tonight's dinner-dance fund-raiser, as Elise asked."

Logan watched Rose glance away, saw her frown. After several moments she took a deep breath, sighed, then met his gaze once more.

"It won't work," she said.

"What won't work?"

''Me—pretending to be someone I know absolutely nothing about.''

She wasn't saying no any longer, Logan realized. He began to smile. This was it. The turning point in the negotiation process. He knew the routine like he knew the curves and twists of Highway 1. What had Donald Trump called it—The Art of the Deal? Well, Victor's tutelage had taught him to master ''the deal'' and all of its variations.

''Sure it'll work,'' he replied. ''You did a great job convincing all of us that Anna is suffering some form of amnesia. Any mistakes you make will be attributed to that. Besides, I'll be on hand to help you over any rough spots. Even though Chas and I both have places of our own, Robert and Elise keep our old bedrooms set up for the nights that family business meetings run late.''

The expression on Rose's face told Logan that, despite his assurances, she still had questions. Taking charge of the situation, he closed the deal with a smile.

''Look, I'll explain everything you need to know as we head back to the house. It'll only take me a few moments to get my tuxedo and a few other clothes. We can stop by your hotel, get your things, pay your bill, check you out, then set you up in Anna's room.''

He turned toward the elevator and pushed the down button. Rose placed a firm hand on his arm. ''I have one condition,'' she said.

The eyes that met his were dark with intent. ''What's that?'' Logan asked.

''If you lie to me or try to manipulate me in any way,'' she said quietly, ''the deal will be off.''

An hour later Rose gazed around Anna's room, wondering what she'd been thinking when she agreed to this charade.

She *hadn't* been thinking, she realized. At least not clearly, or she never would have let Logan Maguire prey on her concern for this unknown young woman and talk her into this insane plan. There was no denying that talking was something the man did well—smoothly, like one of those silver-tongued car salesman, the ones who had you driving off the lot in a car you couldn't really afford, and didn't really want.

She really, *really* didn't want to be here, Rose thought as she stared at the turquoise-and-purple quilt at the end of the bed. The whole thing was just too creepy. In addition to the color scheme and the quilt on the bed, Rose had discovered many similarities, like the collection of Agatha Christie mysteries lined up on the shelves and the rows of CDs above a small stereo system, many of which Rose also owned.

Rubbing her arms to banish the goose bumps, Rose turned at the sound of footsteps. Logan entered the room, carrying her two pieces of soft-sided black luggage. He placed them on the floor, then frowned at her.

"You all right?"

No, Rose wanted to say. I am *not* all right. I don't understand any of this, and I'm sorry I agreed to this charade.

Logan stepped toward her, stopping a scant two feet away. "Second thoughts?"

When Rose nodded, he gave her a tight smile. "Look, everything will go fine. Robert and Elise have left already, and I managed to get these up the stairs without Martina or Aunt Grace spotting me. Stash them out of sight, and no one will have any reason to question you. Okay?"

Rose decided this man must be very good at his job, for even though she wanted to run down the stairway into the street and hail the next car that passed, the quiet confidence in his hazel eyes had her nodding wordlessly. She was rewarded with a wide smile that went quite a ways toward warming away the chills she'd just experienced.

"Don't even think about hiding your bags under the bed," he continued. "A maid vacuums once a week, and unless she wants the wrath of Elise to come down on her, the woman doesn't miss one square inch of carpet. The closet, however, is another matter."

His smile twisted slightly as he gestured toward a set of louvered doors. "I learned that lesson from my own battle with Elise's obsessive neatness,'' he went on. ''Not being orderly by nature, I would just toss my things into the closet and shut the door. On cleaning day, however, I'd leave it open, hoping the maid would think it was her job to straighten it for me. No such luck.''

His half smile awoke a strong memory of a blond boy with a similar grin. Rose glanced at the picture of him as a young boy above the desk. Her lips started to curve, then froze as she realized she'd seen that same image long ago, in the dreams she'd had as a child. Another violent shiver shook her body. Logan's grin faded as he reached out to touch her shoulder.

''Look, everything will work out,'' he said. ''I have some business matters to see to right now, though. In the meantime, why don't you have a quick nap before you need to get ready?''

He turned to leave the room, stopped at the entrance, then swiveled back. ''You should wear Anna's clothes. So there's no point in unpacking your suitcase before you hide it. As for *that*—'' he pointed at the larger of the two bags ''—play it if you want, but make sure the door is locked first.''

''That'' was Rose's travel harp. When Logan first learned what the case held, he'd refused to allow her to take it into the Benedict house. Since Anna had absolutely no musical ability, and it was one of the few areas the young woman hadn't tried her hand at, he said that a harp in her room would be sure to raise suspicions.

Although Rose had been relieved to learn that *something* distinguished her from this person she so closely resembled, she'd informed Logan that the harp was a deal breaker. She made her living playing and teaching the instrument and needed to practice daily to maintain her skills.

At that point Logan had slipped once more into the role of negotiator. After studying her for a moment, he'd smiled slowly. Anna had a collection of harp music, he'd said. In fact, she played her CDs incessantly. So, if Rose locked the door when she was playing, anyone listening would think they were hearing one of Anna's discs.

"Don't worry," Rose told him now. "I'll hide it well."

Logan nodded, then frowned as if he was having trouble remembering what he wanted to say. Then his expression went blank, and his features revealed a bone-deep weariness.

"Jet lag?" Rose asked.

"It shows, huh? Well, I've survived worse. Anyway, we'll need to leave here by five-thirty, so be ready. Oh, and by the way, this affair is ultraformal. I'm sure Anna has something appropriate in there."

He of course meant the closet. After Logan stepped out of the room, closing the door behind him, Anna approached the half-open doors. She vaguely recalled Elise saying something about a dress that was to be delivered, but since nothing of the sort had been brought up to her room, Rose decided she might as well see what was available.

Folding the doors back, Rose stared at the eight-foot-square room filled with clothes and accessories. Item after item hung in neat, orderly rows from each of the rods lining the walls. Rose let her gaze sweep the area from right to left then back again, before taking a deep breath and releasing it with a whoosh. It seemed that the elusive Anna not only owned enough items to fill a small boutique, but all the various-colored shoes to match, resting now in neat pairs on racks beneath the clothes.

Well, Rose thought, at least nothing in *this* area bore any resemblance to the closet in her Seattle bedroom. Of course, those scant five linear feet were more than sufficient, considering the state her wardrobe had shrunk to over the past couple of years.

That was a matter of choice, Rose reminded herself as she spied a set of free-standing white shelves on her left, holding rows of purses and stacks of sweaters. Finding that with a little effort she could drag it forward to make room to hide her luggage, she pulled her suitcase and harp into the closet.

Actually, she'd *almost* owned this many clothes when she

was married to Josh, she thought as she stuffed her carry-on bag in the narrow space she'd created. And she could have taken all of them with her when the marriage ended. But by that point everything had been handpicked by her husband. When she considered that one of the more minor reasons she'd left the man had been his attempt to make her into his own little Stepford Wife, the idea of claiming the clothes as part of the divorce settlement had seemed just a little hypocritical.

Rose placed the harp on top of her carry-on case behind the shelves. After sliding over a floor-length garment bag to disguise the gap between the unit and the wall, she stepped back with a sigh and glanced at the racks of clothes again.

It sure seemed like a lot of stuff. And it wasn't the *stuff* she'd lost in the divorce that she missed. Her main regret was that the happy-ever-after bond she'd thought she was getting when she married Josh had turned out to be only an illusion— one of the many lessons she'd learned in the past two years. Like how much more important loved ones are than stuff.

From nowhere, tears filled Rose's eyes. She blinked them away furiously. She'd promised her mother she wouldn't do this. Promised to remember only the good things, to—

"Were you looking for this, Anna, dear?"

A soft, wavering voice broke the silence, making Rose jump and turn.

An elderly woman with snow-white hair stood just inside the bedroom door. Large, pale blue eyes stared from behind silver glasses. After a moment her thin lips softened into a cautious smile.

"Oh, I startled you, didn't I? I'm so sorry, but this was just delivered, and I thought you might be wondering where it was."

The woman lifted her arms to display a swath of cream-colored fabric encased in a film of clear plastic.

"The delivery boy said that the seamstress was very sorry it took so long to finish your dress." The woman's smile widened. "The fellow must have had dealings with Elise on some previous occasion, because he looked totally *terrified.* I told him she would never know. The gown is here on time for you to wear to your father's dinner, and that's good enough.''

Rose nodded slowly, wondering who this woman might be. Was she a member of the family? Or perhaps the maid Logan mentioned?

"Well..." Rose forced a smile. "Thank you for bringing it up to me."

She reached out to take the garment as she spoke, then held the hanger at arm's length to get a good look at the dress. The fabric was gorgeous, a long sweep of heavy ivory satin. The thick band of pearls sewn along the high neckline and edging the long sleeves were the epitome of understated elegance.

Rose fought off a shiver.

"Oh, that is going to look just *lovely* on you, my dear. I..." The woman paused. Her features grew tight as she went on in a conspiratorial tone that was just above a whisper. "I'm so glad you got home safely. I hope it wasn't something *I* said that got you in trouble. I know I'm not to talk about the...the other one...but sometimes I forget, and other times I just wish I could—"

The woman stopped speaking suddenly and shook her head. A second later she asked, "Do you want Aunt Grace to help you get ready?"

Aunt Grace, Rose thought. Of course. She remembered the photos on the wall and Logan telling her that Grace had been married to a man named Victor. Someone—Elise—mentioned that Victor had died not too long ago, and said something about Grace slipping into some sort of confused state from time to time.

Rose smiled and spoke slowly. "No, thank you. I'm sure I can manage on my own."

"Good." Grace released a satisfied sigh and her lips took on a wry twist. "Your father insists I attend this dinner to-night. I don't do this sort of thing very often anymore, you know, so I'll probably need the next few hours to get myself fitted out properly if I'm to be ready when Nicole and Chas call for me. But you let me know if you need to be zipped or anything.''

Rose found her smile widening in response to the genuine warmth in this woman's pale eyes. When she nodded and said, ''I will,'' Grace turned and left the room.

As soon as the door clicked shut, Rose turned a dubious look to the dress she still held, then hooked the hanger over the top of one of the closet doors. There was something about the garment that she found disturbing, but before she faced putting it on, she had a bath to take.

The walls of the bathroom were the same lavender shade as the bedroom, and the floor was tiled in white. The instant Rose laid eyes on the large oval whirlpool bath in the corner she felt some of the tension slip from her shoulders. In moments she had hot water running into a mixture of bath salts and bubble bath. After twisting her hair into a loose knot atop her head, she entered the tub, stretched out beneath the jasmine-scented bubbles and let the silken water soothe away the rest of her anxieties.

After all, she told herself, what was the point of finding yourself in a fairy-tale world if you didn't take advantage of the fantasy elements that came along with such a place? Especially when she'd only be here to enjoy these luxuries for a day.

It was almost forty-five minutes later when Rose reluctantly left the tub. Wearing the fluffy white robe she found hanging from a hook on the back of the door, she retrieved her makeup bag from her purse and returned to the bathroom to apply mascara and to add some color to her cheeks.

Her hair, she decided with a critical look in the mirror, had benefited from the steam. Her bangs waved softly to just above her eyebrows, and short tendrils had escaped the pile atop her head to twist down along her cheeks. As usual, it looked better haphazardly pinned up than if she'd spent hours fussing with it, so she decided to leave it as it was.

When she returned to the bedroom, she stared at the dress hanging from the door for several long moments before strip-

ping off the protective film. After stepping into the column of
satin and zipping it up, she turned to examine herself in the
full-length mirror located next to the closet.

"Oh, lovely," she said in a hollow mockery of Grace's
enthusiasm.

Lovely, that is, if she wanted to spend the evening in sheer
misery. The pearls at the high, tight neckline chafed and the
matching trim at the sleeves weighed her arms down. The
heavy satin felt tight everywhere although it only skimmed
her body, barely suggesting the curves beneath.

However, the dress *was* very proper looking. Very sedate.
Very boring.

Rose released a frustrated sigh as she studied her reflection.
She looked and felt like Dress-to-Impress Barbie, a role she'd
played more than once. And hated. In fact, she'd even worn
a similar dress to one of Josh's innumerable corporate functions. She'd spent the entire evening in constant fear that she
would drop a bite of food onto her lap and stain the ridicu-
lously expensive thing. It hadn't been a good time.

Rose's eyes narrowed as it occurred to her that she hadn't
had a good time in quite a while. Her mother would *not* approve.

Kathleen Delancey had made her daughter promise to live
life to the fullest, to take any opportunity that came along to
find joy. Well, Rose realized, a political dinner wasn't at the
top of her list of *fun* things to do, but if the quality of this
house and its furnishings were any indication, the function
would at least offer good food, good music and perhaps some
amusing dinner conversation.

But not in *this* dress.

Without a moment's hesitation, Rose slipped the dratted
thing off and placed it on its hanger. Aware that she now had
very little time to finish getting ready, she hung the garment
in the closet, then began to search for something else to wear.

She found at least two dozen formal gowns on the racks,
but nothing looked right. Not the pale-pink lace number, or
the ice-blue floor-length sheath. Certainly not the stark white

thing with the long tulle skirt—not unless she planned on dancing *Swan Lake*.

Aware of time ticking away, Rose rested a hand on yet another champagne-colored dress. It was sleeveless, and looked less rigidly formal than the first one. As she pulled it off the rack, however, something slid onto the floor. Something that puddled in supple folds of shimmering burgundy.

Hooking the beige number back on the rod, Rose bent to lift this intriguing bit of fabric. It felt light and soft to her fingers. Stretchy. Slinky, even. With her breath held still in her chest, Rose grasped the garment by the shoulders. Holding it up, she saw it was floor-length. The burgundy color, however, was an illusion. The gown was composed of two parts. The underdress was a slip of red with a long-sleeve overdress of fine, black net.

Without a moment's hesitation, Rose stepped into it, sliding her arms into the sheer wrist-length sleeves. She struggled with the zipper, but only managed to get it as far as her waist before she gave in to her curiosity and stepped out to study herself in the mirror.

It was perfect. The red slip fell from spaghetti straps to a fairly low scoop. This was made demure by the neckline of the nearly sheer black overdress, which ran in a straight line from shoulder to shoulder. The two fabrics glided together over her curves in smooth wash of burgundy with just enough stretch to promise that she'd be totally comfortable standing, sitting or even dancing.

Dancing.

Rose smiled. Lordy, she hadn't danced in…she couldn't remember. Would there be dancing at this thing? All indications were that the Benedicts weren't afraid to spend money, so the chances were quite good that a band—no, probably an orchestra—would be in attendance.

Stepping back into the closet, Rose headed for the jewelry box atop the dresser in the corner. There she found an appropriate pair of earrings—a single black oval bead to dangle from each earlobe. Searching the racks on the floor for an appropriate pair of shoes, she finally spied a slender black strap peeking from behind a pair of boring beige pumps, and fished out a pair of velvet sandals with heels that were spindly, but not *too* high to be comfortable.

She had just finished shifting a comb and lipstick from her large purse into the smaller black velvet clutch she'd appropriated from the closet shelf when she heard a knock. Hurrying to answer it, Rose realized she was slightly out of breath. When she opened the door to find a tuxedoed Logan Maguire standing in the hall, what little air she had left in her chest caught and froze there.

She'd forgotten what formal attire could do for a man. Even the most average-looking male grew better-looking in a tuxedo. Because she was in higher heels than she'd been wearing when she first met Logan, he didn't seem quite as overbearingly tall. But his shoulders looked even wider, his body more powerful.

Although his features were on the rough-hewn side, certainly lacking the perfection of a male model, Rose had already noticed that he couldn't be described as average, in any way. No, she thought. He was *ruggedly* handsome. Especially with that crooked smile. A smile, she realized, that had suddenly taken on a half-frozen appearance as he stared at her, as if he wanted to stop smiling but felt it would be impolite to do so.

Maybe it was the dress, she thought. Maybe she should have opted for sedate, for boring.

"Is something wrong?" she asked.

Chapter 6

*Is something *wrong?**

Logan stared at the woman before him. Good God, no. Nothing that he could see, anyway. The upsweep of Rose's hair accented the length of her neck, and the long wine-colored dress skimmed her lean curves nicely.

What *was* wrong was his response to her—the sudden rush of blood in his ears, the heavy pounding of his heart, the quick tightening of his loins. Not at all brotherlike. But, he reminded himself with a rush of relief, this woman might look like Anna—well, like some version of Anna that he'd never seen before—but she was a different person altogether. So his reaction was...acceptable. Sort of.

Still, if they were going to pull this charade off, nothing could appear out of the ordinary between them, such as him acting less than brotherly.

Or downright lustful.

Logan drew in a deep breath. *Get your mind on business,* he told himself. Out loud he said, "No. Everything's fine. But we need to discuss a few things while we drive to the hotel. You're ready to go, right?''

When Rose nodded, he frowned. ''Where's your coat? The fog has come in and it's damned cold outside.''

An expression that looked very much like defiance tightened Rose's features. Before Logan could apologize for his brusque tone, she turned toward the closet.

His attention was immediately drawn to the way her dress hugged the curves of her bottom before flaring to the floor, leaving his mouth too dry for speech. He blinked and found himself staring at the low-cut back that revealed so much creamy skin. He then noticed the black bra strap running across her back, and realized the waist-deep vee was not part of the dress's design.

Logan stepped forward just as Rose backed out of the closet. Placing his hands on her shoulders, he said, ''I don't think you finished zipping this thing.''

Her muscles tensed beneath his touch as she said, ''Oh, I forgot. I couldn't reach. Can you do it for me?''

Logan stared at the zipper. He had the oddest feeling that performing this simple act would cross some unseen line. Into what, he had no idea. *And,* he scolded himself, *you don't have the time to be worrying about such things. Just zip the damn thing, and get moving.*

''Just zipping'' proved to be not all that simple. First off, the tab he was supposed to pull was so slim that his large finger and thumb could barely grasp it. For another, when he finally managed to grip the slender wedge, the zipper refused to slide. Instead, the whole back of the dress moved upward, forcing Logan to place his left hand on Rose's lower back to hold the fabric in place.

He was unbelievably conscious of the tempting curve of her derriere just millimeters below his hand, but he concentrated on getting the zipper to draw the edges of the dress together. The moment it reached the neckline, Logan stepped back, breaking contact from the woman as quickly as he would a hot stove.

Clearing his throat, he barked out a quick, "Hand me the coat."

When Rose turned to him, her eyes were large, dark. Before he could determine whether they reflected some of the attraction he was feeling, she blinked. Her chest lifted with an audible intake of breath, and she wordlessly handed him a black velvet garment.

After helping her into the wrap, Logan stepped toward the door. His every muscle was aware of Rose, a scant two feet behind him, as he walked down the stairs, out the front door and into the foggy evening. The cool, moist air cleared his head, and by the time he had her in the passenger seat and was behind the wheel, the strange heat had dissipated, and he felt once more in control.

"All right," he said as he switched on the ignition, "somehow, between here and downtown, you and I are going to have to agree on how to handle things tonight. But before we go, I need to be sure that you're up to this."

He turned to Rose as the car roared to life. In the glow from the headlights he was just able to see her face. Her dark eyes glanced away uncertainly before meeting his, then her full lips twisted into a wry expression as she asked, "I got the impression I didn't have much of a choice."

Logan gave her a tight smile. "Of course you do. The fact that you got all dressed up indicates that you're planning on carrying this thing out, but if you're having second thoughts, I need to know now. With all the emphasis on family values in general and Benedict family traditions in particular, Anna's absence would likely raise some eyebrows, not to mention some questions. On the other hand, if you say or do the wrong thing, other questions would arise that might be more difficult to explain."

"Really. Is Robert's reputation in that precarious a position?"

Logan finished backing out of the driveway and headed down the street before replying. "There are no family skeletons, if that's what you mean. But we're talking about politics.

This race is tight and the primary is barely two weeks away, leaving Robert little time to reassure the voters before they go to the polls.''

He paused as he negotiated a turn. ''When Anna's brother, Chas, called to check on her—that is, you—I explained that although your memory is still a blank, I've convinced you that you *are* Anna Benedict, and that you owe it to your father to make an appearance at this thing to prevent any unfavorable rumors.''

''And he bought that?''

Logan shrugged. ''He knows I've been trained by the best.''

''Really.''

Logan detected a decidedly chilly tone to Rose's voice. Stopped at a red light, he glanced over to find her frowning at him.

''Quite used to getting your way, huh?'' she said.

''In business matters,'' he replied. ''And this *is* business.''

''Let me get this straight,'' she said. ''You were raised by the Benedicts and by your own admission you think of Anna as your sister. But this is *business?*''

Logan frowned. ''Right now it is. When I find Anna, then it will be personal. In the meantime, however, I owe it to Robert to do anything I can to help his campaign. And you've agreed to help me do that. Right?''

He held Rose's gaze until she released a tiny sigh.

''Right.'' She nodded. ''Well then. I guess you'd better tell me what you would like me to do and say. Oh, and the light just turned green.''

Logan gave his attention to the traffic as he spoke. ''Since the spotlight will be on your father tonight, you aren't expected to do much socializing. No one who knows you well expects that of you, anyway.''

''Oh. Am I—is Anna—terribly stuck up or something?''

Logan shook his head. ''She has this thing about crowds. They more or less terrify her.''

And the affair *would* be crowded, he went on. The evening would start with cocktails. People would mill about, walking up to them at random. He would attempt to tell Rose the name of anyone she should recognize before they approached, but in the case of surprise attack, she was to follow his lead. And she wasn't, for any reason, to go anywhere without him.

While Logan described some of the people she was likely to meet, Rose listened quietly. After the seventh name, they all began to sound alike, and she found herself in complete sympathy with Anna and her dread of crowds. Rose shivered slightly as the car pulled to a stop in front of the hotel. What had she been thinking of when she donned this dress, got all gussied up and imagined that this was going to be *fun?*

Had she forgotten those dreaded parties she'd attended with Josh? Those painful occasions where he'd led her over to a stranger, quietly explaining why this person was so damned important, why she should spend hours in their company even if he or she was a self-absorbed snob or an insufferable bore?

Yes, she realized as Logan opened her door and she swiveled to exit the car. She *had* forgotten. Her life, her thoughts and prayers during the past two years had all been focused on the most basic issues of life…and death. So it was completely understandable that the details of those parties had faded in her memory, leaving only the glitter behind.

Making her forget just how much she *hated* glitter.

And there was certainly a lot of *that* commodity here, Rose noted as she stood at the entrance to a huge ivory-trimmed-in-gold room. Glittering chandeliers lit a dressed-to-the-nines crowd. There were tuxedos for the men, with shiny black bow-ties, and shimmering gowns for the women. Glancing around the room, she saw a lot of black dresses, quite a few beige-toned numbers, some royal-blues and even a purple or two.

All very proper looking. Very sedate. Very everything that the dress she wore was not.

Rose's chest tightened and her face burned. She was out of place again, just as she had been at her senior prom, where all the other girls wore the most current off-the-rack styles, while she stood out in the vintage forties gown of pewter-gray satin she'd found at her favorite thrift store.

A sudden, intense panic gripped Rose, urging her to turn and run from the ball like Cinderella as the clock struck midnight. But just as she began to pivot, a large hand came to rest on the small of her back. A breath of warm air rushed past her ear and Logan's deep voice said, "Coming up, on the right is Lila Sanders—a very good friend of Elise."

Rose was so confused by her response to Logan's touch and the shivers raised by his intimate whisper that his words had barely sunk in before the woman in question stepped into view.

"Anna, darling!"

Rose tried not to make a sour face. The woman was tall and thin, dressed in a long purple sheath. Her black hair was slicked back into a low bun and her burgundy lips curved into a practiced, insincere smile that perfectly matched the tone of her *darling*.

Forcing herself to return the woman's smile, Rose replied, "Lila. How lovely you look tonight."

"Why, thank you," the woman simpered.

Rose had forgotten simpers. As far as she knew, normal people didn't simper. But during her courtship and marriage to Joshua Whitney she'd learned that an inordinate number of rich, upper-crustish sorts had mastered that delicate little squeeze of their smile. Perhaps it was something in the Perrier.

"And *your* gown," Lila went on, "is simply—stunning."

Stunning wasn't the word Lila wanted to use, Rose knew. The expression on the woman's face said *outrageously inappropriate*.

"Yes," she heard Logan reply. "She looks great, doesn't she?"

Lila's eyes widened up at him as she raised her eyebrows ever so slightly. "Elise picked it out?"

Logan shrugged. "I have no idea."

"I most certainly did not," a soft voice responded with a frigid undertone that sent a quick chill rushing up Rose's spine.

She turned to find Elise Benedict smiling. It was a cold

smile, tailor-made to go with the ice-blue satin of her dress and the glint of the tiny rhinestones that formed a delicate and very tasteful lattice design on the gown's bodice.

"Everyone knows, of course," Elise went on, her dark eyes holding Rose's, "that I love purchasing clothes for my daughter. But this gown is something Anna came home with last week, something I distinctly recall telling her to return."

Elise's tone implied deep disappointment. Rose felt a well of anger churn in her stomach. Anna was presumably near her own age, about halfway between twenty-five and twenty-six. At this point in life, *no one's* mother should be telling them what to wear, not even the most overprotected and spoiled of little rich girls.

Rose frowned. Somehow it didn't feel right to think of Anna in either of those terms. Perhaps Anna wasn't so much spoiled as ruled with an iron fist. And perhaps that fist needed to be forced open a tad.

"Funny," Rose said slowly, letting her brow pucker in confusion. "I don't recall any discussion regarding this dress. But then, I seem to have trouble remembering all sorts of things lately."

Elise's expression changed so abruptly, from narrow-eyed fury to wide-eyed consternation, that Rose almost laughed as the woman stuttered, "I...I, well, I suppose that's to be expected, with everything that's going on in our lives these days." She turned to Lila. "This campaign is quite intense, as you know. On top of that Anna is getting another degree."

"Oh?" Lila said with a lift of her brow as she turned to Rose. "And what do you plan to do with this one?"

This one? *Another* degree? Rose blinked. Nothing she'd seen in Anna's bedroom had given any indication that the young woman was a scholar—or gave any clue to her interests, beyond harp music and lots of clothes. Aware of the silence following Lila's question, Rose drew on her own experience and said, "Teach."

"Oh, really?" Lila replied with a quick frown. "I thought you already had—"

"Yes," Logan broke in. "She does have her teaching degree, but she wanted to get her masters before she started applying for positions. I keep telling her that she should just jump in, though. She's great with children. And speaking of kids, Anna, I see your friend, Rachel, over there. Didn't you tell me she just had a baby?"

Rose was conscious of his hand resting on her arm. She had no idea if he was making up the business about this Rachel person or not, but she glanced in the direction he'd indicated and said, "Yes. Ohh. I want to get to her before dinner and see if she has pictures."

"I'll go with you. I see Greg Tillis, and I need to speak to him for a few moments."

With that, Logan took her hand and began leading her through the crush of chattering cocktail imbibers. His grasp was firm yet gentle as he guided her toward a four-foot-thick column rising in the corner. When they reached this, he glanced around. His fingers tightened over hers, then he pulled her into the dimly lit area behind the column.

When he turned to stare down at her, Rose couldn't interpret his expression. His features seemed tight, as if he was barely able to control his emotions. Certain that she must have done something to make him furious, Rose spoke quickly.

"I'm sorry. I couldn't resist that crack about not remembering."

Logan's gaze held hers for several moments longer before his lips curved into a wide grin, and he began to laugh.

"You did just fine." He paused to shake his head. "Far better than Anna would have, actually. In the face of her mother's veiled disapproval, she would have turned around, gone home and changed."

Rose blinked, then stared at his wide smile—the one she remembered so clearly from her dreams. Feeling suddenly like a giddy, love-struck teenager, and fearing it showed, she glanced down at the fall of black-over-crimson dress.

"Well," she sighed. "This was probably not the wisest

choice to wear to a political gathering. I should have gone with the sedate ivory dress that Grace brought me.''

Logan gave her a half smile. ''Let me guess, a floor-length satin straitjacket?''

Rose grinned. ''Exactly. *But* I suppose it was…politically correct. I'm afraid I was more concerned with my own sense of style, not to mention comfort. I'm sorry. Maybe I *should* go home and change.''

Logan shook his head. ''You look fine. The dress certainly covers you well enough, although…''

As Logan paused, his gaze swept down her form before meeting her eyes again, making her aware of how the soft fabric clung to her body. The intense admiration in his features, so different from the lighthearted grins she recalled from her dreams brought instant heat to Rose's face.

''Although?'' she managed to ask.

Logan's sudden frown seemed to suggest he wasn't quite sure *what* he'd been about to say. Finally he shrugged. ''It just makes you really stand out in the crowd, which isn't something you would normally do.''

Rose wondered how he could know what she would do, then realized he was thinking of Anna.

''This might draw more attention to you than normal,'' he went on. ''So we have to be careful not to become separated. We can't have you 'winging it,' like you just did, and saying the wrong thing again.''

''I…take it that I'm not—that Anna isn't—studying to be a teacher?''

Logan shook his head. ''I don't know what she's back in school for this time, I'm afraid. Since Victor's death, I've been so absorbed in family business that you and I—that is, Anna and I—haven't spent much time together.''

Rose frowned. ''Victor—he was Grace's husband, right? And his place in all this?''

Logan sighed. ''We don't have time for family history class right now, but Victor was the glue that held the Benedict family together. He was responsible for looking after the family business so that his brother, Charles, could enter politics forty years ago, followed by Charles' son, Robert."

Rose followed this closely, doing her best to connect the names. "Robert," she said. "Anna's father."

"Tonight you have to think of him as *your* father," Logan said with soft force.

His rugged features had tightened. Gone was the warm, amused glint Rose had seen in his eyes only moments earlier. His gaze held hers with a quiet intensity that made her want to reach up, place her hand along his cheek and ease away the worry etched there, to rise on tiptoe and kiss the tight line of his lips, make them soften and smile once more, as they did in her dreams.

She couldn't do that, of course. With a quick, indrawn breath, Rose took one step back and said, "Well, I guess it doesn't really matter if I know all this. If the real Anna had amnesia, she wouldn't remember, either."

"True, but the amnesia story is only for the family. We want everyone else here to think Anna is just fine. That's why you need to stay with me."

Logan took her hand again as he stepped out of the shadows. "Dinner will be served soon," he said. "Only family will be at our table, so we should be safe there."

Safe, Logan thought. There he went again, on his mission to protect the Benedicts. And Anna. But what about *this* young woman? He glanced at Rose as he led her to the banquet room, where already a scattering of people had come to locate their dinner tables.

However, tonight he was more than a little concerned about his own safety. Or should he say sanity? Since the moment Rose Delancey had turned to him on the veranda, she'd brought out something unpredictable in him, some wild part that wanted to break free of the carefully crafted control he'd nurtured since becoming an unofficial Benedict.

And that was crazy. After all, he'd learned long ago to play by Benedict rules. Not that the lessons had been easy to master, considering the life he'd led prior to the accident that killed his parents. Tom and Brenda Maguire had used every spare moment between serving the Benedicts in their respective capacities of mechanic and cook in the pursuit of fun.

But "upstairs" in the Benedicts' world, he'd learned not to run in the house or play the "wrong" sort of music, not to laugh too loud or too long. And after the accident that took his parents' lives, the Benedicts had expected him to concentrate on improving his mind in preparation for service to the family in a much higher capacity.

It had been a very long time since he'd felt even a bit of rebellion—the secret desire to run away and find a home where people laughed. And there was something about Rose that brought those feelings back. Maybe, he thought as he glanced at her, it was because he was asking her to play a role, a role not unlike the one he'd learned to play so very long ago.

And Rose was doing quite well, he noticed. She barely glanced at the sumptuous surroundings as she followed close behind. It was almost as if she were accustomed to all the glitter and glamour, and not just a simple music teacher.

"Do you have everything under control?"

Logan recognized Chas's low, conspiratorial voice. His fingers automatically tightened over Rose's as he turned to Anna's biological brother.

Charles Francis Benedict II had his mother's blond hair and his father's warm-brown eyes. In every other respect Chas resembled the grandfather he'd been named for, with his square, boyish features and charismatic smile—a smile that was a little stiff at the moment.

"Yes," Logan replied in a low tone. "Anna's doing fine."

Chas turned a wide smile to Rose, then whispered, "Glad to hear it, squeaks."

When Logan saw Rose's eyebrows scrunch in puzzlement, he leaned toward her and said softly, "This is your brother, Chas."

"She...she still doesn't remember?"

Logan straightened and forced a smile as he shook his head. "No. But don't frown so. Everything's going smoothly."

Chas's practiced smile returned immediately, but his eyes darkened as he asked, "Are you sure she should be here? Mother said that Dr. Alcott—"

Logan cut Chas off with a quick shake of his head. "She'll be fine. And your father's campaign dinner will be fine, too, just as long as we keep our cool."

Chas glanced at Anna again before giving Logan a quick nod. "Well then," he said in a hearty voice, "why don't the two of you keep Aunt Grace and Nicole company while I circulate a bit. I'll join you as soon as Mother and Father make their way to the table."

He stepped away the moment he finished speaking. Logan watched Chas make his way through the tables, pausing here and there to pat the mayor on the back, shake hands with a city councilwoman.

"He does that well," he heard Rose say.

Logan turned to her, a smile touching his lips. "Yes. Chas is just like his grandfather—a natural at glad-handing."

"Is he a politician, too?"

Logan glanced around. No one was close enough to have heard her question, but he thought it prudent to steer her toward the family table as he replied softly, "Not yet. Right now he's in charge of his father's campaign. Once Robert makes it to the U.S. Senate, Chas will run for local office, just as Robert followed Charles."

Rose continued to watch Chas. "Does he have a choice, or does he *want* to do this?"

Logan leaned closer to her and whispered, "I'll explain more of the family dynamics later. For now just play the part of dutiful daughter, all right?"

As they reached the table he saw Rose shiver ever so slightly. Her eyes were dark with an emotion that looked very close to pain as she glanced up at him. Then she took a deep breath, nodded and lowered herself to the chair Logan had pulled out.

Grace and Nicole were already seated at the table. He concentrated his attention on the older woman. Grace wore a dress of mauve satin with a matching jacket. Logan took the seat between her and Anna, then noticed that the older woman was continuing to stare at the arrangement of pink calla lilies in the center of the table. He leaned toward her.

"Aunt Grace?"

When the woman blinked and turned to him, Logan smiled and said, "You look lovely tonight."

Grace's pale blue eyes gazed at him blankly for such a long moment that his heart sank. Not one of *those* nights, he thought. It was going to be difficult enough watching out for Rose, without worrying about what strange thing Victor's widow might blurt out.

"Oh, Logan," Grace said on an indrawn breath. "I'm sorry. I was just thinking how little things have changed, even with Victor gone. I don't think I've attended a political function in the past forty years where I didn't find myself sitting all alone while my husband hurried around, making sure everything was running smoothly."

Before Logan could reply, a soft voice chided, "Well, Aunt Grace, now Chas is doing the bustling about, abandoning *his* future wife. You'll have to teach me how to handle this."

When Grace turned to the young woman seated on her right, Logan was forced to look at Nicole Cummings. She looked cool and elegant, as usual. The pearls shimmering at the neckline of her sleeveless champagne-colored dress and the pale blond hair swept atop her head emphasized the length of her slender neck. Nicole's opal-green eyes met and held Logan's for a moment, then slid to his left.

"Anna," she said. "Feeling better after your little *adventure,* I hope?"

A glance at Rose's narrowed eyes warned Logan that she wasn't amused by Nicole's slightly tart undertone. Neither was he. Turning to the elegant blonde, he forced his lips into a flat smile that was meant solely for anyone who might be watching as he leaned toward her.

"Cool it, Nikki," he said. "She has no idea what you're referring to tonight, so she can't fight back."

Nicole returned his smile. "So? Anna has always lived in her own world. And she never fights back. When she's not happy with a situation, she just runs away."

Even though Anna wasn't there to hear these words, Logan felt the instinctual urge to defend her. But before he could come up with an appropriate response, Aunt Grace spoke.

"Anna, dear. That isn't the dress I brought up to you earlier today, is it? Oh, I do hope that I didn't add to your problem, confuse you with anything I said. This afternoon *or* the other day when I showed you that—"

Grace shut her mouth abruptly and looked down at her lap. Logan was just about to say something when Rose surprised him by reaching across him to touch the older woman's hand.

"No," she said warmly. "You didn't confuse me at all. That gown didn't suit me, so I chose this one. And it's just as well. The dress you brought up had long sleeves, but otherwise it was almost identical to the one that…"

She paused, then shifted her attention to the woman next to Grace before whispering, "What is your name?"

"Nicole," came the soft, terse reply. "Nicole Cummings. Chas's fiancée."

Rose's eyebrows lifted ever so slightly before she went on, "It was so very much like the one Nicole is wearing that we would have looked like twins. And the gown really looks so much better on her." She smiled at Nicole. "The Ice Princess look suits you to a T."

Chapter 7

"I'm sorry," Rose said softly.

Logan shot her a sharp look as he led her toward the ballroom. The after-dinner speeches had ended, and he was prepared to hold up Benedict tradition, which required family members take to the dance floor to get that part of the evening started.

"You did a very good job," Logan replied in a low voice. "No one has a clue that you aren't Anna."

She gave him a wry grimace. "That's the problem. When Anna gets back, she's going to have to deal with Nicole, and she'll have no idea why the woman is angry at her."

"Oh, that." Logan grinned as he recalled Nicole's restrained fury in the wake of Rose's "Ice Princess" comment. As the band began to play "Getting to Know You," he pulled Rose into his arms and said, "Not to worry. It's not like they got along before."

"Really? Why am I not surprised?"

Logan found himself smiling as he guided Rose around the

dance floor. "Well, actually, they *sort of* got along when I was first dating Nicole."

"*You* were dating her?"

"Yep. Over a year ago. Classic story. Guy reaches his mid-thirties, decides it's time to settle down, falls in love with a beautiful woman who seems completely besotted with him, asks her to marry him, brings her home to meet the family, only to have her decide she'd rather marry the younger brother, three weeks before the marriage."

Younger brother and true heir to the Benedict legacy, he ended silently.

"Witch," Rose uttered in a soft undertone.

Logan laughed, then nodded. "Yes, she is. And for a while what she did hurt like hell. But time not only heals all wounds, it opens lovesick eyes. I count myself quite lucky to have escaped a soulless marriage."

Rose gazed up at him for a long moment, her eyes dark and warm, her lips a soft red as they twisted into a smile. "I couldn't have said it better myself," she said.

She broke eye contact for a moment, then, as if suddenly regretting her words, she glanced at the tuxedoed orchestra and back to Logan as he pulled her into a quick twirl.

"*You* are a very good dancer," she said.

Logan lifted his eyebrows in surprise. He'd never considered himself particularly good at this activity. Elise had insisted he take lessons when she sent Chas, but since graduating from college, he only danced when forced to. It seemed too intimate an enterprise for public consumption, for one thing.

Like tonight. He was acutely aware of the woman he held in his arms, the warmth of her hand in his, the heat building between his palm and the small of her back, the way she brushed against him as they moved. And, for the first time that day, Logan didn't automatically recoil from thinking about this woman in a less-than-brotherly fashion. After all, this wasn't Anna in his arms. It was Rose—a woman he'd only just met, but with whom he'd already argued and laughed, formulated a plan that seemed to be working well and with whom he felt far more comfortable than he'd felt since…

Since losing his parents and becoming a Benedict.

"Am I doing it wrong?"

Rose's question brought Logan back to the present, making him once again aware of the rhythm of her body moving with his.

"Are you doing what wrong?" he asked.

"The dance," Rose responded. "You looked suddenly as if you were in pain. I thought maybe I'd stepped on your toe or something."

"No," he said. "You're very good, too. Where did you learn?"

Her smile faded, her body stiffened in his arms as she replied, "My ex-husband sent me for lessons."

Logan lifted one eyebrow. Rose smiled tightly before going on, "Well, actually, we were engaged at the time. The dancing lessons were all part of a general curriculum to make me acceptable to his family. I lacked—I believe the words his mother used were—'the proper polish.'"

This sounded uncomfortably familiar to Logan. His first date with Nicole was to have been a political dinner, much like this one. She'd begged off, saying she didn't own the right sort of clothes. He'd taken her shopping, then continued to provide her wardrobe whenever she felt she would be "underdressed" or unable to provide the "proper image."

A sudden tightness in his jaw reminded Logan that a few things from that relationship still rankled. Or perhaps what he was feeling was an early-warning system, hinting that Rose and Nicole might be similar.

"I see," he said dryly. "So you got all *polished up,* got him to marry you. Sounds like a lot of work to go through, only to turn around and leave him."

As Logan pulled Rose into another turn, he saw her eyes narrow. "I had my reasons," she replied tightly.

"Good ones, I'm sure."

"Yeah." Rose lifted her chin. "Very good ones. I came to

see that in the long run, I was never going to be what Josh wanted. Oh, I managed the transformation from sow's ear to silk purse, and I won't pretend I didn't enjoy the nice clothes and large house that came along with that. Or the doors that opened for me professionally.''

"Professionally?" Logan prodded.

Rose nodded. "I was teaching school during the day when we met and playing harp on weekends at supper clubs. When the position of harpist with the Seattle Symphony became available, Josh's contacts made it possible for me to get the job I'd been dreaming of all my life." She paused and sighed. "So I suppose his anger was understandable when I gave my notice."

"You quit your dream job? Why?"

Logan's incredulous tone brought back every bit of the frustration and anger Rose had felt two years ago. Her muscles tightened as she met his gaze.

"My mother had been diagnosed with an inoperable brain tumor," she responded flatly. "The doctors said that chemotherapy would shrink the tumor, but would only delay the inevitable. Josh's way of handling my grief was to suggest I put Mom into a critical-care facility—the best that money could buy, of course—then go about my life as an ornament on his arm, making time between corporate functions for an occasional visit with her."

Her eyes narrowed as she went on. "When I told him I intended to spend as much time with my mother as possible, he was furious. Deciding it was unfair of me to put such a crimp in his social and business life, I offered to divorce him. He seemed quite relieved and wasted no time taking me up on my offer."

The music ended as Rose finished speaking. When she tried to step away from Logan, his fingers continued to curve around her fingers, and his arm tightened around her waist.

"I'm sorry," he said.

Somehow she knew that he wasn't talking about the divorce. At her mother's wake, friends and neighbors had offered sincere sympathy, but in Logan's eyes she saw that rarer quality—empathy.

Of course, she thought. He'd been orphaned at ten. He probably knew exactly how much pain she was feeling.

For some reason his silent compassion opened the barrier she'd placed around her heart. With breathtaking swiftness the grief Rose had buried in accordance with her mother's last wishes suddenly flared like a hot flame in her chest, burning upward to curl into a choking knot in her throat. Tears sprang to her eyes, and the flood of moisture blurred her vision, making her blink furiously, as if her eyelids could beat the tears back.

"I think it's time we got out of here," she heard Logan say as he released her waist.

Rose managed to nod, then choked out. "I left my purse at the table."

"Wait here. I'll get it for you."

"No." Rose shook her head. "Anna wouldn't leave without saying goodbye. I'll be okay. Really."

Logan's fingers continued to hold hers as he led her off the dance floor. Rose blinked as she walked, and repeatedly drew in deep breaths which she forcefully released in an attempt to gain control over her emotions. By the time they reached the table, the film of tears had dried. Only three people were sitting there. Grace, once more staring at the centerpiece, and Robert, deep in conversation with another tuxedoed man.

Robert looked up and said, "Well, perfect timing. Logan, this is Sam Lightner. He's a local contractor who has some surplus building supplies for that new shelter. I was just telling him you were the man to talk to."

Logan gave Lightner a wide smile as he shook the man's hand. "Pleased to meet you. I was just getting ready to leave, but I'd be more than happy to speak to you about the matter...say somewhere in the middle of the week?"

Robert interrupted just as the man nodded. "Logan, we have time now, don't we?"

Logan hesitated, then shook his head. "I need to take Anna home now. The strain of the evening is wearing on her."

Robert looked at Rose, his expression instantly one of concern. "Of course," he said with a warm smile. "You get a good night's rest, hon."

As Rose nodded she heard Logan say, "Good night, Aunt Grace. I did tell you that you look wonderful tonight, didn't I?"

Grace blinked, then glanced down at her mauve dress before looking up at Logan. "Yes, you did. Thank you so much. Would you like me to go home with you now, and see to it that our Annie gets to bed?"

Logan shook his head. "You hate the way my Mustang rides, remember? Besides, you haven't finished your cake."

"Oh, yes I have." A blush accompanied Grace's smile as she glanced at the remainder of the dessert in front of her. "This is my second slice."

"Well, you deserve it." Logan straightened. "You know what they say, 'Sweets for the sweet.'"

Grinning widely in response to Grace's, "Oh, you," Logan took Rose's purse from the table, handed it to her and said softly, "Let's get out of here before anyone else wants to trap us in conversation."

Rose fought the exhaustion that had suddenly taken possession of her body and managed a nod. Instantly Logan placed a supporting hand beneath her elbow and led her toward the cloakroom.

The night was thick with fog when they stepped to the covered valet parking area to wait for Logan's car. The chill in the air immediately penetrated the velvet coat, making Rose shiver and reviving her a little.

She turned to Logan. "You know, if you feel you should stay, you can put me in a cab. I'm assuming a maid or someone would let me in the house."

Logan shook his head. "I'm not in any shape to discuss the details of charitable donations and their political implications right now. All the coffee I've swilled to keep me awake and my untreated jet lag is taking over big-time. Besides, I don't really like these shindigs much.''

''Then, why do you do it?''

Logan turned to her with a puzzled frown. ''Do what?''

''The job.''

He was silent for a moment before replying, ''Because I'm good at it, of course. And it's what I was trained for. It's…who I am.''

It was Rose's turn to frown. ''But do you *like* it?''

Logan pulled his gaze away from her to scowl down the street as he shrugged. ''Most of the time. It certainly has its moments.'' As the red Mustang with its black top pulled up, Logan turned to her with what looked like a forced smile and went on in a determinedly lighter tone. ''As well as its perks. The wherewithal to keep a vintage auto in good repair, for example.''

He turned as the young valet got out, exchanged a rolled-up bill for the keys, then turned to Rose with a mock bow and a flourish, saying, ''Your pumpkin awaits.''

Rose couldn't help but smile as she got into the car. Leaning her head against the seat, she stretched her legs out as Logan pulled away. She was aware that Logan really hadn't explained what he liked about his job. Of course, she told herself, this was really none of her business. But if she didn't want to fall asleep, she had to talk about something.

Trying to come up with a safe subject, Rose studied the hood of the car, where the overhead lights painted white streaks on the shiny red surface.

''You did a beautiful job restoring this car,'' she said. ''When did you find the time?''

A wry smile twisted Logan's lips. ''Well, not recently, I can tell you,'' he replied. ''I fixed it up years ago when I was a kid.''

''Looks like pretty advanced work for a *kid*.''

He glanced over, his smile now soft, warm. ''Well, I had a good teacher. Besides, I didn't do all the work myself.''

Rose lifted her eyebrows in a silent question. Logan returned his attention to the road. He seemed to hesitate before he spoke.

"When I was eight my father found this in a junkyard. It was pretty smashed up, but it was a '65—made the year I was born. Dad figured it would be something the two of us could work on together. The plan was to restore it and get me trained as a mechanic by the time I turned sixteen."

He paused. The car roared to a halt at a stop sign. Rose spoke softly over the idling of the engine. "He died when you were ten, right?"

Logan nodded, then shifted into first and sent the car forward. "Yes, but by then Dad had replaced the smashed fender and hood, as well as pulled out the dents in the doors. He'd taught me to sand the metal down, and we'd primered the bare spots. So the car was well on its way when…"

He paused, then took a deep, slow breath before he spoke again.

"Charles was so busy once he won his seat in the Senate that he decided to sell off his collection. Without my dad to guide my attempts to restore the Mustang, it sat in the far corner of the garage until my sophomore year of high school, when I was able to get into auto shop class. I made the car my class project and finished it three days before I turned sixteen. Got an A, too."

Rose thought she saw a flash of moisture in Logan's eye. He turned his head away to look out his window at that point. Seconds later, when he was once more staring forward, the suspicious glimmer was gone.

But Rose was sure she could sense his pain. And it didn't take much insight to recognize the same ploy she used whenever her grief threatened to surface. Respecting his privacy, and unable to force her weary mind to think of a safe topic, she remained silent.

As the car turned off Geary and onto Sea Cliff Drive, Rose saw Logan reach for the remote control device. By the time they angled into the driveway of the Benedict residence, the left-hand garage door was already opening. Logan pulled in, switched off the engine, then turned to her with a smile.

"Well, Cinderella," he said. "Your coach has arrived. And look. It's past midnight, and you're still in your finery."

The teasing glint in his eyes made Rose wonder if she'd imagined that other, sadder glimmer. More likely that was what he wanted her to believe. Either way she thought it best to play along.

"My *borrowed* finery," she said with a lift of her eyebrow. "Mine only until the real princess returns and banishes me, sending me back to my humble abode."

Logan shook his head. "Anna's not the banishing sort."

He slid from behind the wheel. Rose pulled on the passenger door's handle and pushed it gently open. By the time she stepped out of the car, Logan had reached her side and her thoughts had moved on to the reason she was here, in this garage, with this enigmatic man.

"You said that Anna is unpredictable," she said. "Would she be the sort to run off completely?"

"She left twice before," Logan replied. He took Rose's hand to lead her through the garage, dark now that the door had slid shut. "And she always called to let me know she was all right. By the way, while you were getting dressed, I did some checking. There hasn't been any activity on her credit cards for the past few days, but there was a large ATM withdrawal from her account yesterday."

They were inside the house now, walking up a curving stairway to the second floor. "I have a detective friend of mine checking out the location of the ATM. I'm hoping this won't be necessary—that she'll call me tomorrow."

Rose nodded as they began mounting the stairs leading to the third floor. "That would be good," she said.

"Yes," Logan said as they reached the door to her—to Anna's—room. "Then you can go back to being yourself."

"Yes," Rose said with a little smile. "Though, really, playing Cinderella-at-the-ball hasn't been all that bad."

Especially with you *in the role of prince.*

The thought, which flitted so quickly through her mind, thoroughly scandalized Rose. Terrified it might somehow have been communicated through the half-light of the hallway, she turned to grab the doorknob, planning a quick escape.

Almost simultaneously Logan's hand closed over hers. Her gaze shifted to his eyes. Staring into them, she noticed the artistic blending of green and brown, and saw that the fine lines fanning from the corners were suddenly growing deeper.

He was smiling, she realized with a blink. His lips were curving into a bemused grin as his fingers curled around hers, drawing her hand away from the doorknob, then lifting it to the empty space between them. She watched, mesmerized, as he bent to place a butterfly-light kiss on the back of her hand.

How such a tentative touch could elicit such a strong current of energy, tingling up her arm and creating a vibration that resonated deep in her stomach and trembled upon her lips, was a complete mystery to Rose. Perhaps it was because she'd dreamed of this man's face so often, imagined his lips touching hers so many times.

"Good night, princess."

The teasing note in Logan's deep voice, accompanied by that half smile of his, broke the spell that had held Rose breathless. Forcing a bright smile to her lips, she managed to reply lightly, "I suppose the proper response would be, 'Good night, sweet prince.'"

Still holding her hand, Logan smiled even wider. It seemed to Rose that the air between them grew thicker, warmer, more condensed, as if the world around them was suddenly shrinking. As she watched Logan's grin slowly fade, a mixture of apprehension and anticipation stole the smile from her lips.

When his eyes appeared to darken and his head bent toward hers, Rose had no doubts regarding his intent. And even though a voice in her mind whispered that this man was barely more than a stranger, someone she'd known less than a day, Rose found herself breathless to think that he was going to kiss her.

And so she parted her lips in welcome.

It was a magical kiss, not unlike the phantom ones she'd conjured in her imagination after waking from dreaming of this man's smile. His mouth brushed hers gently, then hesitated, lips holding lips in a soft yet firm manner that hinted of understated desire.

Then abruptly the kiss ended.

Realizing that she'd shut her eyes, Rose forced them open just as Logan stepped back. He released her hand, and his lips seemed to struggle into a casual grin.

Rose dredged up what she hoped looked like a relaxed smile as she fumbled to grasp the doorknob. This time she gave it a quick twist. When the door opened, she said, as lightly as her suddenly tight throat would allow, "Good night, Logan."

Stepping swiftly inside, she shut the door with a decided click, then stood gripping the inside knob as she shook her head. What an idiot she was. This was no dream. It was a bizarre, twisted sort of reality in which she was playing a role. A *temporary* role, she reminded herself.

Anna would be back soon, probably the following day. And although Logan insisted that his feelings for the woman were brotherly, several things had happened in the space of the past twelve hours that spoke against this—like the unmistakable male arousal she'd felt as his body lay atop hers when they first met, not to mention the tenderness in the kiss they'd just shared.

And whether Logan was willing to admit this or not, it was almost certain that both were a reaction to *Anna,* not to a stranger named Rose.

Secondhand Rose.

Her high school nickname taunted as Rose reached back to tug at the zipper of her dress—Anna's dress, she reminded herself with silent fury. She couldn't allow those insane recurring dreams to fool her into thinking that Logan had been kissing Rose Delancey. That would only lead to disappointment. And she had too much pain stored in her aching heart as it was.

After carefully hanging the garment where she'd found it,

Rose considered getting her luggage out and putting her own pajamas on. But she had no idea if one of Anna's parents might check on their "wayward daughter" during the night, so she opened drawers in the tall dresser tucked into the corner of the closet. Upon finding a stack of nightclothes, she pulled out a gown made of pink cotton knit and pulled it over her head. Before she went to sleep, however, she wanted something to remind her who Rose Delancey was—needed to bring something of hers into this demented, looking-glass world.

She felt behind the shelf unit for her harp case and drew it out. Pausing to lock the door, she carried the instrument to the bed and sat down. After removing the harp from its case, she balanced the base on one thigh and rested the top against her shoulder.

Her fingers plucked the strings, making music of their own accord. Rose allowed the melodic tune to soothe her taut nerves until the breath moved freely in her chest once again and her muscles began to soften. Only then was she ready to place the harp back in its hiding place and turn to the bed with the strange-yet-familiar quilt. She drew it from the foot of the bed as she slid beneath the covers.

Lying on her back, she floated on the feather bed. The aqua duvet covered a down comforter, which quickly warmed her body. With her head propped up on several pillows, she stared across the darkened room and out the large glass door at the barely visible lights of the Golden Gate Bridge rising and falling within the shroud of nighttime fog until sleep claimed her.

Rose came awake gradually. Lying on her side, she stared at the yellow and pink flowers appliquéd onto the turquoise and purple squares beneath her hand for several seconds, drowsily recalling the previous night's dream in which she had stared over familiar rooftops at Seattle's Space Needle and the city's skyline beyond.

Those images blended with another dream in which she had found the bridge and the man she'd visualized so often before.

With a start, Rose sat up and looked around the room.

Lavender walls, just like home. But this wasn't home. Nor had the previous day or evening been a dream, she realized. When she glanced at the bedside table, the clock told her it was just after six in the morning. Did Anna rise this early? Or was she the sort to sleep till noon? And what about breakfast? Would Anna get up and make her own, or was there a cook to prepare meals, as there had been in the Whitney house?

She supposed she could try to go back to sleep. Or sit and wait until Logan knocked on her door and gave her the day's instruction. Both choices made her lip curl in disfavor. She was too awake to reclaim sleep and too antsy to simply sit, waiting for anyone to tell her what to do.

Rose got out of bed and walked toward the sliding glass door. Not one hint of yesterday's storm nor a shred of last night's fog marred the clear blue sky above the orange bridge. Sun sparkled on the green sea as it curled onto the beach, and suddenly she knew just how she wanted to pass her morning.

In her search for something to wear to bed, Rose had spotted a drawer full of T-shirts and shorts. Turning to the closet, she retrieved one of each, then opened another drawer, full of neatly folded underwear. Rose shut it decisively. She drew the line at wearing someone else's intimates. After retrieving her suitcase and pulling out some of her own underthings, she returned the luggage and her harp to their spots behind the shelf before taking a quick shower and pulling on a pink T-shirt and matching knit shorts. Too anxious to get outside to bother braiding her hair, she ran a brush through the wavy mass to get rid of the worst of the tangles. She didn't bother with shoes, but she did grab a hooded gray sweatshirt she'd found folded on one of the closet shelves.

Rose was glad for the sweatshirt when she stepped onto the deck outside her room, into the chill morning air. She slipped her arms into the sleeves as she moved toward the iron gate. Her bare feet made little noise on the metal steps of the circular staircase. When she reached the tile veranda, she saw a break in the line of brick planters lining its edge, then headed for the opening she assumed led to the cement stairway she'd noticed the day before.

The steps were cold beneath her feet as she took them down a twisting path along the cliff. The sand on the beach was not much warmer, but it was soft, cushioning her feet as she stood deciding which way she wanted to walk. On her left the beach curved beneath the cliff that supported a row of houses, each with their own set of steps leading downward.

To her right a wide swath of sand stretched toward another cliff, and the southern tower of the Golden Gate Bridge. That was the direction she chose, walking along the edge of the water, with absolutely no plan in mind. She only knew that the rhythm of the surf crashing onto the shore on her left, then whispering up and down the damp sand, energized her, much like the music of her harp had soothed her the night before.

Each time her mind started to touch on the subject of Anna Benedict, to wonder how this woman could possibly resemble Rose Delancey so closely, how they could decorate so similarly and yet have such different taste in clothes, how she had come to dream about the view from Anna's window, or more specifically, about a certain man in Anna's life, Rose's muscles tightened. She knew how unlikely it was for two people to look so much alike, but any explanation carried such ugly implications that she immediately turned the thoughts away. She'd heard somewhere that everyone had a double someplace, and Anna must be hers.

Rose concentrated on the music of the sea, on the raucous song of the seagulls wheeling overhead, on the damp sand beneath her feet, until she had cleared her body and mind of the heavy weight that seemed to have seeped into her pores as she slept in Anna's bed.

When Rose finally pulled her attention to her surroundings, she noticed an asphalt parking lot that edged the beach on her right. She stopped to gaze at the grassy area rising behind it, where large cypress trees shaded picnic benches, then realized she was hungry. Hungry enough to turn back.

She walked more briskly on the return trip, and was slightly out of breath as she neared the Benedicts' cement stairway. Lifting her head from her study of the twisted driftwood littering the sand, she was surprised to see Logan walking toward her. He wore a light denim shirt, faded jeans and a dark expression.

Chapter 8

"Something's wrong," Rose said as Logan reached her.

He nodded. "Anna called."

Rose frowned. "If Anna called, how could anything be wrong? Is she in trouble?"

"I don't know." Logan shook his head and released a frustrated-sounding sigh. "I blew it. When my cell phone rang early this morning, it woke me from a dead sleep. I was so groggy I could hardly think straight. When I heard Anna's voice, the first thing I did was tell her how much she'd upset everyone by running off. Then I asked where the hell she was. She said something about wanting me to fly her somewhere, then stopped abruptly and said never mind, she didn't want me to stop her from…"

Logan paused and shook his head again before he went on. "She never finished that sentence. She just said she'd call again when she had all the answers and knew who she could trust. Before I could say another word, she hung up."

His features took on an expression of disgust as he finished, "So much for my well-touted *persuasive* powers."

Rose placed a hand on his arm. "Hey. Like you said, you were hardly awake." She paused before asking, "Is there some way you can trace the call?"

"Possibly," Logan replied with a quick nod. "I called the private detective who checked out the ATM for me. When I told Matt that the call came in on my cell phone, he said it might be traceable, but it would take some time. In the meantime he suggested I check the caller ID record on my home phone, where Anna left those other two messages. I did that. In fact, I just got back from my condo, where I relayed those numbers to Matt. He'll call me as soon as he learns anything."

When Logan paused, he stared deeply into Rose's eyes. "There's something else we need to talk about."

Conscious of Logan's intense gaze and aware of the deep rumble of his voice, Rose felt herself grow suddenly hot, flushed with shame. Oh, Lord, she thought. He's going to talk about that kiss—tell me that what happened the evening before had made him aware that his feelings for Anna Benedict were no longer those of a big brother.

"Before I left my condo," he said, "I received another call."

Rose blinked. This wasn't what she'd expected to hear at all. "Oh?" she managed.

Logan touched her arm. "It was from Dennis—about the DNA tests he ran on the strands of hair from Anna's brush and the sample he took of yours." He paused before saying, "They match."

Rose stared at Logan for several moments as her mind struggled to make sense of this information.

"That's impossible," she said at last. "Yesterday Dennis said that the two sets of fingerprints proved that Anna and I are two different people. I promise you, I *am* Rose Delan—"

Logan placed his palm over her mouth as he said, "Quiet. The wind can blow the sound of voices right up to the house. Now listen, no one is claiming that you and Anna are one and the same. But Dennis says you *are* twins. *Identical* twins."

Rose couldn't have been more stunned if Logan had told her that she was the Queen of England's lost-at-birth daughter.

"That can't be," she said quietly.

"It *is*." Logan spoke just as softly. His gaze was warm with concern as he went on. "And it makes sense, when you think about it. I wondered how two unrelated people could look so very much alike. Your complexion is much paler than Anna's, but living in Seattle means you've been exposed to less sun. You're also the slightest bit thinner and there's something in your eyes, a sadness, a depth, a *something* that I've never seen in Anna's." He paused. "Perhaps because you've so recently experienced a loss."

He was referring to her mother, Rose knew. Her *mother,* she thought, then shook her head.

"No. It's just not possible." Her eyes narrowed. "That would mean my mother gave Anna up for adoption. She would never do such a thing."

Logan held her gaze for several moments before saying, "Rose, that's not the only possible scenario. Each of you could have been adopted by different families. Your mother might not have known you had a twin."

He watched Rose carefully. Her dark-blue eyes grew even darker. Slowly she began to shake her head, but her expression told him she was considering the possibility, perhaps adding up all the similarities that existed between the two women, just as he had.

"Mom wouldn't lie," he heard her breathe. "She never lied to me. She would have told me if...if..."

As her voice trailed off, Logan saw her face go blank. Some instinct sent his hands flying forward to catch her even as her knees buckled. Then he pulled her to him before she could crumple to the sand.

"I'm fine," she protested in a muffled voice against his shirt.

She pushed against his chest, but Logan didn't release his grip on her waist. He held her to him as he spoke.

"I know you are. You're just confused and stunned, and probably a little hungry."

Rose stopped struggling. He felt her chest rise and fall as she took a deep breath. When she shook her head, her soft hair brushed his chin.

"No," she said. "I'm a *lot* hungry. And once I get some food into me, I'll have the brain power to explain to you why this twin thing just can't be."

"All right. Do you think you can make it up the steps on your own power? Or—"

"Yes," Rose said as her hands once again pressed against him. Aware of the warmth where her palms rested on his chest, he released her. She looked up at him, her features tight with determination.

"I'm perfectly capable of making it back up the steps. Especially if I know there will be food waiting for me at the top."

Logan indicated that she should lead the way, letting her set the pace up the 124 steps that he, Anna and Chas had repeatedly counted as kids. He kept a close eye on her, telling himself he was watching for any sign that she might weaken and start to stumble again. But he couldn't deny he enjoyed the sight of the muscles in her legs contracting and lengthening, or watching her round bottom bunch with each step.

When they reached the tile patio, Logan realized he hadn't once felt guilty about taking pleasure in this pastime, that he hadn't once been forced to remind himself that this was Rose, not Anna. And when she turned to him, her eyes dark with questions, he found himself asking how he ever could have confused the two.

Despite the similarities, their expressions were so very different. Anna always seemed to have something of a little-girl-lost look to her, a vulnerable air that probably accounted for his protective, brotherly feelings as much as the way they'd been raised. Rose, on the other hand, gave the impression of being open to the moment, completely willing and able to handle whatever might come her way.

Logan suspected that a certain amount of this was mere bravado. More than once he'd seen anguish attempting to hide beneath the I'm-just-fine smile, like the one she wore now. A smile that clearly expressed her desire to put this "twin" question temporarily aside.

"You *did* say something about food, didn't you?" she asked with a slight tilt to her head.

His suspicions confirmed, and deciding that getting some sustenance into her before they continued their conversation might be a good idea, Logan nodded.

"Follow me. Martina should be in the kitchen, getting breakfast ready for the family. Let's see if I can make up for my failure to finesse Anna this morning, and talk Martina into giving us some homemade takeout."

For one moment Rose's face betrayed the turmoil she was feeling. Her look of panic was quickly replaced by a semi-comical roll of her eyes.

"Good idea. I'd rather not play the part of confused-but-dutiful daughter just now."

Logan gave her a quick smile, one he hoped would convey understanding without the pity she so obviously didn't want. Then, turning, he led the way across the tile patio floor to a white door. He pushed this open and held it, indicating she should enter.

The door shut behind him, closing off the chilly sea-scented breeze. The air that greeted him was warm and filled with the spice of sausage and the sweetness of freshly baked cinnamon rolls. He automatically looked for the colorful plates that had once hung above worn oak cabinets. But Elise had long since replaced the old-world charm of the room with white cabinets and stainless steel surfaces. The only spot of color his glance encountered now was Martina, wearing a bright-yellow T-shirt over an orange skirt, both partially covered by a dark blue apron.

The woman straightened from the open oven door, her oven-mitted hand grasping a baking sheet filled with thick golden brown circles. Her dark hair, streaked with silver, framed a brown face which creased into a smile as her nearly black eyes met his.

"Oh. Been quite a time since the two of you came sneaking in the back door. To what do I owe the honor?"

Logan grinned. "We were hoping we could talk you into fixing us a picnic."

"For *breakfast?*" Martina boomed, lifting one thick eyebrow.

Logan suddenly felt all of ten years old again. Perhaps because Martina had taken on the role of surrogate mother after his parents' deaths had made him a quasi Benedict.

Although Robert truly seemed to consider him a member of his family and treated Logan as Chas's equal, Logan always suspected that Elise thought of him as one of those eggs left in a nest by a foreign species, a chick she had an obligation to raise, but could never truly accept. Martina, on the other hand, had stepped into the role of mother figure as easily as she'd moved from the job of maid to that of cook. She'd secretly seen to it that Logan continued to receive the daily allotment of warm hugs that he'd been accustomed to, along with a dose of discipline when he needed to be put in his place.

Which she apparently figured was the case right now.

"And what's this *we* business?" the woman asked as she nudged the open oven door upward with a raised foot. She placed the baking sheet on a rack atop the white tiled counter as she went on. "Anna knows better than to ask for a special breakfast setup. As do you, young man."

Martina was teasing him, of course. Already she'd opened the cabinet that held the picnic items. "Well," she went on, "I suppose it wouldn't be all that much work to plop some of these scrambled eggs into a wide-mouth thermos."

Logan glanced at Rose. She was standing to his right, her back pressed against a row of cabinets, her eyes following Martina's motions.

"Another container for fried potatoes," the cook continued. "And of course a couple of sweet rolls, to go with your coffee.

While I see to that, why don't you fill these with some orange juice.''

Logan took the two plastic glasses she'd indicated from the counter, filled them, then snapped on their lids. As Martina held out a small picnic basket, he slipped the glasses in place, noting the cook had already packed two mugs, napkins and eating utensils.

Looking into Martina's dark eyes, he smiled again and said softly, ''Thank you.''

The woman's lips firmed into mock severity, then twitched ever so slightly before she shrugged and turned back to the stove. ''Well, off with you two now,'' she said. ''I have *other* people to feed, you know.''

Rose moved to the door. As she held it open, Logan heard the cook say, ''And you be sure to get all that back to me later today, you hear?''

Once outside, Logan faced a decision. The logical thing would be to eat in Anna's room, but some member of the family would be bound to come looking for her there. They could take their picnic down to the beach, but considering the trick the wind had of carrying voices up the cliff, and the very private nature of the discussion he and Rose would soon face, he knew where he *should* take her.

Every muscle in his body tensed at the thought of entering that place. He immediately scowled at his reaction, then forced himself to shrug it away. After all, if Rose could deal with her recent grief, how could he refuse to face a loss that was so much older?

''Follow me,'' he said.

Logan led Rose down the cement steps to the first landing, then made an abrupt right turn to follow a narrow walkway past several windows set into the building's lower floor, and stopped in front of a dark-green door. After pulling a set of keys from his pocket, he fingered them until he found the one he was searching for. He stared at the worn silver key for several seconds before sliding it into the lock, turning it, then pushing the door open and making himself step inside.

Squinting against the dim light, he stared across the room to a small kitchen composed of a bank of oak cabinets with glass-doored cupboards above. A film of dust dulled the yellow dishes, cups and bowls nestled inside. A stainless steel coffeepot and matching toaster sat on the gold-flecked, white Formica counter.

The area was so filled with memories that Logan half expected to see his mother standing at the small avocado-green stove. Aware that Rose had come to a stop just inside the door, he ignored the tightness in his chest and turned to her.

"If you strip the sheet off the couch," he said, "I'll let some light in."

Logan moved toward the wide windows to the right of the door. Unerringly his hand found the slender rope hidden behind the folds of the pale-gold draperies. He gave a tug, and the curtain rings slid over the metal rod, allowing sunlight to spill onto the flower-printed sheets that covered the two chairs arranged beneath the window.

His parents had sat there, night after night, while he did his homework at the table in the far corner—his mother with her knitting needles clicking, his father reading yet another article on carburetor rebuilding. The images were so real, the ache in his chest so painful, that Logan turned to tell Rose they would eat on the beach after all.

She had just finished pulling the sheet off the dull-green sofa that sat opposite the chairs. A cloud of dust swirled up to shimmer in the light. Waving her hand in front of her face, Rose sneezed once, then twice before turning blinking eyes toward him.

"What is this place?"

Despite the pressure in his chest, Logan found himself replying easily, "It used to be my home."

Suddenly it was very important to him that the memories crowding about not affect him in the least. He placed the picnic basket on the draped rectangular shape in front of the couch.

"This apartment backs onto the garage, where my father

worked. Down that hall—'' he pointed to the closed door in the pale cream wall to the right "—is a bathroom and two bedrooms. No long commutes to their jobs for my parents.''

He paused. ''As I explained last night, Charles sold the vintage cars, so a live-in mechanic didn't seem necessary. This place has remained untouched since the day Robert moved me upstairs, with the family.''

Rose seemed to take a moment to digest this information. She glanced around. ''It's a cute little cottage. My mother would have loved it. She liked all sorts of vintage things, and actually had a soft spot in her heart for avocado-green and harvest-gold.''

Logan glanced around, surprised to find himself smiling as he said, ''Well, I can't say it's *my* favorite look. But my mother was thrilled when Charles let her 'update' the place.''

Rose grinned as she finished folding the sheet she'd removed from the couch. ''I'm afraid the color scheme doesn't do much for me, either. But your mom did a nice job in here, considering what was 'in' at the time. You said she worked for the Benedicts, too. What did she do?''

''Cook.'' Logan turned to the basket, opened the wicker lid and started removing containers. ''Martina learned everything she knows from my mother. Especially how to bake. You'll really enjoy these cinnamon rolls.''

It had been a long time since Logan had spoken to anyone about his parents. As he began unpacking their breakfast, he was surprised to find that the tightness in his chest had eased. It was almost as if talking to Rose about the past had worked like a pressure-release valve, allowing him to turn his attention from bittersweet memories to the rumbling in his stomach.

In a matter of moments he had two plates laden with scrambled eggs and potatoes, still steaming from their short stay in the thermal containers they'd been packed in. Rose, he noticed, had poured coffee into two cups and set out the napkins and utensils.

They ate in silence, Logan concentrating on the smells and tastes of his breakfast even as images from the past swirled about him like the dust motes dancing in the sun. He found himself silently repeating the kind words Robert had whispered to him following the accident that had killed Logan's parents, along with Robert's brother, Joe. *The past is the past.*

Robert had assured Logan that he was not an orphan, that he was part of the Benedict family. Of course, Logan knew he wasn't—not truly. But he was positive that the life Robert had given him was far better than any he would have found in foster care as a ward of the State of California. He might desperately miss accompanying his father on his weekly maintenance visits to the private airport where Charles's planes had been housed, discussing the intricacies of life and internal combustion engines with the man beneath the raised hood of a car, or laughing as they teased his mother with grease-blackened hands before dutifully scrubbing them clean. But he couldn't complain. He'd lived the "good life"—good food, good education, good income.

"Oh, you're right."

Logan blinked, wondering if he'd somehow spoken his thoughts aloud. When he saw that Rose was holding a cinnamon roll, obviously savoring the huge bite now missing from it, he relaxed and smiled.

"Good?" he asked.

Rose shook her head. "No—excellent," she said, then took another bite.

Logan glanced at the golden roll, at the flecks of cinnamon atop the drizzle of white icing. The sweet spicy scent that perfumed the air brought with it more mental images of the life he'd spent in this room—his mother quizzing him on spelling words or ironing a patch over yet another tear in the knee of his jeans while his father reminded him, gently, to be more careful, that they weren't made of money.

Logan lifted his cup to his lips and took a quick swig of coffee, as if to wash away the lingering sense of guilt these thoughts stirred up. He lowered the cup, placing it on the sheet-draped coffee table, then looked at Rose.

"I think it's time we discussed you and your sister."

Her sister. Rose froze. The bite of cinnamon roll she'd been chewing suddenly had the taste and texture of clay. And, she found, was almost as difficult to swallow. She took a quick sip of creamy coffee to help the lump flow down her throat, then carefully placed the cup on the table and the last half of the roll on her plate.

"This Dennis person," she said slowly. "Do you think he really knows what he's talking about?"

She looked at Logan as she finished the question. His eyes darkened with an expression of unmistakable compassion as he gave her a small smile.

"He's the head of the forensics department and a brilliant scientist. If he says that you and Anna are twins, then you are."

Rose knew this must be true, although from the moment Logan had dropped that bombshell on the beach, she'd been trying to deny it. With each step up the cement staircase she'd told herself that it was impossible for her to have a sister she knew nothing about.

After that she had focused on everything else—meeting Martina, studying the details of the small room she and Logan now sat in and finally the taste of the food. All this had been a ploy to ignore what her soul and every cell of her body whispered—that the missing part of herself she'd been looking for, longing for all these years, was Anna Benedict.

Her twin.

"But how?" she asked quietly. "And why?"

Rose wasn't even aware that tears had seeped out of the corners of her eyes until Logan reached across to cup her face with both hands, then with his thumbs gently brushed the moisture away.

His eyes held hers for several moments before he said quietly, "I don't know. But I'll find out. You've been lied to. Anna has been lied to. And…"

His voice trailed off. Rose lifted her hands to cover his. Curling her fingers, she drew both pairs of hands down to her lap, where she held his tightly as she said, "And *you've* been lied to."

He nodded slowly. Then he drew a deep breath and pulled his hands from her grasp, placing them on her knees as he spoke.

"We can't dwell on that. We have to look at what we know about you and Anna, then sift through fact and possibility until we arrive at the truth."

That last word seemed to echo in the room. *Truth.* Rose recalled her mother's words, *You must always tell the truth. Truth is more important than beauty, than money. To thine own self be true.*

Again denial curled in Rose's belly as she shook her head. Her mother couldn't—*wouldn't*—have lied to her. Not about something as important as this.

"Rose." Logan had leaned toward her as he said her name. "I need you to help me with this, and if you're still trying to deny the basic fact that you are one of a set of twins, your mind will focus on anything that might back up that belief instead of searching for the clues that will tell us why we were lied to, by whom, and what the exact nature of the lie was— is."

"What do you mean?"

"Well, *were* both of you adopted, or has one of you been living with your true parents? For example, you both bear some resemblance to Robert's great-grandmother, the one Anna was named for."

Rose frowned. "My mother once told me I was named for my grandmother Rose."

"Do you have a picture of her?"

"No. All of Mom's family pictures were lost in a fire that destroyed her home back in Boston while she was away at college, before I was born. She said that all her family was dead by that point, so she never went back there. I do have a picture of her younger sister in my wallet, though. Mom said Aunt Lizzie looked like their mother. She said that's where I got my curly hair."

Rose saw Logan's gaze shift to her hair. She became suddenly conscious of the loose spirals that fell forward over her shoulders to cover her breasts. Aware that he continued to study her, she felt a warm glow flood her cheeks.

Silly girl, she chided herself. Don't go imagining the man is struck dumb with admiration and longing. He's looking for *clues*.

"So," she said on a quick indrawn breath, "it sounds as if either of us could have grown up in our family of origin."

"Or each of you were adopted into families that possessed a couple of the traits we mentioned. I've seen that happen before, you know."

Rose nodded. "As a matter of fact, I do know. I went to school with a girl named Francine Smithers. She was blond, just like her mother and father, while her two brothers had black hair. I couldn't believe it when I learned *she* was the adopted one."

"All right, let's look at other things you two might have in common, starting at the beginning." Logan frowned, obviously thinking back. "According to Benedict family lore, following Chas's birth, Elise suffered a miscarriage, then couldn't seem to conceive again. She went to a fertility clinic somewhere in Switzerland, and once she became pregnant, the doctors kept her there, fearing that a long flight might result in a miscarriage. As it was, Anna was born prematurely. She was only a little over five pounds when Robert and Elise returned with her."

He paused, and a smile stole over his lips as he went on, "I remember how incredibly tiny Anna looked, like a porcelain doll, and thinking how lucky Chas was to get a little sister. Then I remembered that Robert told me she would be *my* little sister, too."

Rose noted the faraway expression on Logan's face, the affectionate—almost worshipful—smile, as if he were once again ten years old, gazing down at that tiny baby. At Anna— who'd grown up with not one big brother, but two, along with two parents, a doting grandfather in Charles and sweet great-aunt Grace.

When she became aware of the jealous tone of her thoughts, Rose blinked. Great, she thought. It had been barely an hour since she'd learned that she had a sister, and already she was experiencing sibling rivalry.

Shaking her head, she focused on the task at hand, searching the past for some clue that would explain their origins and their separation.

"I was premature, also," she said. When Logan's gaze met hers, she went on, "I was barely three pounds, my mom told me. I was in the hospital for over six weeks. She called me her miracle baby."

Rose smiled as she said these words, feeling once again the warmth that had always flooded her when her mother spoke them, something Kathleen Delancey had done every day of her life, right up to the end.

"You were loved, weren't you?" Logan asked softly.

Blinking, Rose met his gaze. "Very much."

She felt Logan's fingers curl around her right hand. "Then whatever we learn about all of this, hold on to that knowledge. Even though Robert tends to spoil Anna, I don't think she has really felt loved, not in the way—"

He stopped speaking abruptly.

"Anna *knows*," he said.

Rose shook her head, confused.

"That's why she left," he continued with growing excitement. "Somehow she learned that she was a twin. That was what made her reassert her belief that she was adopted."

"What makes you say that?"

"The first message Anna left on my machine. She was excited, babbling. She said she'd learned something amazing, something that finally made sense of her life. She wanted me to call her as soon as I got her message, even if it was the middle of the night her time."

He paused, frowning before he went on. "My point is that Anna apparently learned something new, though what that something might have been, I can't imagine. Maybe we should compare the Benedicts with your family. You've told me a bit about your mother. What about your father?''

Rose drew a deep breath before saying, ''I don't have one.''

Chapter 9

Being without a father was something Rose had lived with all her life. However, she could see that Logan was puzzled by her lack of emotion.

"He died before I was born," she said.

"I see." His eyes said he was sorry. "What do you know about him?"

Rose shrugged. "Very little. My mother had a thing about not dwelling on the past. When I was about eight, though, I told her how dumb I felt when my friends spoke about their dads. She sat me down and told me that she and my father met in college. He was a musician from a well-to-do family who didn't approve of her, and they argued. Angry and hurt, she kept the secret of her pregnancy until she was nearly seven months along. When he discovered this, he said he wanted to marry her. On the way to the ceremony, they were in a horrible car wreck. My father was killed, and my mother went into premature labor. Mom said his family blamed her for their loss. They gave her quite a bit of money, then made her promise never to contact them again."

In the moments of silence following these words, Rose heard the echo of her matter-of-fact tone. The quiet sympathy darkening Logan's hazel eyes made her worry that he somehow saw beneath her composure to the sense of rejection that all her mother's love had never been able to banish completely, an ache that now threatened to break open the wall she'd placed around her most recent loss.

She made herself smile. "Mom told me that they did us a big favor. Releasing us that way meant we didn't have to go around scraping and bowing to people who didn't like us. That money paid for the hideous hospital bills that come with keeping a tiny preemie alive, and what was left over enabled Mom to start her own business."

Logan nodded as she finished. It occurred to her that he *had* spent much of his life feeling obligated. But before she could explain that she didn't compare her father's family to the Benedicts, he asked, "What kind of business?"

"A gift shop. You see, Mom learned to work with clay in a commune in Oregon, where we lived the first two years of my life. After that, the two of us traveled the country attending craft fairs, where she sold her wares, until it was time for me to start school. Then she bought an old house in the Queen Anne Hill section of Seattle, and converted the ground floor into a shop. It's called Ridiculous to Sublime."

"And that would be because…?"

Rose grinned. "Because of the things she and her partner sell. Most of Mom's creations are really practical—mugs and dishes and bowls. But she also made some exquisite vases and wall hangings. Those are the sublime. Goldie provides the ridiculous. She creates art from things she picks up at flea markets and thrift shops and the occasional "dumpster dive.""

Rose's smile softened as she recalled the numerous "junking" trips she'd shared with her mother and Goldie—the joy of finding a treasure, like a dusty Art Deco vase or a nearly perfect forties satin jacket, in the piles of unwanted items.

Lost in her memories, she almost jumped when Logan asked, "Is that all your mother told you?"

"About my father? Pretty much. She told me that before she made that solemn promise never to contact my father's family or reveal his identity, she had insisted on knowing their medical history and learned that there were no hereditary diseases for me to look out for. So she considered the subject closed. And since I could see how much it distressed her to talk about this, I never brought the subject up again."

Logan nodded. He was silent for several moments before he asked, "Do you think your mother's friend, Goldie, might know something more about these people—or a possible adoption?"

At the words *possible adoption,* Rose stiffened. "You believe my mother lied about my birth? About my father's death?"

Logan sighed. "I haven't formed any opinion at all. I do know that back when you were born adoptions were often treated as guilty little secrets. And many of them were obtained through less than legal avenues. Your mother's story could be the absolute truth, or one she felt compelled to make up—perhaps in response to a promise she made to someone."

Rose acknowledged this last with a slow nod. "That is something my mother would do. But *if* that were the case, I can't imagine Mom telling Goldie something that she wouldn't tell me. Especially in the last few months, when she knew…"

Clamping her mouth over her words, Rose looked down at her hands. She didn't want to talk about her mother's death now, not in connection with this possible, yet impossible, glaring *lie* about her birth—and about the *other* child born at the same time.

"When she knew she was dying?" Logan asked softly.

"Yes."

Rose heard the tightness in her reply. She felt Logan take her hand. "I know that this may sound odd," he said in a voice every bit as tight as hers, "but there's a lot to be grateful for in that."

These softly rasping words pulled Rose's gaze up. The pain she saw in Logan's warm eyes led her to squeeze his fingers in return and ask, "Because you lost your parents in a flash, and had no time to say goodbye?"

After one tense moment his reply was a brief nod. Rose took a deep breath. "You're right. It was hard…knowing what was coming. But Mom insisted we face facts, grieve together, get past the pain, then enjoy the time we had left together. And we did just that."

She paused as an idea formed. "I think," she said slowly, "that might explain why she didn't tell me I had been adopted, or whatever the true situation was. She didn't want to spoil our time as mother and daughter."

"That's a logical explanation," Logan said. "And it gives us some new scenarios to consider, like the fact that both you and Anna were preemies. Now, Robert and Elise told Anna that she was conceived and born in a fertility clinic in Switzerland. They even showed her the paperwork. I saw it, too. Victor had made all the arrangements."

Logan paused, frowning, before he went on. "I know from personal experience the sort of legal and quasilegal strings Victor Benedict could pull. It would have been simple for him to hide an illegal adoption by claiming that Anna's birth occurred in a foreign country."

Rose followed his words carefully. "So, you're saying that both Anna and I might have been born to someone who couldn't afford to keep two premature babies and gave one up?" She shook her head. "My mother would never do that."

"I'm not saying she *or* Elise did that. I'm thinking that both of you might have been put up for adoption, and the individual or organization that arranged this might have split you up without letting either of the new parents know about the other child." He paused. "Have you ever seen your birth certificate?"

"Yes." The answer came out with a rush of relief. She knew she was Kathleen Delancey's daughter, and now she had proof. "My mother's name was printed on it, and in the space marked Father's Name is the word *unknown*." She frowned. "Now that I think about it, it stated *single live birth,* as well."

"Rose," Logan said softly. "Birth certificates can be altered or faked. *However*—" he lifted one hand, palm out "—all this speculation is getting us nowhere. We need to get down to practical matters. As much as I hate invading Anna's privacy, I think we need to go through her room and see if we can find anything that would tell us what, exactly, she learned before taking off."

He began packing things back into the picnic basket as he spoke. Rose helped silently, suddenly too weary to make any comment. As Logan picked up the basket and started for the door, she followed, feeling as if she was being physically pulled in his wake, as well as forced to examine the past for answers she wasn't sure she wanted, in response to questions she *knew* she wished had never been raised.

Once outside, Logan led her up the steps to the veranda. As she followed, her eyes were drawn toward the bridge and the sight she'd come in search of. The warning *Be careful what you wish for* echoed loud in her mind.

"Hey, Anna, how's your memory today?"

At the sound of Chas's voice, Logan stopped walking and looked up to see the man standing just beyond the top of the steps, the wind ruffling his fine blond hair. Having seen the way Rose nearly sleepwalked as she helped him pack up the remains of their meal, he started up the last few steps and replied for her, "The same as yesterday."

Chas frowned. "Don't you think Anna should see someone about this? I know you feel it's your job to keep everything in line here, but you're hardly qualified to be messing with someone's mind. I think my sister should be treated by someone, preferably in a controlled, safe environment. What if she decides to run away again?"

Logan was mildly surprised by Chas's show of concern. For all his apparent charm, Chas was like his mother, more concerned with how the Benedict family looked to the world than with how anyone was really feeling.

"Anna's not going anywhere," Logan assured him. "She

knows she belongs here, even if she can't remember. Don't you, Anna?''

He glanced at Rose and watched her respond with a solemn nod before turning back to Chas. The man continued to stare at Rose several moments before giving her a wide smile and saying, ''I'm glad to hear it, Squeaks.''

Chas then returned his attention to Logan. ''Is there anything I can do to help?''

Logan shrugged. ''Dr. Alcott said her memory could return bit by bit or all at once. The only thing we can do is expose her to as much of her life as possible, while not pushing her. I guess just being around the family will do the most good.''

Again Chas glanced at Rose. His earlier frown returned as he said, ''Anna, will you excuse the two of us for a moment. I have a business matter I need to discuss with Logan.''

Logan followed Chas to the far corner of the patio, where the man came to an abrupt stop, turned to Logan and spoke softly. ''I'm not sure Anna should spend time with *every* member of the family.''

''What are you talking about?''

''Aunt Grace.'' Chas hesitated. ''You know how she is sometimes—how confused she tends to get? Well, Mother tells me that Anna and Grace were together a great deal recently, before Anna…started having problems. I can't imagine what connection there might be, but maybe, just to be sure, Anna should steer clear of Grace, except when the entire family is together.''

Logan felt the hairs at the back of his neck rise. Carefully controlling his expression, he replied, ''Thanks for the suggestion.''

Chas smiled again. ''Anything to help Anna.'' He looked at his watch. ''Well, got to check a few things with father, then get to campaign headquarters. See you later.''

As Chas headed toward the French doors leading to Robert's study, Logan crossed the veranda to where Rose stood, gazing down at the ocean. She turned to him as he reached her side.

"We need to take this stuff back to the kitchen," he said, giving the picnic basket a quick lift. "We'd also better clean everything and put it away, so Martina won't have our hides. And after that…I think a visit to Aunt Grace is in order."

"Aunt Grace? I thought we were going to—"

"There's been a change of plans," Logan broke in. As he led Rose toward the kitchen he spoke softly, explaining Chas's suggestion that "Anna" be kept away from the older woman.

Rose came to an abrupt halt at the kitchen door. "Ohmigod," she breathed. "Grace. Last night, when she brought that awful dress up to my room, she seemed concerned that she might have said something to bring on my—meaning Anna's—mental confusion, though it made no sense at the time. She said…" Rose paused, thinking back. "Something about knowing it was wrong to have mentioned the *other one*."

Logan's free hand tightened around her wrist. "Are you sure?"

Rose nodded. "It didn't make any sense then, but now, knowing what we do, it makes all the sense in the world. Grace *knows* that Anna has a twin."

"Of course." There was no doubt in Logan's voice. His eyes narrowed in concentration. "She was Victor's helpmate in every way. The others should be leaving the house soon, so we can visit Grace without anyone knowing."

After the quick kitchen cleanup, Rose and Logan watched the car carrying Chas and Robert back out of the driveway. Martina had already informed them that Elise had left earlier, so Logan led Rose toward the house's smaller wing.

"It was originally the master suite for Charles and his wife, Louise," Logan explained as they walked down the dark hall. "Victor took it over after Charles died, leaving the rest of the house to Joe and Robert."

Rose nodded absently, then turned to him. "Can you leave me alone with her?"

Logan frowned. "Aunt Grace? Why?"

"Because now that I think about it, she referred to my—

Anna's—amnesia again at dinner last night. Each time, she abruptly stopped talking. She didn't strike me as being confused or dotty, more like afraid.''

Logan was silent a moment as they turned down the hall leading to Grace's room, then he spoke softly, "You're right. She might not feel comfortable talking about this in front of me. Victor had an iron will, and he used it to keep others in line. I've no doubt that Grace was under strict orders to keep anything she knew about Anna's birth to herself."

When he stopped in front of an oak-paneled door, Rose whispered, "Lovely sounding man."

Logan's eyes narrowed. "He was tough. But then, he had a tough job to do, balancing the financial needs of the family with their drive to serve the public."

Rose felt suddenly cold. "And you think that justifies splitting up a pair of twins? Falsifying—"

"We don't know the facts yet," Logan interrupted. "And until—"

The door flew open at that moment. Logan stopped speaking as Grace's white head appeared near his shoulder. Her blue eyes blinked behind her glasses for several moments before her face crinkled into a smile.

"I thought I heard someone out here. What a pleasant surprise to find it's the two of you." She paused, and her face brightened further. "Did you come to visit *me*?"

Rose saw Logan smile. "Of course."

The anger and fear she'd felt a moment earlier faded as Grace opened the door wider and stepped back into the room. "How utterly delightful. I rarely get guests these days. Please come in. I still keep those lemon cookies you used to like so well, Logan. Make yourself comfortable, and I'll make some tea to go with them."

Rose followed Logan into a salon furnished in dark reds and blues. The two of them sat on a heavy tapestry-covered sofa, as Grace disappeared through a doorway at the other side of the room. The opposite wall was lined with walnut bookcases, some with glass fronts. The shelves not only held books, but knickknacks and several metal file boxes. More of these sat open on an ornately carved wooden desk, along with several large leather-bound volumes that looked like photo albums.

The surface of the dainty coffee table in front of the couch was also littered with papers and ivory file folders, lying every which way atop a square of red leather. Rose stared at the gold-embossed letters peeking out from the stack and read, "aphs." She decided they marked the end of the word *photographs,* and was just about to pull it from beneath the stack of papers, when Grace bustled into the room.

The old woman walked directly to the coffee table and in one quick and amazingly efficient motion scooped up papers, files and album. Straightening, Grace smiled at Logan.

"You take your tea black, right? And, Anna, you take two sugars along with milk?"

Rose nodded numbly. Grace turned, deposited her armload on the desk, then headed through the door.

"That was interesting," Logan said softly.

"What is all this stuff?" Rose whispered.

"I haven't a clue, but if I had to guess, I would say that Grace has begun to go through Victor's papers—the personal files he mentioned to me once or twice. He never told me what they were specifically, only said he'd tell me about them before he retired and handed me the reins."

"He died before that could happen, I take it," she said.

Logan nodded. His expression was closed, giving her no hint to the relationship he'd had with what sounded to her like a cruel and controlling man. Aware of her own need for privacy, she hesitated to pry. But suddenly it was very important to know what kind of influence Victor had wielded over Logan.

A loud whistle echoed from beyond the door Grace had disappeared through. When the noise stopped abruptly, Rose asked, "Were the two of you close?"

"Me and Victor?" Logan turned to her and shrugged. "He wasn't that kind of man. Victor lacked the charm of Charles.

He was…rather self-contained—and direct. When I finished high school, I told him I wanted to study aviation. Elise had never let me forget that I wasn't a *real* Benedict, and I figured I'd eventually need to make my own way. I thought maybe I'd become a pilot, then save up to open my own private airport, like my dad always dreamed of doing."

Rose saw a smile touch Logan's lips as his eyes took on a faraway expression. "But you didn't do that," she said softly.

"No." Logan took a deep breath. "Victor convinced me to study business law—told me I could work for the Benedicts and promised me flying lessons and full use of the company plane if I agreed. Then, after I graduated law school, he informed me that he wanted to train me to take his place."

"And my husband never regretted that choice."

Grace smiled as both Logan and Rose turned to her. She tottered across the room, carrying a wide black tray, which she placed on the table in front of them.

"I left the pot in the kitchen," she said. "Made the tray too heavy. That cup is yours, Logan, the one to the right is Anna's and this is mine. I'll fetch more hot water when we need it."

Grace had pulled a dainty wooden chair with a dark red cushion over to the table as she spoke. She placed two cookies on her saucer, then sat down and looked at Logan.

"I hope *you* don't," she said.

Rose paused in the act of lifting a cookie to her lips, and saw Logan frown.

"You hope I don't *what,* Aunt Grace."

"Oh. You know…regret the way Victor more or less made you give up your dreams to fit his plans."

Logan shook his head. "It wasn't much of a dream."

Grace's pale eyes searched his face for several moments before she shrugged. "Perhaps. I just know that my husband had a way of twisting things around so that a person didn't know *what* they really wanted. Or maybe it was just me."

With that her eyes took on a glazed expression as she lifted the cup and took a slow sip of tea. To Rose it felt as if the woman had once again left the room, even though her body remained in the chair. She gave Logan a quick glance.

He returned a tiny nod, finished the cookie he'd started, took a drink of tea, then suddenly placed the cup and saucer back on the tray. His hand went to his belt, then reappeared, holding a small black pager.

"Aunt Grace," he said. She blinked before looking at him. He held the pager up. "I have to go to Robert's office and call this person back. Keep an eye on Anna, won't you?"

"Of course, Logan."

Rose slowly chewed her cookie as Logan crossed the room. After the door shut, she took a sip of tea. Watching Grace from beneath her eyelashes, she saw that the woman again had that lost expression. Taking a deep breath, Rose placed her cup on the tray and leaned forward.

"Aunt Grace." She spoke just above a whisper. "Tell me about the other one."

The woman continued to stare out the window behind Rose. She drew in a deep breath, then released a sigh. "The little twin? I don't know where she is. Victor frightened—"

Grace stopped speaking abruptly. She blinked and looked at Rose. "I told you something I shouldn't have, I'm afraid. I don't want to make things worse, so—"

Rose interrupted with a shake of her head. "I need to know. I need your help with this amnesia thing. I don't like wandering about in the dark, so to speak."

Grace's eyebrows puckered in concern. "Yes. It must be very distressing. But how can I help?"

Rose lifted her shoulders in what she hoped looked like a helpless shrug. "Tell me what you said to me that day."

Grace glanced away, her lips pursing. Then her eyes once again met Rose's, bright and sharp, as if she were sizing the young woman up. Rose waited, barely breathing. When Grace said nothing more, Rose tried again.

"Aunt Grace, the doctor thinks I'll regain my memory eventually. It would really help me if you'd tell me what we spoke about."

Several long moments passed. Finally Grace placed her cup on the tray, took another deep breath and got to her feet. She crossed the room, returning with the red photo album, which she opened. After flipping through several pages, she placed the album in Rose's lap, and pointed to a picture.

"Two days before you had that argument with your mother, you came asking about some people who worked on your grandfather's first U.S. Senate campaign. I showed you this."

This was a black-and-white photograph of ten people that had obviously been cut from a newspaper. Rose immediately recognized two of them.

Logan frowned as he placed his cell phone back in his pocket. The call had made less of a lie out of his excuse to leave Rose and Grace alone together, but it hadn't made him happy.

He glanced at his watch. Twenty minutes had elapsed. Enough time, he hoped, for Rose to have gotten some explanation from Grace. Turning, he made his way back to the room. When he entered, he noticed that the tray on the coffee table had been replaced by an open photo album. Grace was in her chair, staring out the window behind Rose. She didn't look toward him, even as he approached.

Rose, however, looked up from the album, her face white, her eyes wide and dark with a mixture of fear and confusion. Logan's heart began to pound as he hurried toward her.

"You all right?"

She started to shake her head, stopped, took a deep breath. "Yeah," she said, then closed the album.

"What's been—"

Rose stopped his question with a shake of her head, then stood and turned to the old woman, sitting so very still in her chair.

"Aunt Grace?" Rose said softly. The woman didn't move. "Aunt Grace," Rose repeated, slightly louder.

At this, the white head swiveled, and the blue eyes met Rose's with an expression of mild curiosity.

"I have to leave now," Rose said. "Logan and I really enjoyed the tea. Did you mean what you said, that I could keep this for a while?"

The pale eyes flicked to the album, then back to Rose before Grace nodded. "Of course you can."

"I washed the cups and saucers," Rose said. "Is there anything else I can do for you?"

"No, dear. I think it's time I took a little nap. You'll both come back for another visit, though. Won't you?"

After assuring the woman they would do this, Rose motioned to Logan to follow her out of the room. Halfway down the hall, he started to ask Rose about the album she carried. She shook her head. "Not here," was all she would say. When they reached Anna's room, Rose walked to the bed and opened the album. Her face was still pale.

"I want you to look at this photo while I get my wallet. I didn't want anyone to see my driver's license, so I hid it with my suitcase."

Logan studied the album while she headed toward the closet. The photograph she'd indicated was a black-and-white newspaper clipping. Of the ten people featured in the group shot, he recognized three of the men in the back row.

In the center, smiling the winning smile so much like Chas's, stood dark-haired Charles Benedict, flanked by his two sons, Robert and Joseph. Logan stared at the features of the young men, surprised to find he'd forgotten how much each of them, in their own distinctive way, had resembled their father.

The fourth man in the back row was a tall, lanky fellow with oval wire-frame glasses. The six people sitting in the front row, three girls and three boys, all appeared to be in their late teens or early twenties.

"Grace said this is one of several scrapbooks Victor kept of his brother's various campaigns," Rose explained as she returned to his side. "She said Anna had asked to look through them the day she had her blowup with Elise. Now look at this."

Rose handed him a black-and-white wallet-size rectangle. "My mother gave me this shortly before she died," Rose said softly. "That's her, on the left. The other one is Mom's sister. Aunt Lizzie was supposed to be my mother's maid of honor, but she died in the same accident that killed my father."

She took a deep breath. "The white border around my photo is missing. I always assumed it had been trimmed away to make the picture fit Mom's wallet. But now I see that the shot of the two women was cut out of a larger photograph—the one that was reduced and printed in the newspaper."

Logan glanced between the two prints, and saw that the image in the wallet-size photo was a perfect match to the two girls sitting in front of Charles and his sons. The young woman Rose had identified as her mother had long, straight blond hair, parted in the middle. Her face had the same square shape shared by Rose and Anna. The sister's face was slimmer, but possessed similar features. Her hair appeared to be a light-brown, and was tucked behind her ears to fall in wild curls halfway down the front of her flowered dress—just as Rose's did now. Both sisters had large, wide eyes.

Logan glanced at Rose. Those same-shaped eyes met his beneath a frown. "Look at the newspaper clipping again," she said. "Read the caption below."

The print was faded, but Logan made out the names of the three Benedict men. The man standing with them was identified as Lawrence Wilkins, a professor at the University of California at Berkeley. The six young people were his students, who were working on the Charles Benedict U.S. Senate campaign as part of the Political Science course he taught.

Logan focused on the two girls seated in the middle of the group, read their names, then looked at Rose.

"Elizabeth and Kathleen *Donnelly?*"

She shrugged. "Seems even my last name is a lie."

Chapter 10

Rose spoke far too quietly, as far as Logan was concerned. And too calmly. She looked as if she'd been punched in the gut. He got to his feet slowly.

"We'll solve this mystery," he said as he gently closed his hands around her upper arms, yet again, then urged her to step toward the bed and sit down. When he joined her on the edge of the mattress, she looked at him.

"How? Aunt Grace can't, or won't, help us."

"What do you mean?"

Rose stared out the sliding glass door at the bridge. When she didn't say anything, Logan took her hand.

"Rose, what happened?"

She turned to him, her features tight. "I blew it. I was so stunned when I saw the name Donnelly under the picture of my mother that I forgot all about Aunt Grace's delicate state of mind. I'd been so careful up to that point, too. I got her to tell me that the *other one* was Anna's twin, but when—"

Logan broke in with, "Grace told you *that?* I was right, then. Anna does know about you."

Rose shook her head. "She knows I exist, or that I did, but I'm not sure she has any details. Grace said something that indicated Victor had frightened someone into silence. Anyway, I was doing all right until I saw my mother and her sister sitting in front of Joe and Robert Benedict in that picture. A thousand questions raced through my mind, and I more or less threw them at Grace in rapid-fire. She shut down. She wouldn't talk about the people in the photograph or the 'tiny twin,' or what Victor might have done to cover up this twin's whereabouts. Grace just stared out the window until you arrived."

Logan took her hand. "It's all right. We've got other angles to work on. While you were talking to Grace, Matt Sullivan called."

"The detective?"

"Yes. He hasn't been able to pin down the call from Anna to my cell phone this morning, but he was able to trace the numbers Caller ID recorded on my home phone. The first came from Anna's room early on the day she argued with Elise. The second was recorded *after* she'd taken money out of her ATM, and it originated somewhere on the UC Berkeley campus. So, first thing Monday, when classes resume, we'll head over there."

"And see if this Professor Wilkins is still teaching there?"

Logan fought a smile. Rose was once more alert, questioning. He again noted the difference between this young woman and Anna, who had a tendency to fall into a hopeless depression when faced with adversity.

"Right," he replied. "My original plan was to find out what classes Anna was taking, and see if any of her teachers or fellow students had any idea what she was up to. I don't have much faith in this, though. Anna is extremely private and has few friends."

Rose's dark eyes grew nearly black beneath her frown. "That's…surprising," she said. "And sad. I always thought having all the right things—the clothes, the big house, the important family—would mean lots of friends."

"You were wrong," Logan said softly. "At least in Anna's case. For some reason she never seemed able to connect with people."

Rose nodded slowly, her face pensive. "For some *reason?* I can think of a lot of reasons. How about a controlling mother who is bent on making her into some twisted version of *perfection?* What about a father who is so driven to succeed that he ignores her need for privacy and forces her into situations in which she feels totally uncomfortable? What about a family who jokes about her attempts to find herself?"

She paused to shake her head. "Just how is Anna supposed to *connect* with people, when she's always trying to twist herself into the perfect cardboard figure guaranteed to *please?* How is she supposed to know who she is, when she's been lied to her entire life?"

Logan heard the fury in Rose's voice, along with the anguish she obviously felt for the sister she'd never known. This was not only more fight than he would get from Anna, but more than he wanted to deal with at the moment. And although he knew much of what Rose had said was true, had even had similar thoughts himself, he also cared about the people she was so harshly condemning.

"You make it sound as if the Benedicts are self-centered monsters," he said quietly. "They aren't. Both Robert and Elise are sincere in their desire to help impoverished families. Especially the children."

Rose met his gaze with a look of stubborn opposition. "What about *their* children?" she asked, then frowned and spoke quickly, giving Logan no chance to reply. "Or maybe *that's* the issue. Anna never was their child."

"Well neither was I," Logan countered, holding Rose's gaze. "But they took me in, did the best they could for me."

Old memories surfaced, glimpses into the weeks, even years, after his parents died. Feelings of loneliness, of fearing he would never belong, never fit in. Bits of conversations with Robert, Elise, Victor—lectures on what sort of things Benedicts did not do, how to do the right things. And beneath it all, the fear that if he didn't repay them for allowing him to stay in the only home he'd ever known, he would be forced to leave.

Logan drew in a deep breath, fighting the tight band around his chest, forcing away the memories as he looked into Rose's eyes.

"If Anna felt like an outcast," he said, "then it was my fault. I promised to be her big brother, to help her, to watch over her. And I did all that, but I also spent a lot of time making sure *I* toed the line, so that I would be considered a productive member of the family."

Rose placed a hand on his shoulder. "Logan, it's *their* lies that are at the root of Anna's problems. You couldn't know that Robert and Elise weren't her real parents."

Logan thought about that for a moment, then sat up a bit straighter. "No, I couldn't. We still don't know that. And we won't get the truth if we let ourselves get bogged down in emotional issues."

Rose grew very still. She *wanted* to deal with those emotional issues. They were at the heart of the matter. It appalled her to see Logan so easily turn off the pain that twisted his features when he spoke of *toeing the line*.

But he was right. For the moment, at any rate. They needed to focus on finding Anna, who apparently had at least some of the answers they were searching for.

"All right," Rose said quietly. "We know that Anna called from a pay phone on the Berkeley campus. We now know that my mother and her sister attended the same university, and that they came in contact with the Benedicts through this Professor Wilkins. Anna learned this the day before she left."

Logan nodded and reached in his pocket. He flipped open his cell phone. "I'm going to call Matt and add some work to his load. Give me that album, will you? While he's checking Wilkins out, I'll have him see what he can learn about the other people in the photo. One of them might be able to help us out."

Logan wasn't on the call long before he stuffed the phone

in his pocket. Rose watched him cross the room as if lost in thought, then stop at the rolltop desk and stare at the photos above it.

Rose joined him. "What is it?" she asked.

He blinked, as if waking from a dream, then shook his head as he pulled the top of the desk open.

"Just trying to puzzle things together. With any luck, we'll find some more pieces here." He opened the cover of a gray notebook computer. "Have a seat."

Rose stared at the chair he'd pulled out. "Me? Why?"

Logan finished pushing a series of buttons, then turned to her. "Because of the connection you two seem to share. Something in her files might strike a chord with you that I would miss. I'll stand behind you and read the screen from there."

Rose took the seat as the computer whirred to life. Once it went through its booting routine and reached a blank screen, Logan pulled up a list of files. Glancing through the names, he quickly pulled up one marked, "Berkeley." It turned out to be a collection of downloaded information about general course requirements, so he closed it and continued the search.

A sideways glance revealed Logan deep in concentration. Instead of watching file names moving by, Rose found herself studying the fine creases that fanned out from his narrowed eyes, the firm lines of his mouth. Her body grew aware of his as he leaned forward over her shoulder to work the mouse attached to the notebook. The combination of these sensual stimuli, along with the heated, melting way her body was reacting, had her so completely distracted that she was only peripherally aware of what was happening on the computer screen.

"Well, this looks promising, wouldn't you say?"

Logan turned to look at Rose. She froze, unable to remember ever, in all those dreams of this man, being so very close to those eyes, to those lips. A more recent memory, as fresh as the previous night in the hallway outside Anna's room, captured her thoughts. Her lips recalled the gentle touch of his mouth, and her body softened in remembrance.

The next second, however, she remembered how quickly Logan had broken off the contact and moved away from her. Her face flamed with embarrassment. Reminding herself that Logan most certainly had thought he was kissing Anna, she turned toward the computer to search for something, anything, that might break the moment and keep him from realizing how his nearness was affecting her.

Her eyes locked on the word *twins*.

"Open that file," Rose said.

Her voice had sounded hoarse, tight. She didn't care. Logan knew her well enough by now to know how this subject would affect her. And if he was concerned about her getting "bogged down" in emotion, that was just too darned bad. She wondered, however, just how emotional this was likely to get when the first page of the file popped onto the screen. It was entitled The Minnesota Study of Twins Reared Apart—a research paper that seemed to promise nothing more than dry facts.

Dry to other people, Rose realized as she began reading, but totally fascinating to her. Twins reared apart, she learned, were often more alike than twins who grew up in the same home. They showed a marked similarity in tastes—enjoying the same books, music, colors—possibly because they didn't face the pressure to construct separate identities as twins raised together.

When Rose read that twins demonstrated a marked degree of ESP, connecting them when apart, she glanced over at the bridge outside the sliding glass door. A second later she returned her attention to the text Logan was scrolling through. The pages contained numerous real-life examples of twins who had suffered broken legs at the same time or caught the same childhood disease within days of each other, even though they were growing up miles, even states, apart.

And when she finished skimming the research paper, she found there were other notes, apparently scanned into the file from various books on the subject.

"There's an awful lot of information here."

Logan's voice, coming from so close to Rose's ear, made

her jump. When she turned to him, he gave her a warm smile. "Why don't I print this out? Then you can read it later."

Later, Rose thought, when she was all by herself, when she could take all the information into her heart, the information that proved she had *not* been crazy. Later, when she could let herself revel in the joy of knowing she was not, had never been, truly alone.

"I don't know about you," Logan said. "But I think it's time to get away from all this. We've done all we can for the moment. I really should go into the office and check on a few matters, but what I really need to do is clear my head. How about you?"

Though he hadn't said it, Rose had the feeling that Logan knew just how overwhelming the morning had been for her. Learning she had a twin was just the tip of the iceberg. The whens and whys and whos still remained unanswered. And would, most likely, until they learned something new or found Anna.

"Yes," she said. "I think a mind clearing is a great idea."

"Good. Driving works for me when my brain's gone into overload. That okay with you?"

After she nodded, he frowned. "I'm going to have the top down, so you might want to dress warmly. It's warm for January, but when we get moving, the wind can really bite. While you change clothes, I'll get the car out."

Logan told her to meet him downstairs in fifteen minutes. He shut the door behind him as he stepped out in the hall, leaving Rose to wait while the printer spit out the pages before she exited the computer. Ten minutes later, after braiding her hair, she hurried down the stairs wearing jeans, a lightweight blue turtleneck and carrying the gray hooded sweatshirt jacket.

The Mustang was in the driveway, idling softly. Logan sat behind the wheel, growing warm beneath the sun. He watched Rose close the front door behind her, then walk quickly toward the car. He noticed the sway of her hips as she approached and wondered if he'd made a mistake by asking her to go with him.

This drive was supposed to be about clearing his mind, not overheating his body or fighting an attraction that he couldn't act upon, at least until he had Anna back where she belonged. Then, after all the questions were sorted out and he'd helped the family deal with the situation, maybe then he could turn his attention to Rose and the way she made his heart race, his mind go soft and his body hard.

"Are you hungry?"

Logan blinked at the sound of Rose's question. While his thoughts had been meandering down the very paths he knew were closed off to him, she had taken the seat beside him, closed the door and fastened her safety belt.

Oh, yes, he definitely needed to clear his mind. The question was, how was he to do that with the tempting Rose Delancey sitting right next to him. Perhaps it would be better if he asked her to remain at the house.

But even as the thought crossed his mind, Logan knew he wouldn't do that. Left to her own devices, there was a chance that some member of the family would try to engage Rose in conversation, and she might say something that would make someone doubt that she was Anna. They would learn eventually, of course. Soon, he hoped. But until Anna was safely home, he wanted to avoid that confrontation, along with the fallout he knew would follow.

"Yes, I am hungry, now that you mention it," he said. Shifting the car into reverse, he backed through the open gate, then shifted again and sped forward. "Do you mind fast food?" he asked with a glance her way.

"Not at all," Rose said.

"Good. We'll pick something up at a drive-through, then munch as we make our way north."

"North?"

"Yeah. For some reason Highway 1 clears my mind. Guess it's because the curves take all my concentration—my version of living on the edge."

Rose was quiet a moment. "Does that mean we'll be going across the Golden Gate Bridge?" she asked at last.

Logan glanced over to see that she was frowning. "Is that a problem?"

She turned to him. The frown faded as she smiled and shook her head. "Not at all. I was hoping I'd get a chance to do that. I was just thinking that I've dreamed about the thing so very often from one point of view that it would be refreshing to see it from another perspective."

Minutes later, Logan thought about this as they started across the bridge. As they passed beneath its southern tower, he stowed the now-empty burger and French fry containers in one of the plastic bags he kept in the glove compartment, then stuffed it between the seats to keep the wind from whisking it away.

"Oh! What a *kick!*"

The unmistakable joy in Rose's voice drew Logan's attention. She was sitting up as straight as possible, craning her neck, looking to her right. He smiled, recalling his own first attempt to peer between the orange rails that flanked the bridge to gaze at the island of Alcatraz in the middle of the bay.

"We can stop at the overlook on the other side, if you'd like."

Rose turned to him, her dark eyes shining. "Oh, yes. I'd like that a lot."

She was amazing, Logan told himself. Not a half hour earlier, she'd appeared devastated by the photo that proved her mother hadn't always told the truth, including her last name. The implication had been clear—they would likely uncover even more lies. But Rose had somehow managed to place that concern somewhere in the back of her mind and embrace the moment. This moment.

From what she'd told him, this was the legacy left to her by Kathleen Delancey—*Donnelly*. Whatever else the woman had done, she had loved her daughter to the end of her days, leaving Rose with a resiliency and capacity for joy that touched him in places he hadn't visited in decades. For this was how he'd been raised—by parents who loved life, who dealt with the downside, then grabbed for the gusto the rest of the time. By people who didn't give a second thought to impressing others, status or doing what *looked* right.

As he reached the north edge of the bridge and turned into a parking area crammed with tourists, Logan pushed these thoughts aside. He found himself wanting to experience the moment with Rose. Once the car was safely parked, he led Rose to the edge of a three-foot-high stone wall, then watched her face as she scanned the view, enjoying the look of pleasure and awe that colored her features.

"Look at that *city*," she said. "All white and shining in the sun. It almost looks like some magical island, floating on the water."

Logan turned to survey the scene himself. A slow smile curved his lips. "If you think San Francisco looks mystical today, you should see it when it's surrounded by a low fog. I used to imagine that was how Avalon might have looked."

Logan tensed. He hadn't thought about those drives with his parents for a very long time. It had seemed safer not to, just as it had been safer not to go into the apartment beneath the house, where memories huddled in the dark corners along with grief, waiting to attack.

"Fond of stories of Arthur and his knights, were you?"

Rose's question made him aware that he'd slipped into the past. "Yes," he replied with a smile. "Chas and I used to hold jousts on the beach beneath the house, where no one could see us."

"Where no one could see you?"

Turning to meet her curious gaze, he lifted one side of his mouth in a half grin. "Right. Elise would have had both our hides if she'd seen us wielding wooden swords. Or perhaps just mine. She tended to be a bit overprotective of her children. Her *real* children."

Recalling the anger Rose had expressed in the room on just this subject, and aware that what he'd just said sounded totally ungrateful, he turned away to look toward the car. So much for living in the moment.

"It's time to move on," he said. "Before the afternoon traffic starts up."

He took the time to throw the remains of their lunch in a nearby trash receptacle. Once he was behind the wheel again he switched the motor on, and moments later they were back on the freeway, speeding toward the tunnel that led to Marin County, then passing beneath the arch painted to resemble a rainbow.

In the tunnel's darkness he heard Rose ask, "Tell me, did Elise and Robert treat Anna like their *real* child?"

Logan knew that Rose was finally allowing herself to contemplate the idea that perhaps it was she, and not Anna, who'd been adopted. Logan thought for several moments, knowing how important it was to look through the mist of illusion and get to the truth.

They had reached the sunlight on the other side of the tunnel when he said, "Robert unquestionably treated Anna like his own. He's a busy man, but he spent hours with both of his children, attending functions, going to PTA meetings, sitting at the piano to guide their fingers over the keys." He paused. "I should say *our* fingers. I can honestly say he's never treated me any different from Chas or Anna."

For a moment he considered the woman Robert had married. "Elise's father abandoned her family shortly after they moved here from France. I remember hearing her tell someone that she was too poor to have any dolls when she was a child, so she was thrilled to have a daughter to dress up. I think she would have looked at motherhood the same way no matter *how* said daughter arrived."

Logan nudged the car toward the Mill Valley exit. As the car slowed, he glanced at Rose. "As mothers go, Elise wasn't much for cuddling, and as to fun…well, her idea of family outings ran to museums and art shows and plays rather than picnics on the beach."

As Logan negotiated a sharp turn he suddenly realized how uncomplimentary this sounded, not to mention disloyal. He quickly added, "However, we were all encouraged to find something we especially enjoyed, like my love affair with planes and cars.''

Logan stopped for a red light as he finished speaking. He saw Rose peer forward at the Mustang's shiny hood, then back at the trunk, before sitting back in her seat. ''Well,'' she said. ''It certainly *looks* like a labor of love.''

Logan smiled. ''I spent a lot of hours flat on my back, working on the driveshaft, and many days bent over beneath the open hood, tinkering, tuning.'' One side of his mouth quirked higher. ''Sometimes I could almost feel my dad looking over my shoulder, whispering tips, approving.''

His smile faded, then he sighed. ''He wouldn't be all that happy with the way it's running now, though. I'm hoping the engine just needs a good long run to blow the gunk out. Otherwise I'll have to take it to my mechanic.''

''You won't fix it yourself?''

Logan shook his head. ''I don't have that kind of time. If Anna hadn't disappeared, I'd be in my office filing the papers from my trip to France, making calls to see that everything is running smoothly on the new shelter for homeless families funded by Benedict money or checking on their business holdings. It never ends. Once this matter is settled, I'll be playing catch-up for who knows how long.''

When Rose didn't say anything further, Logan figured the subject of the Mustang was closed. And he was relieved. Talking about the hours he'd spent restoring the car had reminded him just how long it had been since he'd had the time to do anything that was his own.

''That's no way to live.'' Rose spoke very softly. ''My mother said that no job should come before someone's life. The Benedicts shouldn't ask that of you.''

''My job enables me to have the sort of life that few people enjoy.'' Logan was aware that guilt sharpened his tone. ''I meet fascinating people, attend spectacular events and fly a private airplane to places that most mechanics' sons can only dream of.''

He paused, drew a breath, then went on more calmly. ''Besides, the Benedicts don't ask anything of me that they don't ask of themselves. Or, for that matter, anything that they don't have the right to ask, considering all they've done for me.''

Rose didn't respond to that.

The light turned green at that point and Logan pulled forward. The road began to climb, and in moments they were twisting and turning beneath a canopy of trees.

This was what Logan had come to do, he told himself as he focused all his attention on negotiating the frequent switchbacks. He hadn't come to discuss the Benedicts or his job or even the matter of finding Anna. He'd come to clear his mind, not muddy it up with pain or regrets or dead dreams that could never be. So he shifted into second as the road climbed and turned, then back into third, then fourth for the brief straightaways. And before long the tension in his shoulders began to ease.

''Absolutely breathtaking!''

Rose's exclamation came as the road began to dip downward toward the sea. A quick glance told Logan that she was gazing past him, toward the breakers curling onto the shore below. It was a gorgeous view, he knew. He could pull over the car and enjoy it with Rose, but he still had a few tense kinks he wanted to work out.

''I'll stop a bit farther on,'' he said. ''Where we can walk along the beach. But if you don't mind, I'd like to give the car a good hard run through this stretch.''

''Sure,'' she replied. ''It feels good to be outside, in the sun and wind.''

Her words made him aware that the air had become more brisk. ''You aren't too cold, are you?'' he asked, then added reluctantly, ''I can put the top up if you are.''

''No. Please, don't.''

Logan glanced at Rose, saw the dark tendrils that had escaped her braid to dance wildly around her face. A face that was flushed with obvious enjoyment as she lifted it to the sun and smiled.

He shook his head. ''If I had any doubt that you and Anna

were two separate people, this would have convinced me for sure.''

Rose turned to him in surprise. "Why?"

"Anna hates to drive with the top down. She can't stand to have her hair mussed. Or her clothes. And God forbid she should break a fingernail."

"Not the outdoor type, huh?"

Logan considered the question. "Actually, at one point Anna was something of a tomboy. She ran track during her freshman year in high school and made the varsity team as a sophomore. Then Elise enrolled her in a modeling school, where they indoctrinated her on things like how to wear her hair, along with the proper way to stand and sit and walk. If I remember correctly, her running career ended shortly after that."

"Jeez. Elise sounds like Josh."

Rose shivered, then glanced at Logan. The landscape beyond had changed from pounding surf to an inlet of some sort. Ducks floated on the calm water and two white egrets waded on their long legs near the road.

Logan's eyebrows lifted as he shot her a quick, dark glance. "How do you mean?"

She smiled, fully aware it was a sad smile. "I met my ex-husband at a fancy French restaurant, where I was playing harp," she explained. "After we started dating, Josh began taking me shopping on a regular basis—places like Nordstrom's. He knew how much I liked clothes, and after we became engaged, he promised to buy me an entire new wardrobe if I would get rid of all my thrift-shop and flea-market finds."

She paused to shake her head. "It was the answer to a young, middle-class, working-woman's dream. It didn't occur to me that I was giving up some really unique items in return for all those new, perfectly matching overpriced things. After the divorce, I didn't really regret leaving those clothes behind. Mom and I had a great time poking through secondhand stores to refurbish my wardrobe. Thrift shopping is my version of big-game hunting, you see. I get a big kick out of stalking great deals, like finding a Ralph Lauren at a fraction of retail.''

Rose watched Logan's lips form a slow grin, then she turned forward to watch the road. When she realized that they'd left the coast altogether and moved inland, she almost reminded him of his promise to stop near the ocean. But suddenly she didn't have the energy for a walk. Besides, she was enjoying the grassy rises on either side of the road, the trees that twisted up toward the blue skies, the hum of the motor and the sway of the car as it took the curves.

She had no idea she'd even closed her eyes, let alone fallen asleep, until she became aware of Logan's hand on her shoulder and his voice saying, ''Hey, Rosie. Time to wake up.''

Opening her eyes, Rose discovered Logan's face was very near. The memory of those moments outside the door to Anna's bedroom caused a tingle in her lips. With the languor of sleep still blanketing her mind, warming her body, she wondered if she might have dreamed that moment in the darkened hallway. No, she thought as the heat of remembered contact flooded her. That kiss had been real. And so was this moment, with Logan's face close to hers, his features shadowed by the sun behind his left shoulder.

In an attempt to ignore the shiver of anticipation coursing through her body, Rose frowned and asked, ''What time is it?''

''A little after six.''

''Six o'clock in the *evening?*'' Rose sat up with a start. ''How long did I sleep? Where are we?''

''Whoa.'' Logan's hand pressed gently against her shoulder. He smiled as he said, ''We're in Jenner-by-the-Sea. You fell asleep hours ago, and I didn't have the heart to wake you. Besides, I was enjoying the drive. However, I haven't forgotten that I promised you a good long view of the ocean. Okay if we combine that with dinner?''

Rose became aware of the whisper of waves breaking onto the shore. But when she glanced toward the sound, she could see only a blue sky streaked lightly with flat, thin clouds. Once again she tried to sit up straighter. This time she caught sight of a wide band of water—a river, she guessed—bisecting the beach then running right into the ocean. Beyond the shoreline, the sea stretched away, dark green-blue, glittering beneath the lowering sun.

"You hungry?"

Without looking away from the view, Rose nodded. Once she was out of the car, however, she turned to follow Logan toward a wood-and-glass structure that hung over the edge of a cliff.

"It's going to be a beautiful sunset," Logan said as he held the door open. "And, unless things have changed a lot, the food here is every bit as good as the view."

When Rose glanced at him, he went on, "I used to come here with my parents."

The words came out with such ease that Logan found himself blinking with surprise as he followed the hostess to a table by the window. He took a seat across from Rose, noting that the location provided views of both the sea and the river flowing into it. Then, glancing around, he saw that the dining room was just as he remembered, a high wood-beamed ceiling above walls of glass. It was as if nothing had changed.

Except that his parents weren't here with him.

Logan took a deep breath. He rarely spoke about his parents, certainly never about the private times they spent away from the house. Yet, after the waitress took their order, when Rose turned to him and asked if his parents were able to get much time away from the Benedict house, he found himself explaining that whenever the family was out of town, the Maguires were free to take their own vacations.

"We only went to Southern California once," he said. "The obligatory trip to Disneyland when I was about eight. The drive back up, through Big Sur, Carmel and Monterey, was gorgeous. But my father preferred the northern coast. So whenever my parents got a decent block of time to travel, we headed up this way. We always stopped here."

With perfect timing the waitress chose just that moment to

bring their food. In wordless agreement both Logan and Rose ate in silence. Logan found himself savoring every succulent mouthful of his lobster and each bite of soft sourdough bread.

"Is the food as good as you remember?" Rose asked.

Logan swallowed a sip of wine. Gazing out the window, he saw that the wispy high clouds had begun to turn the lightest shade of pink.

"Every bit," he replied slowly. "Nothing about the place seems to have changed at all."

"Has it been a long time since your last visit?"

"I don't usually have the time to drive up this far." Logan paused. There seemed no point in being evasive. "Actually, I haven't been here in over twenty-five years—since the last trip I took with my parents, the summer I turned ten. You should have seen the sunset *that* night. It was spectacular."

Logan stared at the soft pink of the high clouds outside the restaurant window. Suddenly his memory overlaid the view with billows of crimson and tangerine clouds that stained the sea beneath to match. The image hit Logan with a suddenness that took his breath away, opening a window onto a time he'd shut away, a moment that now seared his heart with a mixture of joy and pain.

"What a wonderful memory," he heard Rose say. "Something really special to take out when you get lonely."

Logan frowned. His shoulders tightened as he turned to her and said with quiet force, "I am *never* lonely."

Chapter 11

The wounded expression in Rose's eyes made Logan realize just how sharply he'd spoken. Clearing his throat, he went on more quietly, "The Benedicts took me in without hesitation after my parents died. I've always been cared for, always been surrounded by people. I've had no reason to be lonely."

Instant sympathy colored Rose's features. She took a quick breath before saying, "That was a poor choice of words on my part." She then reached across the table to cover his hand with hers. "What I should have said was that it was a lovely memory to take out when you find yourself missing your parents."

Missing them. Logan gazed at the awareness, the empathy in Rose's dark eyes, eyes that seemed to say she knew exactly how he felt.

He had no idea how that could be. He'd been so very careful to show the world he was fine, that he deeply appreciated everything the Benedicts had done for him. Yet, although he felt he had no right to feel lonely, he'd been just that, so very much of the time. Somehow Rose had managed to see this, and it seemed silly now to deny it.

"I have lots of memories of my mom," Rose was saying. "Many little things from my childhood, and many more that I purposely stored up during the past two years. Mom saw to that. She didn't want me to feel all alone after she was gone. She wanted me to be able to get on with my life, without wasting a lot of time grieving."

Logan wanted to ask Rose how she could talk about her recent loss with such ease, but the tightness in his chest held the words back. Instead he nodded to acknowledge her words, then said stiffly, "We should be heading back to the city. There are several things I should be working on."

He stood, leaving the amount of the bill and a generous tip in the black folder on the edge of the table, then led the way outside. When they got to the car, however, and Rose moved toward the passenger side, Logan reached out and took her hand.

No matter what she said or how she said it, the look in Rose's eyes had told him she was indeed missing her mother and feeling the pain that came with loss. He had no words to offer her, no experience other than that of denial, pushing pain away. The only thing he could give her was his time, along with the soothing scents and sounds of the ocean.

"We haven't taken that walk on the beach yet," he said.

She turned to him, and after a moment's hesitation she nodded.

Still holding her hand, Logan led the way down a narrow rocky path to the sand, where he stopped to remove his shoes. After Rose had taken her sandals off, he shoved both pairs beneath an overhanging bush and took her hand again.

Strolling silently toward the faintly pink remains of the sunset, they reached the undulating line that separated dry sand from wet. Three feet in front of them the weak remains of a wave slipped back into the sea. Farther out, more waves curled and crashed before smoothing into a film of white, bubbly foam that slid up the glassy dampness to hover and tremble before again retreating to the sea.

Logan realized that pushing his car through the twists and turns as he drove up here might have eased the tension from his muscles, but the motion of the sea was soothing his soul in a way the long drive had failed to do. Or maybe that feeling was a product of the quiet, nonjudgmental sympathy he'd seen in Rose's gaze.

Slowly he felt the tightness in his chest ease. When he turned to Rose in the twilight, he could see that she was also staring at the waves. Recalling the way in which he'd abruptly ended their conversation in the restaurant, he said softly, "I was rude. I'm sorry."

She turned to him, a look of surprise on her face. "I'm the one who should apologize. I guess playing the role of Anna for the past day and a half made me forget that you hardly know me well enough to discuss your personal life."

Logan shook his head. "It's not that. I don't talk about my parents. Never have. With anyone."

Rose looked at him, her eyes wide, dark and soft. "Not even Anna?"

"Especially not Anna."

"Why?"

Logan took a deep breath. "When Robert and Elise took me in, they gave me things my parents never would have been able to afford—along with the advantages that came with a degree from an expensive university and introductions to the right sort of people. I never wanted any of the Benedicts to think I was ungrateful."

Rose shook her head. "I can't imagine they would mistake grief over the loss of your parents as ingratitude."

Logan gazed into her eyes for several moments, searching for words to make her understand. "The Benedicts don't see emotions in the same way as most people," he said at last. "The first ten years of my life were full of love. And laughter. I knew how good I had things, despite the cramped quarters I shared with my parents and the teasing I suffered because

my folks couldn't afford to dress me like the wealthy kids I
went to school with. But my mom and dad were always there,
whereas Robert and Elise were often gone on business trips.
Each night my parents read to me, and both hugged me before
I went to sleep, while Chas, often as not, was put to bed by
a maid. I felt—''

Logan stopped speaking. He didn't really know what he felt,
and he was afraid that the glitter in Rose's eyes as she gazed
up at him indicated that she was thinking he must be crazy.

''You felt guilty,'' Rose finished in a soft, quavering voice.
The glimmer in her eyes shone more brightly as she lifted a
hand to his cheek and went on. ''You, sweet man, didn't want
Chas, and later Anna, to see the depth of your grief and perhaps realize that you had experienced something that they,
with all their money, never had—lots of time with people who
gave you lots of love.''

Rose's hand was warm where it rested on his cheek. In her
eyes, sympathy and understanding shimmered behind her
tears. Tears for his sorrow, tears he could never allow himself
to shed.

Even now he was aware that he was shoving the old grief
deep into the tightness of his chest, refusing to let it rise and
break the surface of his control. It was enough, he realized,
that Rose was crying for him. The relief was palpable, allowing him to draw a deep, soothing breath, smile and say,
''Thank you.''

But, he realized, words alone weren't sufficient to express
the wave of gratitude he felt for the understanding she offered,
for the ease she'd brought to his soul by giving voice to the
emotions he'd locked so tightly away.

Lifting his free hand to her cheek, mirroring the action she'd
taken only a moment before, he bent forward to place his lips
on hers. He felt them tremble beneath his touch. He wondered,
as he lifted his head a second later, whether the vibration sig-
nified a further expression of sympathy and shared grief, or
held the beginnings of desire.

He had no trouble identifying the physical need that swept

through his own body, urging him to lower his mouth to claim hers again, to slide one arm around Rose's waist and pull her to him as the hand touching her cheek eased along the side of her face to cup the back of her head, allowing him to deepen the kiss even further.

As Logan's arm tightened around her waist, Rose became aware that what had started as a sweet kiss was now becoming something altogether different. Passion, desire, longing flowed from Logan's lips to hers. A tight ache swelled within her chest, then spread throughout her body in a pulse that mimicked the rhythm of the sea.

Rose let her hand glide from Logan's cheek, the stubble rough against her palm as it passed, to curl her fingers around the back of his neck. Her lower arm rested on his shoulder for support as her body melted into his. The kiss intensified further as Logan brought his tongue into play, sliding past her parted lips, entering the recesses of her mouth to communicate a growing desire, which her body answered with more heat. A deep ache grew in her breasts where they pressed against his chest, then spiraled lower and lower.

Against her closed eyelids Rose suddenly saw the famous image of Burt Lancaster and Deborah Kerr embracing in the surf. Any moment now, she thought, the passion flowing between her body and Logan's would pull them down, onto the beach. And with the waves crashing over them, they would—

The fantasy ended in a gasp as a wave struck their legs to splash upwards in a fountain of icy water. Together she and Logan stumbled backward, but the damage had been done. Already the rogue wave had begun to recede, leaving them drenched from head to toe, staring at each other in stunned surprise.

The wind deepened the cold, chilling her wet flesh, yet when Rose saw one side of Logan's mouth quirk into a smile, she smiled back. She stared at his wet hair, saw water drip from it onto his nose as he began to laugh. A drop of moisture trickled down her face to find its salt-flavored way into her own mouth as her laughter joined his.

Then Logan grasped her hand. "God, it's cold," he said. "Let's get back to the car."

He pulled her up the beach as he spoke. Rose hurried beside him, missing the heat that had fevered her flesh before the wave interrupted their kiss. Her shivers were growing stronger as they paused at the bottom of the path just long enough to grab both pairs of shoes from their hiding place and raced up the path to the car.

Logan tossed the shoes into the back seat as they reached the passenger side, then turned to Rose. As she shuddered before him she noticed that his white shirt was now plastered to the hard curves of his chest. A tiny thread of heat battled the chill dancing along her arms as she lifted her gaze to his. His eyes, however, were focused lower. Aware that her turtle-neck must be clinging to her breasts, accentuating the tight bud her nipples had formed against the cold, the thread of heat running through her pulsed a little stronger.

At that moment Logan's eyes met hers, dark and hard. His lips came down on hers swiftly, hot and demanding. Rose matched the intensity with all the force of her being. Heat flared higher, but still she found herself shivering as Logan broke off the embrace.

"We're going to freeze to death if we keep this up," he said.

Rose noticed that he had a grin on his face as he reached down to open her door.

"Get in and get that damned window up," he said, then stepped toward the back of the car.

Rose lowered herself to the seat and closed the door. As she rolled the window up, she heard the trunk open then slam shut. She turned toward the driver's side as Logan reached his door, saw him pause to toss a large, floppy square of fabric into her lap, before he got behind the wheel.

"Wrap yourself in that while I get the top up," Logan instructed.

"That" referred to the plaid blanket he'd thrown at her. With practically senseless fingers, Rose unfolded the wool, then pulled it up to her chin, letting it drape around her arms and flow down her legs to mid-calf.

Somehow the tiny amount of protection this provided from the biting ocean breeze only made her shiver more. When the convertible roof came forward to lie on the windshield frame, the breeze was cut off completely. Still, she shivered. The engine roared to life. Rose glanced toward Logan to see a blue-and-gold beach towel draped over his shoulders and upper arms—rather scanty-looking protection against the damp and the cold.

"Here," she said. "Help me turn the blanket sideways, so both of us can get under it."

Logan's hands tightened around the steering wheel as he shook his head. "No. The best way to warm us up is to start driving and get the heater going."

He was backing up even as he spoke. A quick turn of the wheel and a click of the stick shift had them moving forward, then roaring onto the road. Rose waited, shivering. Several minutes passed before he reached for the dashboard and slid the lever marked Heater. Instantly warm air caressed her feet. A few moments later she felt the heat slide through the fabric of the blanket.

Even so it was several miles later before she felt warm enough to let the blanket slide to her lap. She glanced at Logan. His hair was still plastered to his forehead, except for a few dry locks that fluttered in the air flowing out of the heater.

Without thinking, she reached across to smooth these errant strands back. The quick glance and half smile Logan sent her way heated her much more effectively than the blast of warm air coming from the floorboards. She returned his smile, then dropped her hand to her lap and rested against the seat.

"We're in for a long ride back," he said.

"That's all right," she replied. "Then I'll get to see the scenery I missed while I was napping."

"Afraid not. I'm cutting over to Highway 101 to take the inland route. It'll get us home faster. And out of these wet clothes."

A heavy silence followed these words. Were they just an innocent reference to their recent drenching, Rose wondered, or was there a deeper, more suggestive meaning? She shot another glance toward Logan, then drew a deep breath. She wasn't sure she was ready for anything deeper. Not tonight. Already things had moved faster than she was comfortable with.

Despite the fact that she'd seen this man in her dreams for most of her life, she didn't really know him. She was aware of an emotional bond that she didn't understand, a bond that went beyond the obvious physical attraction. And given the romantic sensation she'd always experienced upon waking from one of those dreams, her response to Logan in the flesh—where he was real, solid, charming and oh, so appealing on so many levels—was completely understandable.

Or it would be, if not for the fact that once upon a time she had been just as attracted to Josh Whitney, had thought *he* was the man of her dreams. That relationship had most certainly turned out to be a nightmare.

She'd had two years to gain distance from that fiasco, and had come to see her own part in the failure of her marriage. It was now clear that she'd been so besotted by Josh's good looks, his charming ways and high-powered lifestyle that she'd overlooked the clues that might have warned her away. Her mother had always impressed upon her the need to be open to new experiences, so it had only seemed natural to let Josh instruct her in how things were done "on the hill," where everyone had been wealthy and cultured for decades, where setting a proper table, choosing the proper attire for each and every function and discussing the proper subjects with the correct political spin came as naturally as breathing.

And if it had been just a matter of learning about wines and which of these should be served with what food, things would have been fine. But it became very clear that Josh wanted more from her. He wanted a wife who thought *exactly* as he thought on each and every subject, who dressed according to *his* taste, always. A wife who would be happy to associate only with his friends, who would be willing to sever all past ties, even to her mother. Maybe *especially* to her mother—who still dressed in tie-dye and jeans—regardless of how little time the woman had left in this world.

Logan could turn out to be just as controlling, she warned herself as they crossed the Golden Gate Bridge. The high-rise buildings of San Francisco on her left glittered with a thousand lights against the black sky. She shifted her attention to the man sitting next to her, studying Logan's profile, the way his eyes narrowed as he concentrated on the traffic in front of them. Did those green-brown eyes see *her,* she wondered, or simply a reflection of someone else.

Logan's explanation of the way in which he'd controlled his grief over his parents' deaths indicated that he'd mastered the art of hiding his true feelings, even from himself. What other emotions might he have shut away in some forgotten part of his heart? For all she knew, he might even be in love with Anna, despite his insistence to the contrary. Because he'd grown up playing the role of protective big brother, it was possible that he'd buried any romantic attraction so deep that he could only act upon it in the presence of someone who looked like Anna.

Her twin.

Rose shivered. The thought didn't please her one little bit. She wanted to believe with all her heart that she'd dreamed about this man over and over again for a reason—that they were meant to be together, that when they kissed, he'd been thinking of *her.* But she had to admit that the things she'd read today regarding the almost extrasensory link many twins reported suggested that when she'd dreamed of the Golden Gate Bridge, or of Logan, she had been seeing whatever Anna had been looking at.

"Home at last."

Logan's words woke Rose to the fact that they were passing through the open gates that guarded the Benedict house. The far left garage door finished sliding up as they approached. A moment later she was sitting in the dimly lit enclosure, her senses suddenly attuned sharply to the man sitting next to her. Her heart was beating wildly despite the warnings from her mind to retreat quickly before anything resembling the passion that had flared between them on the beach had a chance to spark to life again.

The garage door rumbled shut behind the car as Logan switched the engine off. In the ensuing silence, he suddenly became aware that Rose and he had not spoken one word on the two-hour drive back to the city. He tried to tell himself that he'd been intent on negotiating the narrow roads between the coast and Highway 101 in the dark, then on keeping an eye peeled for signs of cruising Highway Patrol cars as he pushed the speed limit by several miles per hour.

It had seemed very important to get back to the house as soon as possible. It hadn't occurred to him to question this need, but now he realized it was an attempt to escape his feelings. After his parents had died, he would ride his bike, long and hard, whenever the loneliness or the grief threatened to overcome him. Pedaling as fast as possible, pushing himself up the surrounding hills and weaving in and out of traffic had dulled his sense of loss. Once he learned to drive, the car had become his source of solace in exactly the same way. Driving cleared his mind, he had told Rose. Now he realized it also numbed his heart.

The click of the passenger door handle surprised Logan out of his thoughts. Seeing that Rose had turned toward the half-open door, he placed a hand on her arm. He thought he saw her hesitate one second before she turned to him. Their eyes met and held.

Logan wanted to thank her—for opening a door to himself that had probably been shut far too long. But with those words would come a flood of emotion that he wasn't ready to deal with right now, not with everything that was going on with Anna. Not with what he sensed growing between him and Rose.

So, once again he resorted to action. Leaning toward her, he lowered his lips to hers. He planned a simple kiss, one he hoped would express all the things he couldn't bring himself to say right now, one that would communicate his inability to do so, and his desire that she understand.

With the touch of her lips, however, a different kind of desire flared. Deepening the kiss, he reached across to her waist and pulled her closer to him. He thought he felt a moment of resistance from her, but a soft moan escaped her throat, and she leaned into the embrace.

"Logan?"

It wasn't Rose's voice calling his name, Logan realized. It was Elise—speaking, he guessed, from the door at the far end of the garage that led to the house. As the woman said, "Anna?" he pulled back from the kiss. Seeing Rose's eyes widen up at him, he gave her a quick smile and whispered, "Follow my lead."

Turning, he exited the car. "Elise," he said to the woman standing thirty feet away. "Is something wrong?"

The question seemed to take the woman by surprise. She frowned, then shook her head. "No. I was wondering if something was wrong down here. I was in the living room when I heard your car drive up. We haven't seen you, or Anna, all day. How...how is she?"

Logan fought a smile as Rose chose that moment to make her entrance, rising from the car on the opposite side.

"I'm fine," she replied. "Logan took me for a long drive."

"I see." Elise's sharp eyes shifted to Logan. "Is this your idea of therapy?"

Logan nodded slowly as he closed his door and started around the car. "You know how Anna likes to go to Stinson Beach and lie in the sun. I thought a drive up there might stir some memories."

"Oh. Well, did you have any luck?"

Aware that Rose was looking to him for guidance, he shook his head. "No. Even being hit by a wave and getting a mouthful of salty water didn't help."

The reference to that wave brought back every sensual moment of that kiss on the beach. Logan stepped toward Elise, mentally cursing the woman for showing up at the door, for interrupting those moments in the car, for making sure that nothing further would happen between him and Rose now or most likely the rest of the night.

He knew Elise all too well, recognized that she had decided to play the role of concerned mother this evening, and once he followed her up the narrow set of stairs that led to the foyer, with Rose at his heels, he knew why. Robert and Chas stood beneath the crystal chandelier, waiting, with Nicole behind them. When Rose stepped onto the marble floor, the two men glanced at each other as if wordlessly confirming a previous agreement.

"Anna," Chas said. "We've been worried about you."

Logan watched Rose glance from Chas to Robert, her features tight with confusion. "Have I done something wrong?" she asked. "I didn't say anything last night to cause a problem, did I?"

"Well," Elise replied. "You did raise some eyebrows with that dress."

Robert shot a reproachful glance toward his wife before looking at Rose again. "As far as I know, last evening went well. But we were hoping that your memory would have begun to return by now. The next few weeks are critical to the campaign, and I was hoping you could help out."

The hesitant look on Rose's face told Logan she was unsure of her next line. "Robert," he said, "you know that Anna has never cared much for social engagements."

Chas stepped forward. "We do know. But Stephen Dahlberg just announced plans to set up a special task force to provide schooling and health care for indigent children if he's elected, something the Benedicts have been involved in for years. Tomorrow morning Dad is speaking at the family center we opened last year. Having the entire family present would serve to emphasize the Benedict tradition of service."

Logan turned to Rose. He was certain that the last way she wanted to spend a Sunday morning was listening to political speeches. But if it had been Anna standing there, he would have had no qualms about suggesting she help her father in this way.

"You can do that, can't you, Anna?" he asked.

Rose's dark-blue eyes widened, whether in anger or terror he wasn't sure. He found himself holding his breath until she shrugged.

"I guess so," she said, then turned to Robert. "All I have to do is sit at the table, right? I won't have to speak or anything?"

"Not at all," Robert replied with a warm, affectionate smile.

"Well, you *will* be expected to carry on a conversation with the others at your table," Elise interjected.

"But I'll be sitting next to you," Logan followed quickly. "To prompt your memory as new people approach, and head off confusing questions, just like last night."

Rose nodded slowly. Logan turned to the other four people. "What time do you need us to be ready?"

Chas replied, "We're to arrive at nine, so to allow for traffic we should all meet here, in the foyer, by eight-fifteen." Reaching back for Nicole's hand, he continued. "Which means the two of us should head back to the apartment and get some sleep."

Logan glanced at his watch. "Jeez. It's almost eleven already. No wonder you were concerned about us." He glanced at Rose. "Time to get you up to bed."

The words must have sounded as suggestive to Rose as they did to him, because her face grew suddenly pink. She nodded wordlessly, then turned toward the stairs. After bidding a quick good-night to the others, Logan followed Rose up the stairs, catching up with her just outside Anna's room. He took her hand as she reached for the doorknob.

"We need to talk," he said softly.

In the glow of the small light at the top of the stairs, he saw her look up at him, her eyes dark, unreadable.

"I know," she whispered. "But not now. Not all of that

was an act down there, you know. I really *am* tired, in spite of dozing off in the car.''

Logan continued to hold her hand a moment, debating if he should insist they talk for just a bit, to clear up any misconceptions that might have grown out of the day's events. But when she drew her hand from his fingers to twist the knob and open the door, he stepped back and said simply, ''Good night. Sleep well.''

The following morning, when Rose came down the stairs to join Logan in the foyer, the dark circles under her eyes told him she hadn't slept well at all.

''Are you okay?'' he breathed as she reached his side.

She looked up at him as her shoulders lifted in a shrug. ''I'm a little sleep deprived,'' she replied softly. ''A dream woke me in the middle of the night. I…thought I was home again. When I couldn't get back to sleep, I got on the Internet and looked up more information on twins. It was three o'clock before I shut the computer off, and I had to get up at six to wash my hair, dry it and make the blasted stuff look right.''

She'd pulled the ''blasted stuff'' back into a tight French braid, and used some substance to hold her bangs and the loose tendrils back from her face. The severe style perfectly complemented the pale-blue jacket she wore over a straight, knee-length skirt. A scoop of embroidered white cotton filled in the jacket's deep vee demurely. A single pearl stud decorated each earlobe, and a matching string encircled the base of her neck.

''Do I look like hell?''

Logan grinned. ''No. You look perfect in that outfit. *Very* Annalike.''

Her quick frown surprised him, but before he could ask Rose if he'd said something wrong, Elise's voice cut across the foyer.

''Now, *that's* more like my girl.''

Chapter 12

"Oh, and you're wearing your great-great-grandma Anna's jewelry," Elise continued as she descended the stairs, followed by Robert. "What a wonderful touch."

Rose lifted her hand to the strand of pearls. When she'd picked the clothes she was to wear, her intention had simply been to look the part of Anna. Quiet. Understated.

Of course, considering that Anna had purchased the red-and-black dress, Rose wondered if the former track star Logan had described didn't sometimes rebel at this image. But Rose had decided it was up to Anna whether she continued to dress as her mother dictated or chose to please herself. Today Rose would go with the former, if only to make things easy on herself.

Easy depended on one's definition of the word, Rose decided three and a half hours later, as the limousine carrying Anna's family pulled back into the driveway. It hadn't been at all easy to smile constantly and listen to people praise her "father's" plans for the state, to carry on polite conversations with perfect strangers about subjects totally foreign to her or to stay awake through the seemingly endless speeches. She was aware that the breakfast meeting had given her only a taste of what candidates must go through to win an election, but it had greatly increased her appreciation for their stamina. She was exhausted, and it wasn't even noon yet.

Only two things had kept her from running out of the room, screaming. The first had been the young girl sitting next to her at breakfast. After a slow warm-up period, shy, ten-year-old Denise had confided that the ribbon holding her blond ponytail was the first new one she'd had in the three years since her father lost his job. During Robert's speech, he used Denise and her family as successful examples of the program he'd put in place the previous year. They now had a home in one of the self-help apartment buildings the Benedicts had helped to fund, and Denise's father was now employed as the building manager.

The other compensation had been Logan's presence and the frequent smiles he sent her way to let her know she was doing a good job of being Anna. But even the warm glow that she felt each time she received one of those smiles couldn't keep Anna's beige pumps from pinching her toes, or ease the pain in her skull from having tightly braided her hair in search of perfection.

Not only did she feel like an impostor, she was beginning to resent the way everyone so easily accepted her as Anna. So when the car pulled into the driveway, she was dying to run up to Anna's room and change into something more comfortable, something that would make her feel more like herself. But Elise had called ahead to Martina, so the minute the family walked into the house, lunch was served.

Breakfast was now a faint memory, as far as Rose's stomach was concerned, so she responded to its empty growls and joined the family in the dining room. From her seat next to Logan, she had a glorious view of the Pacific Ocean as it approached the bay, and, of course, of *her* bridge. Anna's bridge, she reminded herself as she ate the lasagna—Anna's favorite food, Elise reminded her—surrounded by Anna's family and Logan, Anna's surrogate brother.

Anna, Anna, Anna, Rose thought. Then, realizing how much that sounded like Jan Brady's famous, "Marsha, Marsha, *Marsha*" lament, she laughed, choked on a piece of lettuce and began coughing uncontrollably.

She was vaguely aware that Logan was slapping her back, and when he handed her a glass of water, she took several sips. As soon as her throat was sufficiently soothed, she turned watery eyes his way.

"Thank you," she croaked.

"You okay now?" he asked.

Rose nodded.

"You look tired."

This came from Robert. When Rose met his concerned gaze, it struck her that this man truly did care about his daughter. It occurred to her that Robert would most likely be frantic if he knew that Anna was missing, off on her own, who knew where. And with his money and contacts he would most likely be able to have her located and returned in no time.

"Anna," Robert said softly. "Why don't you go up to your room and take a nap?"

Rose glanced at Logan. She suddenly wanted to have the private conversation with him that she'd turned down the night before. Perhaps it was time they admitted the charade they were involved in and see if the authorities could locate Anna, bring her home and put an end to all the lies.

"Logan and Chas," Robert continued. "While she naps I have several business matters I need to discuss with both of you."

Rose yielded to the inevitable with grace. What she had to say could wait an hour or two. "You know," she said, "a nap sounds like just the thing."

And it was. By the time Rose climbed the stairs to Anna's room, her weariness was pulling at her like a heavy weight. She barely had enough energy to remove the skirt and jacket, hang them up, then kick the hated heels into the closet. She would put them on their proper rack later, she decided as she grabbed a thin cotton robe from a hook.

Sliding her arms into the sleeves, she belted the wrapper at her waist as she crossed the room to her bed. *Anna's* bed, she reminded herself as she slipped beneath the covers. And this is Anna's pillow, she told herself as she laid her head upon it. I'm in Anna's world. Rose doesn't exist here.

It was nearly four in the afternoon when she woke. She stared at the digital readout on the clock by the bed and drew in a deep breath. Sitting up, she glanced around the room and shivered.

She'd had a lovely dream. She'd been back at the home she'd shared with her mother in Seattle, standing behind her harp and staring out the large picture window at the Space Needle, rising at the foot of the hill in front of the buildings that comprised the Seattle skyline.

She'd been *herself,* again.

Longing to capture that feeling while awake, Rose went to the closet and pulled out her harp, then took it to the bed where she began to play. While her fingers alternately plucked and stroked the strings, her soul settled down. Closing her eyes, she conjured up the image of home, of her room high above the city, of the teddy bear missing half its fur that her mother had purchased at an antique store, the pillowcases embroidered with flowers, collected from various garage sales.

As she drew her fingers over the strings at the end of the last tune, the vibrations in the air seemed to complete the healing, to restore Rose to herself. When she opened her eyes again, however, she found she was back in Anna's room, surrounded by Anna's things. She frowned, gazing out the window where fog had crept in to completely shroud the beach in gray and render the Golden Gate Bridge a mere shadow.

She needed to get out of here.

Rose stored the harp away, then opened her suitcase and pulled out a pair of black leggings and an oversize turquoise sweatshirt. She knew this outfit looked far too bright to have been pulled from Anna's neutral-toned closet, but at the moment she needed to be in her own clothes, her own skin. If someone saw her and demanded an explanation, she would come up with something, but at the moment, all she could think of was getting out of the house.

Once she was dressed, she slipped out the door and made her way down the iron steps leading to the stone balcony. Holding her breath, terrified that someone inside the house would see her and cut off her escape, she crossed the herringbone tiles, then hurried down the cement steps to the beach and started walking.

The fog was wonderful, muting the colors of sea and sand, turning the sky into a thick soup of gray that swirled around her as she walked along the base of the cliff. Her bare feet dug into the cool, dry sand with each step. The act of moving, combined with the soft whisper of waves breaking onto shore, finished the soul soothing that the harp had started.

The sheer wall on her right came to an abrupt end, like the corner of a building. As Rose continued on, she noticed several trees rising up a gentle slope. About ten feet to her right, a man wearing a brown baseball cap and a denim jacket sat on a weathered wooden bench. Behind the bench, a dirt trail wound upward, then disappeared into the trees.

Rose turned and stepped toward the path, thinking she might follow it just to see where it led. But when she glanced up the steep incline, she decided she didn't have that kind of energy. She just wanted an easy stroll, so she turned to the left and continued walking toward the southern tower of the bridge.

"Anna, what do you think you're doing?"

She turned toward the deep voice. Her brief detour had taken her within five feet of the wooden bench. The man she'd noticed sitting there was now standing. He had lean, craggy features and dark, sharp eyes.

"I've been here three afternoons in a row, waiting for you to get back to me. And now you just walk away?"

Rose's heart began to pound as the man approached. When she realized he was only an inch or so taller than she was, some of her panic subsided. He appeared to be in his late twenties. As Rose studied his face, she thought he looked vaguely familiar, much the way Robert and Elise had when she first encountered them.

Could his face, like theirs, be connected to images she'd seen through that extrasensory connection she seemed to share with her sister? If so, how was this man connected to Anna? A boyfriend, perhaps? Someone Anna's parents disapproved of, requiring clandestine meetings?

It was obvious she couldn't just come out and ask him. So she decided to act the role of stuck-up rich girl, even if she wasn't sure this did Anna justice. Standing just a tad taller, she lifted her chin and asked, "*I* was supposed to meet you here?"

The man gave her a tight smile. "Yes. You were going to give me an interview."

Rose knew where she'd seen this man now. He'd been among the crowd of reporters covering Robert's speech this morning. She remembered the intense way he'd stared at her during Robert's speech and that he'd begun to step toward her just before she was ushered to the car to return to the Benedict house.

She didn't know what his connection to Anna might be, but from things Logan had said about her twin, she doubted that Her Shyness would have agreed to speak to a reporter—about her family or anything else. Rose imbued her voice with every bit of that doubt as she repeated, "Interview?"

This time the man grinned, a rather charming grin, she had to admit. "Okay," he said. "Can't blame a guy for trying. So, no interview. But you did say you'd look into those rumors for me."

Not for the first time, Rose fervently wished that Anna had kept a journal. Maybe then she'd have *some* clue what this man was talking about. Considering that this was a reporter, someone who would be more than delighted to launch an investigation into the strange behavior of Robert Benedict's daughter if she were to slip up and say the wrong thing, this wasn't good at all.

As the silence stretched between them, Rose saw the man's grin fade. "Look," he said at last. "I don't want to cause any problems for your father. Actually, I prefer him over Dahlberg. But, the fact is, if Robert Benedict fathered a child out of wedlock twenty-five years ago, the public has a right to know. Especially when you consider how he parades his 'family values' about."

Rose fought a shudder. Twenty-five years ago. The man was talking about her—and her twin.

"Anna." He took another step toward her, his tone conspiratorial. "I could tell you wanted to learn the truth, too. So what did you find out? Did Robert have an affair with one of the Donnelly girls?"

The Donnelly girls. Rose felt the very center of her body grow cold as she remembered the caption beneath the newspaper clipping in Grace's scrapbook. The fact that her mother had been identified with a different last name was something she hadn't had time to consider much, let alone come to terms with. And now this man was suggesting that her mother had had an affair with Robert. That *he* was her father?

"Why now?" The words were out of Rose's mouth before she even finished thinking them. "Why are you investigating this now? Rob—my father has been in politics for *years*."

The man frowned. "I told you the other day. I've only recently moved to California. I grew up in Chicago, where my dad transferred to Northwestern University from the University at Berkeley almost twenty-six years ago. When I got hired at the paper, I was assigned to cover Robert Benedict's primary campaign. When I called my dad, he said he'd worked Charles Benedict's campaign when he was in school here, and suggested I should check into—I think he called it 'the *almost* scandal.'"

Rose instantly knew who this man's father was—the skinny guy with the glasses in the newspaper clipping bearing the image of her mother and aunt. She drew a slow breath. The caption had said his name was Scott something. Scott Miller. Well, at least she knew this fellow's last name. But what, exactly, had his father told him? And how was she supposed to ask without clueing him in to Anna's "amnesia"?

"Do you mind telling me," said a voice from behind Rose, "what something that may or may not have happened in the past has to do with the issues that Robert Benedict and Steven Dahlberg are debating *today?*"

Rose turned to see Logan striding forward. He stopped at her right side to tower over Mr. Miller.

The reporter glanced up nonchalantly. "You're Logan Maguire, aren't you?"

"Yes."

"I know about you. Victor Benedict's protégé. The family watchdog. Pleased to meet you. I'm Scott Miller."

The man offered his hand. Logan ignored it. "Well, Mr. Miller, as the 'family watchdog' I'm here to tell you that you're trespassing."

"I'm not on your property."

"Not physically, but you are invading our privacy. And then there's the matter of slander."

"Hey…" Miller held his hands up as if to ward off a blow, but he hardly looked worried. "I believe in doing a thorough job. I'm just trying to follow a very old trail to see whether there's anything to the story my father told me."

"Which is?"

"My father was enrolled in the same political science class as the Donnelly sisters. He told me the class was divided into groups and assigned to volunteer for various primary campaigns when the January session started. The six students designated to answer phones and send out flyers for the Charles Benedict campaign formed a deep friendship. The primary was held in June back then. After Benedict won, the group broke up and headed their separate ways over summer break. The following fall, Dad saw one of the Donnelly girls coming out of one of her art classes, where she was met by Victor, Joe and Robert Benedict. Curious, he waited until the men left, then approached her, intending to ask if she planned to work with the Benedicts for the November election. Two things became immediately obvious. She was crying, *and* she was pregnant.''

His last word hung in the air for several moments. Logan broke the silence. ''I'm not seeing any scandal here. Surely the young woman had a boyfriend and—''

Miller cut Logan off with a shake of his head. ''My father asked around. No boyfriend. Also, shortly after this, both Donnelly girls suddenly dropped out of their classes, and disappeared. When he asked around, no one, not even Professor Wilkins, could tell him why. I tried talking to the professor, but he's *still* not talking. Robert hasn't returned my calls, so, I thought the family might be able to offer an explanation.'' He paused. ''I'm just looking for the truth.''

Logan shook his head slowly. ''Not buying it, Miller. What you're looking for is a sensational story, and you're attempting to confuse Anna into providing it. Since you are such a *thorough* fellow, why don't you trace the records of Anna's birth. You'll learn that she was conceived and born in a fertility clinic. Print that if you want, but it's old news.''

Rose was impressed. Logan had as much admitted to her that he thought Victor had falsified Anna's birth records, but now he'd spoken of them with such conviction that he'd nearly convinced *her* of their validity. And, apparently, this had also persuaded Mr. Miller to drop this line of investigation. For the time being, anyway.

''I'm sorry I bothered you,'' the man said to Rose, then turned and started up the path.

Logan watched Miller for several minutes. When the reporter disappeared into the trees, he turned to Rose. Her face was nearly white. Hardly surprising, considering all that had happened to her the past two and a half days.

Logan took her hand. She glanced up at him and gave him a tiny smile. ''Thanks for coming to my rescue,'' she said, then frowned. ''How did you know I was down here?''

''I saw you through the window in Robert's office, tiptoeing across the veranda. Fortunately, he and Chas were bent over some papers at the time. As soon as I could conclude our talk, I came after you.'' He sobered. ''Just barely soon enough, it seems.''

''In the nick of time. I had no idea what the man was talking about at first. Worse, once I realized he was a reporter, I was afraid I might say something that would make him think Anna was nuts and give him a *real* story.''

''Well, you seemed to be doing a pretty good job. I came around the corner just as he said something about Robert having an affair. I ducked back against the cliff so I could listen, afraid I'd break in and say the wrong thing.'' He paused. ''Interesting story he had to tell, but I don't think we should discuss it here. You okay to start walking back to the house?''

''Sure.''

They turned, and Logan slid one arm across Rose's shoulders. As they strolled along the base of the cliff, he felt her arm sneak around his back and her fingers grip the side of his shirt. They walked along in companionable silence, with only the sound of waves whooshing onto the sand on their right, until Rose spoke.

''Aren't you concerned someone might see us, walking like this?'' She glanced up at him with an uncertain expression. ''Not that I mind the support or the warmth. But is it normal for you to walk arm in arm with Anna?''

He shook his head and smiled. ''Hardly. But this is where Chas and I used to stage our mock battles. I know for a fact that we're too close to the cliff for anyone to see us. And I also know that the fog muffles our voices. Best to talk softly, though.''

They didn't talk at all for several moments, just walked in companionable silence until Logan asked softly, ''How did you come to talk to that fellow, anyway?''

Rose turned to him. ''He was sitting on that bench,'' she replied quietly. ''He said he was waiting for me—for Anna. He referred to the old newspaper clipping, the one from Grace's scrapbook. It seems he showed a copy of it to Anna three days ago and wanted to know what I'd—what *she* had found out."

She paused and shuddered. "It was so surreal. I came down on the beach because I needed time to feel like *Rose* again. When he addressed me as Anna, I felt lost, confused. Almost as if I couldn't remember *who* I was. Logan…" She stopped walking and stepped away from him.

Logan stopped, also, and turned to Rose as she went on. "I was thinking, during lunch, that we should let the family know that I'm not Anna. Doesn't Robert have contacts with the police? Couldn't they find her more quickly than you can?"

"Maybe," Logan replied.

He took her hand and began walking slowly, considering her words. As they drew near the house, he said, "I'm concerned that calling the police in might let the media get wind of this. Considering our encounter with Mr. Miller, I'd rather not take that chance. At least until we've exhausted all our leads."

They'd reached the smooth wall that formed the base of the stairs leading up to the house. Logan stopped walking again and turned to Rose. She gazed up at him for several seconds, her eyes dark.

"I suppose that means I continue to play Anna."

Her features revealed no emotion, but Logan heard a thickening in her lowered voice that spoke of reluctance and perhaps doubt.

"You're doing a good job," he said with a smile.

"Maybe too good. The whole thing is getting a bit creepy. I feel…haunted, sort of."

Rose drew in a deep breath, which ended in a choked laugh as she went on. "It's so weird. I told you about growing up with the sense that I was missing a part of myself. Well, when I looked through that information on twins who'd been separated at birth and were eventually reunited, I learned that they had all expressed the same feeling of being not quite whole."

Rose paused. Logan watched her lean against the wall and gaze past him, toward the ocean.

"As a kid," she said softly, "my favorite movie was *The Parent Trap*. I thought it would be great to look like someone else, imagined how much fun it would be to trade places, to fool all my friends and hers."

Her dark eyes shifted to Logan's. "It isn't fun at all. It's lonely. And sad. I feel as if I'm disappearing, that no one can see me. Mostly, I worry that…" She hesitated over the words, then with a tight frown, went on. "I worry that when you're kissing me, you're actually thinking of Anna."

Logan could hardly believe his ears. "Are you kidding?" he asked. "Rose." He turned, placing his body between hers and the view of the sea, forcing her to look up at him. He gazed intently into her blue eyes as he went on, "I do care, deeply, for Anna. But believe me, never have I even *considered* thinking about her as anything other than my little sister. Not once have I ever had the slightest inclination to hold her in my arms or to kiss her or felt the desire to—"

Logan broke off. He didn't want to tell Rose what he desired. The words would sound crass. Only action would do. So he lowered his mouth to hers, then gently forced her back against the wall, pinning her there with his body, deepening his kiss and increasing the contact between their forms until she could have no question in her mind just what it was he wanted to do with her.

As his body grew even warmer against hers, and the ache of desire intensified, Logan felt his heart swell. From the moment he'd encountered Rose on the third-floor deck, he'd felt the strangest connection with this woman, a connection that went deeper than pounding blood and tightening muscles. With Rose he'd discovered a union of mind and spirit he hadn't experienced since the day his parents had been ripped out of his life.

A sharp pain shot through Logan on the heels of that thought. He ignored the ache. This was not a moment to mourn the past, but to grasp the present, savoring each kiss, each contour of Rose's softness as he lost himself in the feel, the taste, the scent that was her.

Rose was aware of the cement wall against her back, rough and cold. Logan's body, pressing against the front of hers, was firm and hot. Trapped between the two, she was a swirl of heat and sensation—Logan's lips on hers, his hands on her arms, his hips communicating his need, her body responding.

"Rose."

Her name was half moan, half whispered tribute as Logan ended the kiss and slowly pulled away. Rose opened her eyes wide to gaze up at his. They were not just warm, she saw, they were dark with intent, expressing hunger as clearly as did the hardness of his body.

A thrill shivered through her.

The sensation raised a thousand questions. Was the connection she'd dreamed of with this man for so many years just physical, or did it go deeper? When would she know—*how* would she know—if this man was capable of loving her, the *real* Rose, not just the one caught in a role that restricted what she said and how she said it?

There were too many questions, and that kiss had drained her of all energy, leaving her only able to whisper, "Now what?"

Logan continued to gaze at her for several seconds, eyes dark, his breathing quick and shallow. Then one side of his mouth quirked up. "Well," he said quietly, "I doubt if we could slip into either my bedroom or Anna's without being seen. But I suppose…" He stopped, smiled widely and raised his eyebrows. "Oh, *you* mean how we should go about finding Anna?"

He waited for Rose's weak smile before going on. "Well, tomorrow Professor Wilkins should be teaching. I think a trip to Berkeley is in order. Now, as to whether you can bear to keep up this charade for another day or so…well, I'll understand if you can't. In fact—"

"I can do it," Rose interrupted. Her chin came up. "It's not killing me, you know, sleeping in a luxurious bed, dressing in designer clothes, being served delicious meals. I just want to be sure that while I 'suffer' in the lap of luxury, Anna isn't in some sort of danger.''

Logan considered these last words. "You know," he said slowly, "I'm not all that worried about Anna. When she called me yesterday morning, she didn't sound afraid. She was excited, then angry at me for not giving the answer she wanted."

He turned to stand next to Rose. Leaning lightly against the cement wall, he stared at the towering cliffs on the other side of the bay, thinking back to that call. "Now that I think about it, I would say she sounded better than she had in a very long time. Defiant. Decisive. Almost sure of herself."

Rose considered his words, then nodded. "All right, then. I'll play her part for another day. But if we don't find anything out after we get to Berkeley, then—''

"Then I go to the police," Logan finished.

He stared at the waves rolling onto the beach some fifty yards in front of them, forcing his attention from the heat still rushing through his veins.

"We have some more information to consider now," he started slowly. "We need to examine the facts—those we know and those we don't."

He turned to look down at Rose. He'd been mulling over those facts on and off all day. It was time to make her aware of the directions his thoughts were taking.

Rose gave him a puzzled frown. "All right," she said. "We know that Anna and I are twins. It's obvious that we were separated at birth. We know that my mother—''

Logan interrupted her with a shake of his head. "We don't *know* who either of your parents are," he said gently.

"*I* know that Kathleen Delancey was my mother," Rose said through clenched teeth.

Logan's jaw stiffened, but he controlled his response. Time would tell on this matter, and they would deal with that subject when the truth became known. Experience in negotiating had taught him not only to pick his battles, but to pick *when* he chose to fight them.

"All right," he said. "We know what made Anna question

Aunt Grace. We know Kathleen and Elizabeth's last name was Donnelly and that they worked on Charles's first campaign for U.S. Senate. The picture in the paper proves that both young women knew Joseph and Robert Benedict.''

An image of that picture appeared in Rose's mind. She said slowly, ''If you're thinking that one of those two men fathered a set of twins, then my money is on Joseph.''

''Interesting,'' Logan said. ''I had the same thought yesterday when you showed me the picture and I remembered what you said about your father dying in a car accident—''

''At about the same time as Joe Benedict,'' Rose finished. ''Remember, I told you that my mother was big on the truth. If, for some reason, Mom felt compelled to lie, I'm willing to bet that she would keep the story as close to the truth as possible.''

Rose watched Logan consider this. When he nodded, she went on. ''Okay, then. Let's see if there are other connections. Mom also told me that my father was a talented musician. There's a big piano in the living room. Did Joe play it?''

''Yes, he did. Along with guitar and saxophone. In fact, he belonged to a band. However, all Benedicts play several instruments. It's a requirement.''

Rose frowned. ''I thought you said Anna had no musical talent.''

''She doesn't.'' Logan shook his head. ''She's not the only one.''

Rose had been desperate to disprove a fear she didn't want to admit—that her life had been built on as many lies as Anna's. But something about Logan's wry expression made her tight lips soften.

''Might we be talking about you?'' she asked. ''What instrument do you play?''

''I took piano lessons,'' he replied stiffly. ''I wouldn't call what I do *playing* the thing. But then—''

Logan didn't need to finish the sentence. Rose knew the following words would have been, ''I'm not a real Benedict.'' She wanted to say, *Thank goodness for that,* but she was now well aware of Logan's need to give loyalty and service to the family who'd taken him in. To her mind this exaggerated sense of duty was as sad as being alone. Or worse. At least alone, a person had the freedom to find their own way.

But what would she know? She'd been surrounded by love all her life. Then, the first time she found herself really alone, she'd gone running off to fill the emptiness.

And now wasn't the time to discuss either of these issues. They had more pertinent matters to deal with.

"Okay," she said. "If all the Benedicts play the piano, you're thinking that my mother could have been speaking about Robert *or* Joe when she was telling me about my father."

Logan gave his head a quick shake. "Robert was married at the time and had a child," he said. "And it was Joe who was killed in that car heading to Reno, Nevada, land of quicky weddings."

Rose blinked.

"Logan," she breathed. "I was born in Reno."

Chapter 13

Logan couldn't have looked more stunned if Rose had told him she'd been born on Mars.

"Reno. I should have thought of that earlier," he said slowly. "I must be failing Detective 101. I guess because you said something about growing up in a commune in Oregon, I just assumed…"

Rose placed her hand on his arm. "It was a reasonable assumption," she said. "I've been rather forceful in insisting that my mother always told the truth, so we've been focusing on the idea that Anna's birthplace was a lie. The *only* lie, that is." Her throat tightened. "It's obvious now that they've come from all sides."

She stared down at her bare toes, poking out from a bed of sand. Soft sand, just like the foundation of her life, appearing solid, yet so ready to shift in the breeze, wash away with the tide.

She felt Logan's warm fingers cover the hand she'd placed on his arm, then give it a squeeze. She blinked back the moisture blurring her vision and looked up.

"I think maybe we need to sort through our facts," he said. "You mentioned you'd seen your birth certificate. Do you remember the name of the hospital?"

"Washoe Medical Center."

"Well, that's a match. Joe was taken there by helicopter from the accident site in the mountains near Donner Lake. He died shortly after he arrived."

Knowing that Logan had lost his parents in that same accident, Rose hated to ask the next question.

"That was the eighteenth of October, right?"

"No." Logan shook his head sharply. "October eighth."

His eyes had the lost, wounded look of a ten-year-old boy trying to keep his emotions at bay. She understood, because this evidence of yet another lie had reawakened her own anguish and formed it into a painful knot in her chest.

Facts, Rose, she told herself. *Concentrate on the facts.*

"My birth certificate states I was born on October eighteenth," she said softly.

"Well, that's an easy thing to change," Logan said. "Presuming, as we must, that someone wanted to cover up the birth of a child on the day her father died. If I'm right, I'm sure that we'll learn that Anna was *not* born in Switzerland, nor is her birthday October *twenty*-eighth."

"So," Rose said softly. "Not only is my last name not Delancey, but my birthday is a lie, too."

She was aware of Logan taking her hand as he spoke. "Well, at least it wasn't a self-serving one. I'm beginning to wonder if there was any truth to the fertility-clinic story. Elise had family in France that she occasionally visited. I do know that when Robert took me and Chas to greet Elise and little Anna at the airport, there were reporters everywhere. If the two of you were born somewhere in the middle of October, it's rather interesting that Elise didn't arrive until two days before the November elections—just in time for some sympathetic press coverage."

Rose considered this, then shook her head. "I don't get it.

Why all the lies, all the secrecy? Joe was single. He was apparently on the way to marry my mother, so…''

Rose grew very still. "Oh, dear," she said. "My mother told me that her older sister died in the same accident as my father. Aunt Lizzie was to have been Mom's maid of honor."

"Where are you going with this?"

"Remember when I told you that my mother would never have allowed a set of twins to be separated? You suggested my mother might have adopted me without being aware that a twin existed. Well, we now know that car accident killed four of the five people in that car, because my mother told me that Aunt Lizzie died in the same wreck as my father. My mother must have been hurt, though. She could even have been unconscious for a couple days. I'm wondering if Victor saw this as a chance to give Robert and Elise the child they wanted, and simply *stole* Anna from my mother."

Logan took a deep breath. "I don't know. Most of Charles's political ambitions were based on a long family tradition of service to the public, which went back to Lucas Benedict discovering all that silver. Victor felt it was his duty to aid his brother in this endeavor, and was every bit as devoted to helping Joe and Robert follow their father, eventually. I guess if he felt that Robert's relationship with Elise was threatened by her inability to…''

When he paused, perhaps to consider his next words, Rose gave voice to her thoughts.

"No. It was the election. Victor had probably been none too happy to learn that one of Charles's sons had fathered a child out of wedlock. And with Joe dead, he knew he had to give my mother at least one of the twins, along with lots of money to keep the scandal out of the papers."

Logan turned to her with a sigh. "You may be right," he said. "But we're still missing quite a few pieces of the puzzle. I think we—"

"What the *hell* are you two talking about down here?"

The deep voice, coming from just above Rose's head, made her jump and turn as Logan's hand released hers.

Chas was leaning over the iron railing, his blond hair shining, a frown darkening his brown eyes. She was aware of Logan next to her, every muscle tense as he no doubt wondered, as she did, just how much Chas had heard.

"Have you forgotten that it's family dinner night?" Chas went on without waiting for an answer to his first question. "Martina is getting ready to serve, and Mother is furious. She sent me to look for you."

"I'm sorry." Logan started for the stairs. "You know how Anna used to love running on the beach. I thought a jog along the shore might...*jog* her memory a little. We were just catching our breath."

Chas stood in the center of the step several feet above them. He turned his dark eyes to Rose. "And did you remember anything?"

Rose shook her head.

"That's too bad," Chas said. "Well, something's bound to come back to you eventually. In the meantime we need to get up to dinner."

He turned as he spoke, and Rose forced her tired legs to hurry behind him. As she climbed alongside Logan, he took her hand. Her flesh tingled, reminding her of those earlier moments when he had pinned her against the wall and kissed her breathless.

She was in that state again by the time they reached the top of the stairs from both the climb and the memory, along with the sudden realization that Chas would have seen that embrace, that kiss, if he'd come looking for them even ten minutes earlier. She pulled her hand from Logan's fingers mere seconds before Chas turned to her.

"Anna, you should change clothes. I'll tell Mother that you'll be right down."

Chas glanced at her sweatshirt, then gave Rose a tiny conspiratorial smile that made her wonder if, when they were younger, he'd covered for Anna in a similar manner. Still too out of breath to speak, however, Rose nodded and headed toward the circular staircase leading toward her room.

It took only minutes to remove the sweatshirt and pull on a long turtleneck sweater, made of the softest lilac cashmere, over her black leggings. She brushed the remaining sand off her feet, slipped them into a pair of black velvet flats, then rushed down to the dining room.

The rest of the family was already seated—Robert at one end of the table, Elise at the other. Rose took the chair between Logan and Aunt Grace, opposite Chas and Nicole. After breathing a quick apology for being late, she forced her attention to her salad, composed of oh-so-fashionable baby greens, English cucumbers and hothouse tomatoes.

As she ate, Rose only half listened to Nicole and Elise as they discussed the latest addition to the wedding plans. Her own awareness kept shifting to Logan, sitting on her right, and the warm electrical sensation she felt in his presence. Moments later she found herself considering the new bits of information she and Logan had learned that day—what they might mean and where they might lead. Then her thoughts returned to Logan again, to the kiss they'd shared—what it might mean and where it might lead.

Rose was so lost in those memories that she gave a little startled jump when Martina reached down to remove her gold-edged plate and replace it with a larger one, which contained a generous slice of roast beef, tiny grilled new potatoes and asparagus drizzled in butter.

If Martina had learned to cook from Logan's mother, Rose thought as she ate, Brenda Maguire must have been quite a chef. Deciding to get maximum enjoyment from each bite, as her mother had taught her, Rose paid scant attention to the conversations exchanged across the table.

That is, until she heard Logan say, "Yes, Anna will be going to class tomorrow."

He was looking down the table at Elise. "It has the advantage of being familiar to her," he went on. "Without the expectations that come with being at home, where she feels she *should* recognize people and things. Anyway, we'll be leaving early tomorrow morning, so I'll come back here and spend the night again.''

"Come back?" Robert asked. "Are you going someplace?"

Logan nodded as he glanced at his watch. "In fact, I should be leaving right now. I promised to deliver some papers.''

Chas lifted his head. "Anything I should know about?"

"No." Logan pushed his chair back and stood. "Do you remember Robert Summers? He and I hung around for a while at Stanford."

Chas frowned. "Premed student? Fairly good at darts?"

"That's the one. Well, I ran into him last week. He's establishing a new partnership and asked me if I'd go over the agreement. He has his own lawyers, of course, but if you recall, he was always rather anal-retentive about checking and double-checking details." Logan paused. "I guess that means he went into the right field.''

Chas frowned. "What field would that be?"

Logan carefully shoved his chair back toward the table. "Proctology," he replied.

Without waiting for a reaction, Logan turned and left the room. Seeing the stunned look on the faces of those around her, Rose lifted her napkin to hide her smile, then faked a cough to cover her laughter. Her amusement faded, however, when she realized that Logan had left her completely alone with Anna's family.

Her first instinct was to escape, but a crystal bowl filled with chocolate mousse had just been placed in front of her. Deciding that the treat was worth the risk of being asked a question she couldn't answer, Rose waited till she'd swallowed the last bite before asking to be excused so she could go to bed.

The following morning Logan dressed quickly in a tan T-shirt, jeans and his favorite brown leather jacket. Outside Anna's bedroom door, he knocked softly. Rose opened the door, wearing jeans and a white T-shirt. As she stepped into the hall she flicked her turquoise sweatshirt defiantly over her shoulder.

"I'm ready for school."

He wasn't so sure she was ready for anything. Her voice sounded weary, and her smile was on the brittle side. Before he could comment on this, however, she turned toward the stairs. He followed her down, but once they were in the garage, with the door to the foyer securely closed behind them, he took her hand.

When she turned in surprise, he asked, "What's wrong?"

She gave her head a quick shake. "Nothing. I had a hard time getting to sleep again, what with wondering what we might learn today and worrying about how much of our conversation Chas heard yesterday."

The same thoughts had crossed Logan's mind. He gave her a small smile. "I know. Chas is hard to read. He has the Benedict knack for hiding his thoughts behind a charming smile. But he's also impatient, so I really doubt he'd been standing above us for very long. Certainly not long enough to see…"

He paused. Again he decided it was a time for action over words, so he leaned forward and angled his head to capture Rose's mouth with his. She stiffened for just a moment. Then her lips softened beneath his, her hands stole up to his shoulders as he encircled her body with his arms and pulled her to him.

Logan kissed her for several long, slow moments. When he caught himself wondering if the two of them couldn't steal away for another day at the beach, someplace private where they could continue to explore the feelings growing between them, he realized he had to stop. Now. There were, unfortunately, too many mysteries to unravel, and too little time to do this.

Reluctantly he withdrew his lips from hers. Resting his forehead against hers, he said, "We have a long day ahead of us. You up for it?"

Her eyes gazed mistily into his for a moment, then shimmered with focused energy the next. She nodded. Logan dropped a light kiss on her nose, then pulled away, letting his fingers slide down her right arm to grab her hand and lead her to his Mustang, waiting in the far stall.

He didn't speak to her again until they were driving down the foggy streets. "There's been a change of plans," he told her with a quick glance. "We aren't going to Berkeley."

Her eyes reflected surprise. "Why not?"

"Well, it seems that Professor Wilkins has taken a sudden leave of absence."

"How do you know that?"

"I made that story up about having to deliver those papers last night. Matt called on my cell phone while you were upstairs changing for dinner. I could hardly talk then, so he asked me to go to his office after dinner, where he could fill me in on the latest things he'd turned up."

"On a Sunday night?"

Logan gave her a tight smile. "Matt's a hungry guy, and the P.I. business he shares with his cousin is still in the building-up process."

Spotting a takeout restaurant, Logan turned in to place an order at the talking menu, then moved forward to collect their breakfast. When they pulled back into traffic, he was too busy eating with one hand and driving with the other to continue the conversation.

It wasn't until he was on the freeway heading south that Rose asked, "Logan, are you going to tell me what you learned?"

"Well, other than the fact that Wilkins is not available to answer questions, I learned that Anna was *not* finishing up a degree. Matt was trying to see if he could get the location of the pay phone Anna used to call my answering machine, so he checked university records to see what classes she was taking. It seems she'd declared a whole new major. Art."

"Art," Rose said softly. "My mother studied art in college."

Logan glanced at her. "Well, the field isn't entirely new to

Anna, either. A couple of years ago she attended one of those schools for interior decorators. She did several houses before dropping the business.'' He paused. ''Anna used to draw all the time when she was a kid, too. She stopped in junior high. When I asked why, she said that her teacher hated her work. I told her the guy was nuts, that her stuff was really good, but the damage had been done.''

''Jerk,'' Rose said, her voice low and harsh.

As Logan started down the exit ramp, Rose said, ''I didn't mean *you*. I was referring to that teacher. I hate it when people put down someone's efforts to create, no matter what the medium. The learning process is so darned fragile, especially in the beginning. It requires patience and encouragement, not harsh instructions in what someone thinks is the *right way* to do something.''

Logan felt Rose's anger. Recalling her gentle hand on his cheek as they stood on the beach up at Jenner, he could imagine the patient encouragement she gave her music students. He wanted to ask more about her business, but realized there were more pressing matters to discuss at the moment.

''Matt had also managed a partial trace on the call Anna made to my cell phone. It originated in Reno.''

Rose turned wide eyes to his. ''Where in Reno?''

''Apparently tracing calls from and to cell phones is a tad tricky, so Matt's still working on the details. But I can guess.''

As Logan turned off the street into an open gate in the chain link fence, then stopped in front of a small toll booth. He glanced over to see that Rose was staring ahead. Her expression suggested that she was too involved in her busy thought process to notice the stretch of blacktop in front of them.

''Anna learned from Grace that she has a twin,'' Rose said slowly. ''Scott Miller gave her the connection between our birth and Joe's death. So she must have gone to the hospital to get more information.'' She turned to Logan. ''Perhaps in an attempt to locate me.''

''My thoughts exactly.'' Logan flashed his ID to the man

leaning out the booth's window, then returned it to the inner pocket of his jacket as he stepped on the accelerator.

"So," he said. "We're going to that hospital in Reno. Have you ever flown in a small plane?"

Again he glanced at her, smiling as he watched her blink, stare at the wide expanse of tarmac, dotted with private planes tethered at various spots.

"No," she said as she turned to him. "But I'm guessing that's about to change."

Logan grinned. "I think you'll enjoy it. The ride isn't anything like taking a commercial flight. It's one hell of a lot more fun."

It took a little longer than Logan had hoped to get the Cessna out, run his preflight check and get clearance from the tower at the private airfield where he stored the company's private airplane. But as he sat at the end of the runway, fingers lightly curving around the controls, he gloried in the feel of the aircraft vibrating beneath him like a cheetah readying its muscles.

Minutes later, after receiving the okay for takeoff, he gunned the plane down the runway. The moment the wheels left the pavement and the large metal bird became airborne was as thrilling to him as it had been the very first time.

"Have you been flying long?"

Rose's obvious attempt at sounding unconcerned brought a quick grin to Logan's lips.

"Since I was five. Charles Benedict took me and Chas up one day. It was the most amazing experience of my life. I went up as often as possible after that, started studying about flight and got my license as soon as I was legally able. I promise you," he said as he turned to her, "I have a lot of flight hours under my belt. You're safe with me."

Rose smiled at him. "I trust you." A second later the smile faded and she said softly, "That's rather amazing, you know. I spent half the night remembering the total trust I had in my mother's honesty and wondering just how much of what she told me might turn out to be a lie. I should doubt everyone and everything around me, yet here I sit, trusting a man I've known only a few days with my life.''

Logan's own smile disappeared as he came down from his ''pilot high.'' He wanted to say something that might ease the pain and sorrow shadowing Rose's features. But he had to call the tower, report his heading and check altitude and speed. By the time he was finished with all that, the moment had passed.

And he wasn't all that sure he *could* offer Rose any assurance. His own world had been rocked by the deceptions they'd uncovered. He'd known Victor had no problem using the power of the Benedict name to protect the family's reputation. But when training Logan, Victor had made it clear that this very reputation required that all dealings be kept within the law. Now it seemed that Victor felt it was ''within the law'' to falsify birth records and perhaps bribe or threaten others into silence.

Where that left him, as Victor's successor, he had no idea, other than that he'd been trained to see that Robert Benedict gained the power he needed to help people less fortunate, and he still felt honor bound to fulfill this duty.

''Logan?'' Rose's soft voice interrupted his thoughts. When he glanced toward her, she asked, ''Just what are we going to do when we get to the hospital?''

''Well, when we land, I'm going to call Matt and see what else he may have turned up. He told me he'd try to get the names of some of the doctors and nurses who were working there at the time Joe died. Maybe one of them will remember just what happened. *And* be willing to discuss it with us.''

Less than an hour later, Logan was radioing the Reno Municipal Airport for landing clearance, then he had to concentrate on the quirky air currents that were making for a less-than-smooth approach. After landing and taxiing to a stop in the area designated for tethering the aircraft, he switched the engine off and turned to Rose.

''Well?'' he said expectantly.

Like someone coming out of a trance she jumped, then

blinked and turned questioning eyes to him. When she didn't say anything, he asked, "How did you like the flight?"

Rose gazed at him a moment longer before twisting her lips into an expression of chagrin. "I guess I liked it fine," she replied at last.

"Oh, what high praise." Logan gave her a wounded look, then smiled gently as he touched her arm. "I know. You've been preoccupied with a thousand questions. But we're here now. With luck, we'll get some answers soon."

Logan asked Rose to wait in front of the small building for the arrival of the rental car he'd arranged for while he called Matt. He returned just as the pale-blue midsize vehicle stopped in front of the building.

"The hospital isn't far away," Logan said, once both of them were belted into their seats.

While he drove, he told Rose that the private detective had learned that at the time of the accident Washoe Medical Center had possessed the only newborn intensive care facility in the area, and this was where a woman in premature labor would have been taken. He frowned as he finished relaying this information to Rose.

"What's wrong?" she asked softly.

"Well, Matt said he was able to get the clerk to check for records pertaining to Kathleen and Elizabeth Donnelly. There wasn't a thing under that last name, however. When he checked for your birth on the eighteenth, again nothing came up."

Rose was silent as Logan took a right turn, following the blue sign marked Hospital Parking. They were halfway up the ramp when she said, "You told me that Victor Benedict was very powerful."

Logan nodded. As he pulled into a parking space he said tightly, "Yes. I've little doubt he had something to do with this. But knowing that doesn't help us much."

He opened the door and got out of the car. Rose did the same, then walked next to him toward the hospital doors. "What are we going to do here then?"

Logan sighed. "Walk around and keep our eyes peeled. My guess is that Anna was here a couple of days ago. She must have questioned a few people. We need to watch for anyone who seems to recognize you. Let's start with labor and delivery—or whatever it is they call it."

Rose had her doubts about Logan's plan, but when they stopped at the nurses' station in the obstetrics area, a petite blonde wearing pink scrubs looked at Rose and asked, "Did you find Dottie?"

Rose drew in a quick breath. Trying to remain calm, she repeated, "Dottie?"

"Yeah. The other day, you were looking for Dorothy Reynolds. I told you that you could find Dottie in with the newborns."

"Oh…yes. Yes, I found her. Thanks."

With that, Rose smiled and walked away from the counter, aware of Logan at her side, walking rapidly toward the sign marked Newborn Nursery.

When they reached the wide bank of windows separating the hallway from a roomful of plastic isolets, Rose noticed that only two were occupied. Her gaze lingered on the tiny pink face above a blue-swaddled body, then the brown baby with the full cheeks and thick curly lashes wrapped in pink.

When she looked up, she met the surprised gaze of a woman with short, dark hair in pale-green scrubs. Her dark-brown eyes held Rose's a moment before she turned to a tall Hispanic woman wearing a matching smock and pants. The two spoke briefly, then the first woman walked toward the door at the end of the windows and pulled the door shut behind her as she stepped into the hall. Rose noticed that the nurse's name tag said Dorothy Reynolds.

"Anna," the woman whispered. "What are you doing here? I told you all I could the other day."

Rose drew a slow, deep breath and said what she hadn't been able to say to anyone other than Logan for days now.

"I'm not Anna. I know I look like her, but I'm—"

"Rose," the woman broke in.

A shiver raced through Rose's body as she stared at the woman. "How…how do you know my name?"

Up close, the fine web of wrinkles around Dorothy Reynolds's eyes belied the impression of youth Rose had seen though the nursery window. The lines around the nurse's mouth deepened as she pursed her lips and glanced over her shoulder.

When her gaze once again met Rose's, she said, "Because that was what your mother named you, right before she died."

Logan saw the color drain from Rose's face. He placed an arm around her waist.

"Nurse Reynolds," he said softly. "Is there somewhere we can talk?"

The woman nodded, then opened the nursery door. "Cindy, I'm going to be in the cafeteria for a bit. Page if you need me."

Once the three of them were seated at a round table near the windows overlooking the parking lot, Logan saw Rose's cheeks had pinkened, and the glint of determination had returned to her eyes.

"I want to get this straight," she said. "Tell me *everything* you know about the night that I—that Anna and I—were born."

After taking a deep breath, Dottie Reynolds explained that Elizabeth Donnelly had been unconscious and in critical condition when she was care-flighted from the top of the mountain to the hospital that October night. Recognizing the severity of her injuries, the trauma team had performed an emergency cesarean section to give both mother and child the best chance at life.

The fact that Liz delivered *two* babies had surprised all concerned, especially her sister, Kathleen Donnelly. Not as severely injured as any of the others in the wrecked car, she'd been transported to Reno by ambulance, arriving over an hour after Liz. Kathleen had been ushered into the intensive care unit, where Dottie Reynolds was in charge of watching Liz battle her life-threatening injuries.

Dottie told Kathleen all she knew, that three other people in the car containing the sisters had died, along with the driver of the huge jackknifed truck that had started the chain reaction. A middle-aged man and woman in the front seat had been declared dead at the scene. The young man, Joe Benedict, had seemed fine aboard the helicopter that flew him and Elizabeth to the emergency room. But moments before he reached the hospital, his condition had taken a sudden nosedive. He'd been bleeding internally from a ruptured spleen and liver, and he died even as the trauma team opened him up.

Dottie had watched Kathleen's features twist with grief and sympathy as she gazed at her unconscious sister. From the moment Kathleen walked into the room, she'd never once looked away from Lizzie, except to glance up in surprise when Dottie revealed that Liz had delivered not one baby, but two. And it was only moments after this that Lizzie regained consciousness. When the young woman opened her eyes and saw her sister, she smiled. Then fear touched her features.

"The baby," Lizzie had said. "How is the baby?"

"Fine," Kathleen had replied.

Before she'd been able to tell her sister that there were two babies, one weighing a little over five pounds and the other not quite three, Lizzie had smiled, then blinked. As her eyelids drooped she grabbed her sister's hand.

"Boy or girl?" she'd asked. Kathleen replied, "Girl. That is—"

Lizzie had cut her sister off with a shake of her head and opened her eyes wide. "Roseanna. Name her Roseanna—for our grandmother and her father's..." She'd swallowed and said, "Joe's grandmother. And promise to take care of her."

"Of course," Kathleen had replied. "I'll help out while you get better, but—"

The heart monitor had gone off at that moment. Lizzie's eyes had remained open, staring vacantly. Though nurses and doctors had rushed in with machines, paddles and meds for her IV, within fifteen minutes it had become clear to Dottie Reynolds that the tiny twins down the hall were now orphans.

Chapter 14

"Well, now at least I know that *some* of the things my moth—that Kathleen told me were true."

These were the first words Rose had spoken since leaving the hospital. She'd been completely silent on the drive back to the airport, sat wordlessly next to Logan during takeoff and hadn't uttered a sound until they'd flown over the Sierras and he'd turned the plane south.

"I always knew that I'd been named for her mother, Rose," she finished. "Kathleen said that Grandma Rose had helped make my quilt. That is, of course, the quilt that Anna and I share. Another mystery that Dottie was able to help us with."

The nurse had explained that Kathleen and Lizzie had been napping under the large quilt in the rear of the car at the time of the accident. Kathleen had brought it with her in the ambulance, and covered her sister with it until her body was taken away.

Seeing that the young woman was close to going into shock, Dottie had asked about the quilt. Kathleen said that their mother had helped Lizzie put the quilt together the summer that their parents died. Later, when Kathleen had finally agreed to separate the twins, it was on the stipulation that half of the quilt go with Anna.

"That means my mother *did* make my quilt," Rose said softly. "My real mother, that is."

Logan noticed a hardness in Rose's voice that he'd never heard before. He glanced at the instrument panel. Assured that the plane was on the correct heading, he turned to her.

"You once told me that if it turned out Kathleen had told any lies, she would have kept the details as close to the truth as possible. She also told you she'd made a solemn vow never to tell anyone about the man who fathered you. We now know who she made that promise to."

Logan's jaw tightened over these last words. Nurse Reynolds hadn't pulled any punches as she'd described Victor Benedict's arrival at the hospital. Dottie said she'd never been able to learn exactly what strings he'd pulled, she only knew that all the charts pertaining to Kathleen, Lizzie and the two babies had suddenly disappeared.

The next thing Dottie knew, Victor was making arrangements to take the twins from the hospital. When Kathleen learned of this, she'd moved in like a mother tigress. Not only was she the children's aunt, Dottie heard Kathleen tell Victor, but Lizzie had asked *her* to take care of her baby. Kathleen would not go back on the promise she'd made to her sister.

Victor had replied that the twins were Benedicts, and would be raised as such. He'd said that his niece-in-law, Elise, had recently miscarried the child she'd conceived in the Swiss clinic. He would have no problem keeping this information private and passing the twins off as Robert's and Elise's. As such, they would be well taken care of and treated to advantages that an unemployed twenty-year-old student, like Kathleen, could never offer.

Considering all the power at Victor's disposal, Dottie believed that the only thing that prevented the man from whisking both babies off in the plane he'd had fitted with special incubators was Rose, the tinier twin. The girls had shared the same amniotic sac, proof that they had developed from a single egg, but apparently Rose hadn't received the same nourishment in the womb. She was barely over three pounds and having difficulty breathing. Taking her from the hospital would have meant endangering her life.

Victor's wife, Grace, had stepped in at this point. The woman had suggested that Anna, who was much stronger, could be sent to Elise in Switzerland. Kathleen would receive Rose, along with sufficient funds to raise and care for the child. Provided, of course, that Kathleen promised never to tell a soul what had transpired.

"Nurse Reynolds is very kind." Rose spoke so softly that Logan could barely hear her over the hum of the engine. "And very brave."

"What do you mean?" Logan asked.

Rose turned to him, eyes narrowed, glittering. "Victor Benedict threatened to ruin anyone who revealed anything about my—our birth. She had no way of knowing if his successor might carry out that threat."

Logan greeted Rose's fiery expression with mixed emotions. The information they'd received from the Reynolds woman had stripped Rose of her two most cherished beliefs, that Kathleen Delancey had been her mother and that the woman had been incapable of telling a lie. The silence Rose had wrapped around herself after leaving the hospital made him fear that she'd slipped into a dark, emotional hole.

Her current show of anger was a welcome sign, but it wasn't without its own problems. Logan had admired Victor's devotion to family, had been trained to fill the man's shoes. Right now he wasn't sure he was comfortable with the fit.

"Let's not get sidetracked," he said at last. "The important issue at the moment is Anna. We know now that she was in Reno on Saturday and that she learned what we just did. This gave her all day yesterday to return home and start demanding an explanation of her family."

"That's what I'd be doing," Rose said. "*If* I thought anyone there would tell me the truth."

Reaching over, Logan closed his fingers over hers. They felt cold as ice. Turning toward her, he saw that she'd once again shrunk into her seat to gaze ahead, her eyes wide, her expression bleak.

"You aren't alone in this," he said quietly.

It was several seconds before Rose turned those dark eyes to him. "I know. If you were't here, I don't know what I'd be doing."

Logan gave her a wide smile. "I do. You'd be storming the gates of the Benedict house, *demanding* an explanation."

Rose stared at him a very long moment. Her eyes narrowed as she took a deep breath. She seemed suddenly to grow taller and straighter in her seat.

"You're right," she said. "And that is just what I intend to do when we get back to the house."

An hour and a half later Logan braced himself for an argument with Rose as he turned onto Sea Cliff Drive.

She'd sat silent and stiff next to him on the ride from the airport, as if mentally preparing herself for battle. He understood her need for answers, even applauded her desire to take the bull by the horns and demand them. But he didn't agree with the timing. He wanted to be sure of all the facts before confronting the Benedicts and, more important, he wanted to have Anna on hand when this took place.

Upon pulling into the garage, he noticed that each of the family cars were in their places. Switching the engine off, he turned to Rose, half-afraid he would be forced to grab her to keep her from leaping from the car and marching indignantly into the house.

The woman seated next to him, however, lacked any hint of the fire and fury that had fueled her walk across the airport tarmac to the Mustang; who had belted herself in with understated violence and asked just how long it would take to get to the Benedict house. In her place sat the woman who'd left the hospital like a sleepwalker, the wounded soul who didn't know what to believe or, what was more important, *who* to believe.

Logan was accustomed to seeing Anna overwhelmed with self-doubt. Rose was another matter. From the moment they'd met she'd been asserting herself. She might have occasionally expressed confusion and doubt, but never had he seen her look so very lost.

He glanced toward the door that led to the foyer. For all he knew, the entire Benedict family was inside, waiting for him to appear and tell them if "Anna's" proposed visit to Berkeley had brought up any memories. He would have no trouble coming up with a story to stall their questions, but one look at Rose would tell them something was wrong.

The last thing he needed at the moment was for them to call in Dr. Alcott and begin another round of questioning. There was a small door on his left that led out of the garage and to the stairs along the cliff. He considered taking Rose for a walk on the beach, but another glance at the young woman indicated she was too drained for that.

Almost without his will, his gaze shifted to a door in the wall in front of him. This was the entrance his father had used to enter their apartment after a long day of tuning engines and polishing hoods.

What's the problem, Maguire? he chided himself. *Afraid of ghosts?*

Truth be told, he was—a little. When he'd taken Rose to the apartment before, he'd imagined that he could feel his father's presence in the big chair near the front door, he could have sworn he'd caught sight of his mother standing at the stove, for just one second, wiping her hands on her apron. The brief moments of pleasure he'd felt had been swiftly replaced by pain, sharp and deep.

But now that he thought about it, what better place to take a woman grappling with the pain in her past? If she could face ghosts with composure, so could he.

Logan got out of the car, walked around and opened Rose's door. She looked up, her eyes puzzled beneath a faint frown.

''Time to go in,'' he told her.

Wordlessly she swung her legs to the side, then exited the car. Logan took her hand and led her to the door directly in front of the car. As he put the key in the lock, he noticed that Rose didn't seem the least bit curious about where he was taking her.

Once inside, Logan hesitated. Four doors opened off the hallway that ran along the garage wall. All were closed now, accounting for the total lack of light. Rose still hadn't said a word. Her hand lay limply in his grasp as she stood next to him in the dark. Logan stepped forward, right hand extended until his fingers encountered a metal doorknob. With a twist, he pushed the door open, then took one step into the room, aware of a deep chill in the air as he looked around.

Two narrow windows with drawn shades on the opposite wall let in only the dimmest of daylight. To his left a toy chest sat at the foot of a twin bed, which was draped in a faded red comforter printed to look like a low-slung race car—a gift from his parents on his tenth birthday, two months before they died.

A flood of memories struck Logan directly in his chest— the party held on the patio in his honor, the game of pin-the-hood-ornament-on-the-Mustang that his father had created in the workshop, the cake his mother carved and decorated in the shape of a Mustang convertible.

He reached to the right of the door, fumbling for the light switch, surprised to find it was located lower on the wall than he remembered. When the overhead bulb lit up, revealing just how empty the room really was, Logan immediately switched it off again.

Taking a deep, steadying breath, he pulled his attention from the empty ache in his chest and turned to Rose. She stood next to him, gazing at the dimly lit room, but obviously not really seeing a thing. There was no hint of the curiosity that normally lit her features, none of the fire that normally needed banking so she could convincingly impersonate Anna.

He'd seen a similar expression on his own face following

the loss of his parents—a young boy staring into the mirror, telling himself that he was doing fine, that his heart wasn't breaking, then repeating Robert's encouraging words, *You're a Benedict now. Benedicts don't cry.* Robert—who had just lost his younger brother, his very best friend in the world.

For the first time in his life, Logan fought against the instinct to swallow the pain that came with these memories. Rose was in trouble, and she needed what he'd never given himself—permission to grieve the loss of the woman who'd so recently died, as well as the loss of her own innocence and faith.

Logan turned to Rose, placed a hand beneath her chin, then tilted her head up, forcing her eyes to meet his.

"Rose?" he said softly, letting the pain he was feeling color his voice. When her large eyes widened slightly, he said, "Go ahead." His voice was hoarse with the effort to contain his own emotions. "Cry."

Her eyes darkened. "No." Rose shook her head. "I *promised* I wouldn't. I promised to move on, to find joy in every moment, to be hap—"

Her mouth clamped shut. Logan watched her features harden as she blinked furiously.

"Rosie," he said softly, forcing the words past the tightness in his throat. "Do you remember when I told you that I was never lonely? Well I lied. I lied because I allowed people to convince me that everything was okay. My parents were dead, but I was safe, warm, well fed. To grieve was to be ungrateful, I felt, and I convinced myself sorrow could be shut away, eventually forgotten."

The ache in his chest had continued to grow as he spoke, so that now he could barely breathe. Tears filled his eyes. He let them flow as he forced himself to continue.

"I know better now. I've learned that unexpressed grief only hardens, festering in a hot lump just beneath the surface. That if you can't feel sorrow, you can never truly feel joy. I'm sure Kathleen wouldn't want that for you, that she would tell you it's all right to cry."

Rose gazed into Logan's eyes for several moments, the words *all right* echoing in her mind. What did *all right* feel like? She must have known that, once upon a time. But now it seemed that *all right* existed in some far distant past, before she'd met Josh and had mistaken attraction and a need to ''belong'' for love, before she acknowledged the mistake she'd made in marrying him, before her mother got sick, then—

That woman hadn't been her mother.

Rose felt her breath catch in her suddenly tight chest, clog her suddenly aching throat. She blinked hot tears that hadn't been there a moment earlier. *All right* had been a lie. Her whole life had been a lie, told to her by a woman who had *claimed* to be her mother.

Except, in the past three days, *she* had become the liar, ignoring the emerging facts to tell herself that this couldn't possibly be so, that some mistake had been made. Or, if someone had lied, it must have been the Benedicts. Kathleen Delancey *was* her mother, who must have been told she had only one child, who had never known she had another daughter, one named Anna.

Rose blinked as it occurred to her that in some ways, all this was true. It had been Kathleen *Donnelly* who had lied, a woman Rose had never known. So that made everything *all right*. Didn't it? That meant there was no need for the tears falling onto her cheeks, no reason for the sob that ripped from her chest and exited her throat with a deep, guttural cry. No need for Logan to take her into his arms, to hold her, his body shuddering as violently as hers, murmuring in a soft voice that broke repeatedly as he urged, ''Let it out, Rosie. Don't fight it. Just…just let the tears…come. It's…okay. Let it out.''

With a loud sob, Rose did just as he asked. More sobs followed, and soon she lost all sense of time and place as the anger at the lies, the grief at losing the only mother she'd ever known shuddered through her body. She was aware that, at some point, Logan eased her down onto the twin bed, where he continued to hold her in his arms. But she had no idea how long she'd been crying before the sobs slowly began to subside. She knew only how she felt. Emotionally spent. Drained. Exhausted.

Three quick breaths, coming in rapid succession from deep within Rose's chest, brought her eyes open. She must have dozed off for a moment, she realized. She'd dreamed of home again. Of gazing over the rooftops at a clear blue sky punctuated by the Space Needle, Mt. Olympia rising in the distance.

But she wasn't home. She was in San Francisco, in Logan's arms. Where she belonged. Where she felt love. She'd come looking for something to fill the empty space in her spirit. She'd found it—love—in this man's generous, wounded heart.

Placing her hands on his chest, she pushed away from him. The arms gently surrounding her relaxed just enough to allow her to lean back, yet remain within the circle of his embrace as she looked into his face.

His cheeks were streaked with moisture. For a second Rose wondered how *her* tears could have gotten onto his face. Then she remembered what he'd been saying about grief festering and realized she was seeing remnants of the tears he'd been holding in since his parents died twenty-seven long years ago.

When Logan's eyes met hers, they gazed at each other in wordless communication, letting the individual moments of grief they'd just shared settle and ease as they reached for healing. Another sigh shuddered through Rose, then she smiled.

"Thank you," she said.

"No," Logan replied. "Thank *you.*"

There didn't seem to be any need for further words. Which, Rose decided as Logan bent his head to hers, was just as well. She gave herself fully to his kiss, returning it with every part of her heart, hoping that this physical gesture would communicate the love she felt for him. It didn't matter that she'd known him only a few days. The moments of emotional intensity they had just shared had been the most intimate of her life, touching her deeply, changing her at some level she didn't quite understand.

However, she felt too emotionally vulnerable to allow the heat flowing through her body to pull her into a physical intimacy she wasn't quite ready for. Slowly, reluctantly, she pushed on Logan's shoulders. His lips left hers slowly, his eyes looking down into hers for a long moment. When the chilly air in the unheated room sent a shudder through Rose's body, his lips twisted wryly.

"I suppose it is too cold to stay down here for any length of time," he said. "Besides, I think we need to go upstairs and face the music before someone notices my car and thinks to look for us in here."

Rose let her head roll onto his shoulder. "I suppose. The Benedicts will probably wonder why we didn't come in right after we arrived. What story can we make up?"

She felt Logan shrug. "We can leave through the apartment's front door, go up the steps and enter the big house through the kitchen. We'll tell them we took a walk on the beach before coming in for dinner."

Rose frowned. "They'll want to know why we did that, what we've been doing. I don't know if I'm ready to get into what we learned in Reno, if I can manage to—"

Her words were silenced by the touch of Logan's fingers on her lips.

"We'll wing it," he said as he sat up next to her on the edge of the bed. "We don't have to confront them with all that tonight, anyway. I think we should hold off until we find Anna."

Rose frowned. Logan braced himself for a fight as he stood.

But the next moment her eyes narrowed, as if she were remembering something. Then her eyes widened and she grabbed his hand.

"Logan," she said in an urgent whisper. "I know where she is."

"Anna?" He knew his tone was skeptical.

Rose gave him a vigorous nod. "Yes. She's in Seattle. At *my* house."

"Rose—" he placed a hand on her shoulder "—how would Anna find—"

"The same way I found this place," Rose replied, then stood and went on, "The dreams. I told you about coming here, searching for the view of the Golden Gate Bridge I kept dreaming of. You remember what that article said about twins having a high degree of ESP? Well, I think that Anna and I share—" She paused. "No. Somehow we *exchange* dreams."

"Okay," Logan said slowly. "I get the part about you dreaming of the bridge, but how does that make you think that Anna is in Seattle?"

"Because, ever since Saturday afternoon, I have been dreaming of the Space Needle. When I'm home, I look at it every day while playing my harp. I thought I was just homesick, but now I realize that I've been seeing what *Anna* is looking at."

Logan shook his head. "I still don't understand how Anna could be sitting in your house, looking out—"

"I *told* you," Rose interrupted. "I bet that all these years *Anna* has been dreaming of the Space Needle, just like I dreamed of the Golden Gate Bridge. After talking to Dottie Reynolds, I bet Anna decided to go looking for me before confronting her family about my existence. Now I have to go find her."

Logan stared into Rose's eyes for several seconds. It was a long shot, a very *unlikely* long shot. But it was all they had.

"Okay. Back to the airport, then. I can have us in Seattle in three hours."

A little more than three hours later, Rose sat tense and excited in the back of a taxi as it turned up the hill leading to the house she'd shared with Kathleen "Delancey". The slight drizzle that greeted their landing in Seattle had deepened into a steady downpour, limiting visibility. But as the peaked roof of the yellow Victorian house finally came into view, Rose's sense of anticipation blossomed.

The narrow house towered above her as she got out of the

car. All the windows were dark, except for the square panes on the left side of the second floor and the dim light from the two low-wattage bulbs that lit the windows on either side of the front door.

It was just after seven o'clock. The shop closed at six on Sundays, so Goldie was probably long gone. Anna, then, would be upstairs. With this thought propelling her, Rose hurried through the white picket gate and up the walkway through the rain. By the time she reached the porch covering the wooden steps, her turquoise sweatshirt was nearly drenched. Logan had paused to pay the cab driver. As she fitted her key in the lock, his dash up the cement behind her was reflected in the oval of heavy beveled glass set in the oak door.

Logan reached her side just as the door clicked open. The bell attached to the top of its frame issued a welcoming tinkle. Rose stepped into what had once been the old house's parlor and now served as the gift shop's main showroom.

The familiar scent of potpourri wafted toward her from the ceramic bowls her mother had made to display Goldie's unique blend of petals. For one moment Rose closed her eyes and let herself luxuriate in the comfort she found at being here. It was almost as if the renovated furniture Goldie had specialized in long before it became "shabby chic" and the beautiful items her mother had so lovingly created had recognized her arrival and were welcoming her back.

Then the moment passed.

Rose opened her eyes and took Logan's hand in hers. "There's a set of stairs behind that." She pointed toward the rear of the dimly lit room, where a wrought-iron screen blocked off a wide doorway. "Stay close to me," she said softly as she stepped forward. "I know my way, and I don't want you to knock anything over."

It was Rose, however, who did the knocking over. About three feet in front of the screen, she ran into a low table, sending it crashing to the ground. When she bent to set it right, she felt around to see what might have fallen off and broken. She frowned when her searching fingers encountered nothing, knowing that Goldie never let any horizontal surface remain empty.

Her frown disappeared as anticipation drew her up and sent her moving forward again. Without mishap this time she led Logan to the iron screen bearing a sign that warned, No Shopping Beyond This Point, pushed one panel inward, stepped around, and started up the wide staircase.

At the top of the landing, Rose's keys jingled in her trembling fingers until she found the one that would admit her to the only home she'd ever known. She pulled hard on the old-fashioned latch handle, then gave the door a quick shove and smiled at the familiar *crack* it made upon opening.

Entering a small vestibule where framed flower prints decorated every inch of wall space, she hung her purse on the coatrack in the corner, then turned to make her way into the living room. She flicked a light on the wall before entering the furniture-crammed area and crossed toward a narrow door.

Rose was quite aware of Logan following close behind her as she approached her bedroom. The door was open, and without even turning on a light, she could see that the neatly made bed was empty. She turned then and approached the door to the room that had been Kathleen Delancey's. She hesitated before knocking. When there was no answer, she pushed it open.

Again the room was empty.

Rose suppressed a shudder and bit her lip at the painful reminder of the woman whose loving spirit had once filled this room. She felt Logan's hand on her shoulder and turned to him with a sigh.

"I guess I was wrong about Anna being here," she said.

"Maybe not," he said softly, then took her hand and pulled her back into the living area.

"Did you leave that on the sofa?"

The burgundy couch he referred to was huge, like something out of a Sultan's palace. Rose remembered the day she, her mother and Goldie had found the ratty-looking item in the back of the thrift store, the effort it had taken to get it up the stairs and into the room, the hours she and Kathleen had spent upholstering it in a deep wine-colored velvet.

Now she noticed that the collection of tapestry pillows were all bunched up at the sofa's far end. And in the center lay a twisted blanket made of faded shades of turquoise, purple, yellow and pink.

Her quilt.

Chapter 15

"I don't remember leaving it out here," Rose said slowly as she stared at the quilt. "But I was rather...spacey following Mom's funeral—lying around a lot, watching TV, wrapped up in it. When I made the decision to go to San Francisco, however, I shifted into high gear. I must have forgotten to put it back in my room."

Logan's eyes held hers. "I can see how that could happen."

Rose knew he meant every word, that he understood exactly how disoriented she had been, how lost. She didn't feel that way now, though. She felt emotionally cleansed, warm, safe and at home. Not just because she was back in Seattle, but because this man had made it possible for her to release her pain and see each moment fresh again.

Just as Kathleen would have wanted.

Thinking of the woman, Rose glanced around at the walls where Kathleen had turned discarded windows into multipaned frames to hold a variety of pictures and photos, where old mantels formed shelves to hold a collection of Roseville vases, and a grouping of mirrors with slightly chipped gilt frames reflected the lights of Seattle, just outside the wide window.

"I know it looks like a rather cluttered antique store," she said as she turned back to Logan. "But we—"

Logan cut her off with a shake of his head. "It's great," he said. "Whose idea was it to stick a plant in that bird cage?"

"Mom's. She felt birds should be in the air. Plants didn't mind being boxed up so much, she said."

Logan nodded absently, then turned to her. "You told me that you could see the Space Needle while you were playing the harp. Where is it?"

"Up in the attic," she replied. "That's my area—to practice and teach my students. Mom's kiln and all her materials are in the basement."

Again Logan nodded. He stepped over to the wall opposite the couch to stand in front of the deep shelves that held an old stereo system and rows of record albums.

"Who collected these?"

Rose crossed the room to join him. "Mom. She didn't just let them sit around gathering dust, though. She played them all the time."

Logan's head was tilted to one side as he studied the slender spines. "My parents loved music, too," he said. "They had the radio or the stereo going all the time when we were together in the evening. More often than not, they'd end up dancing—sometimes to rock and roll, other times to big-band music."

He pulled one album out as he spoke. Seeing the title brought a soft smile to Rose's lips. "That was one of her favorites."

Logan's head came up. "You're kidding. Mom and Dad's, too."

Rose gave him a skeptical glance. "No...Jimmy Durante? Really? I thought Mom was the only one. Most people I meet only know him as the comedian with the big nose and his signature lines 'Hot-cha-cha,' and 'Good-night Mrs. Calabash, wherever you are.''' She glanced at the album cover, then up to Logan. "Would you like to listen to it?"

His eyes grew dark. For one second she thought he was going to shake his head. Then he shrugged. "Sure."

Rose stepped over to the old phonograph, removed the record from its jacket and slipped it onto the turntable. After switching it on, the black disc began to spin, and she carefully placed the needle down on the outer rim. A second later the achingly sweet strains of violins filled the air, followed by Durante singing, "Make Someone Happy."

The entertainer's raspy voice and distinctive phrasing had accompanied homework and housework alike, and the memories filled Rose with sudden warmth.

"Would you like…" Logan started.

When he didn't go on, Rose turned to him. His eyes were dark with what looked like longing. Rose felt her breath catch in her throat. "To dance?" she finished on a whisper. "Yes, I would."

Logan gave her a slow smile and moved toward her. Simultaneously placing one hand on her waist and taking her hand with the other, he pulled her to him. Then they were moving, their bodies swaying to the slow, rhythmic music. Moments later the song ended, but it was only a second before the orchestra was again playing and Durante was singing about smiling when a heart was breaking.

Rose felt her heart swell as the pain of missing her mother blended with the joy of having found love. And it was the man holding her in his arms who had taught her that these two emotions could exist side by side. She wanted to thank him for those moments in his old bedroom, but her heart was too full. If she spoke now, she would cry again, and there had been enough tears today. Now, this minute, she wanted only the joy.

She looked up to meet Logan's hazel eyes. Just as their bodies were effortlessly moving in perfect unison, so, it seemed, their minds were running along the same lines. Logan's head bent toward hers. Rose tilted her face to his. Their lips met and clung, at first gently, tenderly, then hungrily, almost savagely. Desire swept through Rose as Logan stopped dancing and drew her into a tight embrace. She gasped as he slid one hand down to cup her bottom, then lift her feet from the ground and urge her hips toward his.

Rose gripped his shoulders and arched toward him as they continued to kiss. Several moments passed before she realized that Logan had let her feet touch the ground again, that his hands had moved to her waist, were working on the buttons of her jeans.

She felt not one second of embarrassment—only the sense that being in this man's arms was where she belonged. And the belief that *this* time that feeling was not an illusion. In the three and a half days she had known Logan, she had come to see that he was not only capable of understanding and sharing emotions, but admitting to them. What other man would allow himself to release his own long-held grief in order to help ease hers?

And beyond the sense that loving this man with all her mind and body—here…now—was the right thing to do, it was what she wanted. Both need and desire twisted through her, hot and insistent as she eased her body away from Logan's, granting him easier access to her zipper and buttons, while she began to disengage those items of his.

As fingers brushed sensitive skin, their lips maintained nearly constant contact, holding, clinging, parting for brief gasps to swiftly, hungrily rejoin and connect on an even deeper level. Her turquoise sweatshirt joined his tan T-shirt on the floor, then his hands gently held each side of her face, while his lips repeatedly claimed her mouth.

They stepped out of their jeans in perfect unison. Naked legs brushed naked legs in a caress that led to a flesh-pressing-flesh embrace. They stood in the center of the room, kissing, touching, exploring each other until Rose thought her heart would explode with joy and her legs would give way under the sensual assault that had her head spinning and her blood coursing through her body with dizzying speed, drawing all strength from her lower limbs. Just as her legs began to buckle, Logan lifted her, stepped to one side, laid her on the wide velvet couch and joined her without breaking their kiss.

When Logan's lips did lift from hers, Rose waited for their return, and when this didn't happen, she opened her eyes in protest. In the dim light filtering through the window, Logan's eyes met hers, dark beneath a frown. She felt her own brow tighten. Her heart fluttered, not with passion this time but with dread.

He didn't want her.

Rose held her breath, waiting for him to tell her this. Her heart pounded several times before he spoke.

"Is this going too fast for you?"

Rose stared at him, stunned, while her body screamed that things weren't proceeding fast *enough*. But she knew Logan wasn't referring to what her body was experiencing, he was talking about her heart, asking if she was really ready for their relationship to move to a deeper intimacy.

Jimmy Durante was singing, "I'll See You In My Dreams." A soft smile curved Rose's lips. She had seen Logan in her dreams many times, but that was no longer enough. She wanted to make that dream connection real, in every sense of the word. Her heart answered his question, growing warm and large in her breast. But she knew she had to say the words.

"Not at all."

Logan's frown disappeared as a smile creased his face. His gaze held hers one second longer before he once again captured her mouth in a long, deep kiss that sent blood reeling through her head and heat spiraling down through her body to pool and build into a tight longing ache.

It was an ache that Logan seemed to share and was more than willing to ease. Rose felt him gather her to him with a combination of tenderness and urgency that both pierced her heart and piqued her desire. Opening herself to him completely, she greeted their union with a combined gasp and moan, then smiled at the deep groan of pleasure that escaped the lips still kissing hers.

So *this* was making love.

The thought flew through the sensation-laden void that Rose normally regarded as her mind. Silly thought. She'd done this before. She'd been married, for goodness sake.

But that had been only sex, she realized. Never had she been held so tenderly, loved so thoroughly, brought to the physical *and* emotional peak where Logan was taking her now.

When Logan began moving against her more quickly, the wild, pulsing sensations racing through her body wiped all thoughts, even involuntary ones, from her mind. Her body took over, responding to the increased rhythm, matching Logan move for move, breath for ragged breath, climbing and climbing, then soaring, soaring, soaring.

When Rose again became conscious of her surroundings, she realized that Logan was still holding her in his arms. They lay spooned together on their sides, her back pressed against his body. Something light yet warm covered them. The quilt.

The sofa beneath her was so familiar. Rose knew just where all the soft spots were, all the lumps. The couch felt the same, but she felt different—whole, for the first time in her life, as if giving her heart and body to this generous, caring man had healed that hole in her heart at last.

A soft *shh, shh, shh,* whispered from the record player across the room. Logan's breathing was slow and even. The two sounds blended in a soothing rhythm that urged Rose's eyelids to close and promised to lull her back to sleep.

Until her stomach growled.

Her eyes flew open, hoping that the deep, satisfied breaths fluttering over her neck indicated that Logan was too deeply asleep to have heard.

"You know," he whispered in her ear, "I find that I'm rather hungry, too."

Rose buried her face in the pillow beneath their heads. Logan grinned and tightened his arms around her, then closed his eyes to savor the complete sense of contentment that claimed every part of his being.

He couldn't remember ever feeling so at ease with a woman in the moments following shared intimacy. Maybe, he thought, it was because he'd shared with Rose the emotions he'd kept bottled inside for so long, something he'd never done before. And maybe *that* was because he'd never before been in love.

Logan blinked, then stared across the room, lit softly by the dawn.

Love. He knew what love was, of course. He'd been given more than ample servings of it daily, during the ten years that he'd lived with his parents. But in the world of the Benedicts, that kind of open and vulnerable emotion was too fragile to exist within the parameters they'd created to deal with society, politics and business. Somehow, in trying to order his inner life to theirs, he'd lost touch with his heart.

Until Rose Delancey slipped into it, with her saucy smiles, the joy she took in living, and her open, warm soul.

With her, he had found the part of himself he'd locked away long ago. And, he suspected, more hidden parts were bound to come out in response to further exposure to her smile, her warmth. Like his inner imp who had refused to let that stomach growl go by without comment, and who now was not about to let Rose hide her embarrassment in the crook of her arm.

Leaning forward, Logan nuzzled her ear, then caught the soft lobe between his teeth and began to nibble gently. He heard her gasp, felt a shudder run lightly through her form. Suddenly the hunger he'd felt moments ago had nothing to do with his stomach and everything to do with wanting a second helping of Rose. Gently but firmly he turned her to him, then leaned forward and kissed her parted lips.

The complete surrender with which she greeted him reawakened the fires that had been banked by their earlier joining. Apparently those fires were going to need quenching once more, considering they'd flamed brightly to life in his body with a suddenness that seemed to engulf Rose, as well.

She arched up to Logan as he pulled her closer, granting him access as quickly as his need climbed higher. Her body rocked along with his, sharing and participating in an exchange of pleasure and passion that flared quick and hot in a searing joining of body and soul.

After, as he rested on his back with Rose's head on his shoulder, Logan forced his breathing to slow. He felt her shiver. He reached for the quilt to draw it over them, then drew a deep breath.

Right before *his* stomach growled.

Rose giggled and angled her face up to his. He grinned down at her.

"I do think it might be time for us to eat," he said.

Rose arched her brows. "Time to refuel? Good idea. I don't think I have the energy to do—"

Logan silenced her with a deep kiss. He heard a soft moan that sounded like half protest and half pleasure. Grinning, he pulled back.

"Oh, we could probably manage," he said. "But then the paramedics would have to be called to cart us off and set us up with intravenous glucose. Better to feed ourselves, I think, and then…"

He purposely left the sentence unfinished. Watching Rose blush again brought another grin to his lips and the beginning of temptation to his body.

Rose saved him from any attempt to give in to that temptation by sitting up abruptly. She held the quilt in front of her body in a gesture of modesty that once again had him grinning.

Until he saw the serious expression tightening her features.

"Hey." He reached up to close his hand gently over her arm. "What's wrong?"

"Anna." She turned to him. "We…I forgot about her."

Logan sat up more slowly. "You're right. I suspect she's returned to San Francisco. We need to get back there. But I prefer not to operate machinery six miles above the earth on an empty stomach. Maybe we should fix something to eat before we go."

"Fix?" Rose turned to him. "As in *cook?*"

Logan couldn't prevent his surprised response. "You *don't?*"

Rose shook her head. "No." A second later she was the one with the surprised look. "You mean Anna *does?*"

Logan pushed himself into a seated position. "Absolutely." He bent forward to retrieve his beige T-shirt. After slipping it over his head, he went on. "Martina taught Anna the basics. Later she studied at Cordon Bleu."

"In *Paris?*"

"That's the one."

Logan was pulling his jeans on as he spoke. He stood, pulled the zipper up and turned to Rose. "Where's the kitchen?"

Rose stared at him for several seconds. "*You* cook, too?"

He let one side of his mouth quirk up. "My father was in charge of showing me how to tune an engine. Mom made sure I knew my way around a kitchen."

Rose seemed to digest this, then nodded slowly. "Go through that door, then make a quick left. I'll join you as soon as I'm dressed."

A few moments later, when Rose entered the kitchen, she found Logan standing in front of the open refrigerator. "I doubt if you'll find much in there," she said as she crossed the room. "Even at the best of times, I don't do much shopping, so—"

Rose stopped speaking as the refrigerator's interior came into view. The normally empty shelves held more food than they had in months. On the top rack she saw a half gallon of milk, a carton of eggs and a wedge of cheese. Lower shelves held romaine lettuce, celery, the remains of an onion and half each of a red and green pepper.

Logan looked over his shoulder. "I take it you didn't buy this stuff?"

"No." Rose stared at the food. "And maybe I *didn't* leave the quilt on the couch, either." Her eyes met Logan's again.

"Anna," they said together.

Logan closed the fridge and turned. "Let's go. We can do

drive-through on the way to the airport. We should be able to make it back to San—''

"Wait." Rose grabbed his arm as he strode toward the door. She responded to his questioning glance with a hurried explanation.

"Goldie will be arriving at eight to open the shop. There's no way she wouldn't have known someone was up here, although I'm guessing Anna did what I tried to do, bluffed her way into convincing Goldie that she was dealing with me. There's a good chance Anna mentioned where she was going, or gave Goldie some information that might keep us from another wild-goose chase."

Logan frowned for several moments, then nodded. "Well, in the meantime we should eat. There's the makings of a pretty decent omelette in there."

Rose gave him a wide smile and moved toward the doorway. "Great. If you don't mind, though, I'm going to jump into the shower while you cook. I'd only be in the way here."

Rose returned fifteen minutes later. Her hair hung to her waist in half-dried ringlets. She'd chosen an ankle-length skirt printed in purple and lavender with a short-sleeve cropped cotton sweater of bright pink. All in all, she felt more like herself than she had in days.

The kitchen, however, didn't seem all that familiar, what with the wire whisk and omelette pan sitting on the blue tiled counter. Heck, she didn't even know she *had* an omelette pan. Also, the papers that had littered the table beneath the small window at the end of the narrow room were now neatly stacked on the nearby hutch. In their place sat two plates filled with cheese-oozing omelettes.

The coffee machine was just sputtering out the last drops of that fragrant, life-giving substance. Logan stood next to it, and the minute he saw Rose he pulled the clear carafe from the spout and poured a cup of coffee. Rose grinned as she wrapped her hands around the cup and headed for the table.

"Oh, this is *heaven*," she said after her first bite of egg.

"Your mother was a *very* good instructor. Have you ever thought of cooking for a living?"

After swallowing, Logan laughed. "Yes, actually. When I was twelve or so I thought it would be great to own one of those old diners attached to a gas station. I wanted to call it Logan's Pit Stop—fill your stomach while you fill your tank."

Rose grinned. "Hey, that could work. People pay small fortunes every day at drive-through espresso places. You could specialize in those wrap things, so people could order while filling their car, then eat on the road."

Logan shook his head. "I don't think so. Besides, I already have a job."

Sure he did, Rose thought, one that ate at his soul and kept him too busy to refuel. As Rose took another bite of omelette she found herself wondering just how long it had been since he'd had any real time to himself. Although the past few days had been relatively free of business concerns, Logan had essentially still been working—trying to locate the Benedicts' runaway daughter and prevent a scandal.

And she could see by the frown creasing his face and the way he glanced repeatedly at his watch that he was once again on the Benedict clock. She wondered if he had any idea how much of his soul he'd given to these people. But now was not the time for such questions. After all, his main concern at the moment was less business and more personal—Anna's well-being, a concern she shared.

So Rose finished her breakfast in silence. She was gazing at the coffee carafe, considering a second cup, when she heard a muted *thump* echo somewhere on the first floor.

She glanced at her watch. "Goldie's here."

She got to her feet. When Logan stood, too, she placed a hand on his arm. "I think I should speak to her alone before she meets you."

Logan nodded. "I was going to clean up the kitchen."

Rose had started toward the door. She stopped and stared at him. He was going to *clean?* Good grief, she couldn't remember Josh setting foot into the kitchen, let alone making a meal and washing up after.

"Uh...thanks," she said weakly.

He answered with a grin and a nod. "If you don't mind," he said, "after I'm done in here I thought I'd take a quick shower myself."

"Of course." Rose turned toward the door again, speaking over her shoulder. "There are plenty of towels in the closet next to the bathroom, and I left you lots of warm water. Come on down when you're done, and I'll introduce you to Goldie."

When Rose reached the screen at the bottom of the stairs and peeked around, she immediately spotted Goldie Lander's brassy blond head bent over a table, writing on one of the ivory cards that served as a price tag.

Rose slipped into the room with a bright, "Hi, Goldie! I'm home!"

The woman straightened with a jerk, making her beaded necklaces rattle sharply. A loose tunic-top of orange and yellow silk fluttered around her thin body as she turned, and her green eyes widened with surprise as she stared at Rose.

"So soon?" she asked.

"Soon? Goldie, I was due to fly back yesterday afternoon."

Rose realized, suddenly, that she should have called to let Goldie know about the change of plans.

"No." The woman shook her head. "You returned from San Francisco *Friday* afternoon. Then you left again yesterday—after I gave you those letters."

Goose bumps tingled over every inch of Rose's body.

She had guessed right. Not only had Anna been here, she'd obviously kept her identity to herself. Perhaps for the same reason Rose had tried that ploy, because she realized no one was likely to believe the truth.

"Goldie," she said softly as she crossed the room. "I have a real wild story to tell you. Sit down and just listen, please?"

Goldie did as Rose asked, sitting in the wicker rocker with the peeling white paint and the beautiful needlepoint cushion. Her green eyes alternately narrowed and widened as Anna gave the most brief and concise explanation of the past few days she could manage.

When she stopped speaking, Goldie's pleasant features reflected a mixture of relief and comprehension. "So. The young woman I spent the last several days with was *Anna*. My God, she asked so very many *strange* questions, I thought that she— that *you*—had lost your mind. Not that I didn't understand, what with Kathleen…"

Rose nodded in Goldie's long pause, then reached over to take the woman's hand. "You said something about letters."

Goldie nodded. "That's right. Sunday afternoon, out of the clear blue, you—Anna—asked me about the last name Donnelly. I was near speechless."

"You? Speechless?"

The two women shared a grin, then Goldie shrugged. "I know, amazing concept. But you have to understand, I never expected that name to come up."

"You *knew* about that?"

"No." Goldie shook her head emphatically. "I had only heard the name one time. It was about three months ago when Kathleen…when she knew she didn't have long. One day she handed me a thick manila envelope, then asked me to put it somewhere safe and *only* to show it to you if you were to ask about that name."

"What happened when Anna asked about it?"

"Well, I told her about the envelope and explained I'd put it in my safe-deposit box. I promised to get it yesterday, as soon as the bank opened."

Rose's impatience was growing by the moment. "And?" she prompted.

"*And,* I did just that. I brought the envelope here. She opened it, and two thick packets of paper fell out, each tied with a purple ribbon. One had the name Rose written on it. The other said Anna."

"What did the letters say?"

Goldie reached over and touched her arm. "Honey, she

didn't read them. She shoved them back in the envelope and said she had a plane to catch.''

The huge straw hat protecting Rose from the sun flopped in the wind as the Mustang turned onto Sea Cliff Drive. Her fingers closed convulsively over the quilt in her lap as her emotions careened from excitement to fear, from hope to dread, depending on the scenario currently playing in her imagination.

''Will Goldie's plans affect your life much?''

Logan's question startled Rose out of her thoughts. She turned to him with a puzzled frown. ''You mean selling off all her merchandise and traveling? No. It makes perfect sense. Goldie always had a bit of the gypsy in her, was always talking about her plans to see the world—someday.''

She paused. ''We never know how much time we have. I'm glad Goldie is doing what she feels is important. As to the shop, well, I make my living with my harp. Maybe I'll rent the lower space out.''

Logan nodded as he pulled into the driveway. As the garage door opened, Rose saw that all the other vehicles were in their places and braced herself for battle. The Mustang had barely pulled to a stop when she got out, hugging her purse and the quilt to her chest. She was halfway to the door leading to the foyer before she felt Logan's gentle, restraining hand on her shoulder. She turned to question him.

''Slow down,'' he said with a half smile. ''Before you go marching in there, I think we should get the lay of the land.''

He paused. His frown told Rose he was working out a plan.

''Okay,'' he said finally. ''Let me go in first. Stay by the door here and listen. If anyone asks where you are, come in and join us—without *that*.'' He glanced at the quilt, then looked into her eyes again. ''However, if it sounds as if Anna is already here, I want you to go up the back way to her room and stay there until I can figure out how to handle things. I'll engage the family in conversation so they won't see you go past the French doors. All right?''

Not really, Rose thought. She was sick of sneaking around. But the plan made sense, so she nodded.

Logan guided her over to the door. He turned, dropped a quick kiss to her lips, gave her a tight, lopsided smile, then opened the door and stepped into the foyer. Rose took a deep breath as she held the door open a scant two inches. She heard nothing but Logan's footsteps for several moments. Then Elise's voice.

"Logan, where have you been? Anna's been up in her room since late yesterday afternoon and refuses to speak to any of us."

Rose had heard enough. After quietly closing the door, she made her way across the garage to the side door that led outside. Her feet echoed softly on the wrought-iron steps that ran up the side of the garage, tracing the route she'd taken the day she'd first arrived at this place.

Just inside the gate leading onto the veranda, she paused to take a deep breath. Then, counting on Logan to keep his promise to distract the occupants of the living room, she crossed in front of the French doors without so much as a sideways glance.

She was nearly out of breath by the time she finished running up the circular staircase to the wooden deck. She stood on the top step to draw cool sea air into her tight chest, before she turned toward the sliding glass door leading to Anna's room. Rose remembered, at that moment, that she didn't have a key to this door. There was nothing to do but knock, then wait, anticipation flowing through her like a jangling electrical current.

A moment later a figure approached to stand on the other side of the glass.

It was like looking into a mirror. Rose saw her own features, hair pulled back from her face as she'd worn it on Sunday. She was again wearing the thigh-length pale-blue turtleneck she'd worn to dinner on Sunday night. Eyes that matched her own stared back, filled with the exact mixture of wonder and fear and joy that she was feeling.

The ocean behind Rose sent a soft breeze to chill the flesh on her arms, already tight with goose bumps, as that image stretched a hand out toward the side of the door. It slid open, and the illusion of the mirror was gone. The figure standing before her was flesh and blood, smiling uncertainly before she spoke.

"You must be Rose."

"And you must be Anna," Rose replied.

"I've been looking for you for days," they said in unison.

Both women fell silent. They stared across the four feet of space that separated them for several moments. Rose thought, later, that she was the first to move toward Anna. But if that was so, then Anna was only a second behind, stepping toward Rose. When they were a foot apart, they opened their arms at exactly the same second, then enfolded each other in a tight embrace, with the quilt trapped between their bodies.

Chapter 16

The hug lasted for several long, wordless minutes. When the two women at last parted, Rose blinked the moisture from her eyes just in time to see Anna wipe a tear from her cheek.

They each released a choking laugh, then Anna asked, "Where have you been?"

"In Seattle," Rose replied. "Looking for *you.*"

"How did you know to look there?"

"Because of that." Rose turned to point at the bridge. "I came to San Francisco because I've been dreaming of it for years. After learning that I had a twin, and discovering that you'd recently found out about my existence, it took a while to realize that I was dreaming of the Space Needle, not because I was homesick, but because you were looking at it." She paused. "You went to Seattle after speaking to Nurse Reynolds, right?"

"Yes!" Anna nodded enthusiastically, her eyes wide with surprise. "Because *I* had recurring dreams about the Space Needle."

Rose nodded. "I figured that. But how did you ever find the house?"

"The harp."

"The harp?"

"Yes. In my dreams, the image of the Needle was usually set within a frame that had the shape of a harp, and I was looking through a set of vertical strings. Before I left Reno, I stopped at a bookstore and bought a Seattle guidebook to study on the plane. I found an area called Queen Anne Hill that looked as if it would provide the perspective that matched my dreams."

Anna paused, took a breath, then continued in the same rapid-fire delivery.

"After landing in Seattle, I went to a phone booth and looked under harps. When I determined that the address for Harps 'n' Chords was in the Queen Anne Hill area, I took a cab to the location and hurried into the shop on the lower level. At that point it suddenly occurred to me to wonder *what* the owner would think when I asked, 'Is there a window somewhere in this building that overlooks the Space Needle? Oh, and by the way, does it by any chance happen to have a harp sitting in front of it?'"

Rose smiled, recalling how she'd hesitated in front of the Benedict house, feeling silly to ask to be allowed on the balcony to look at the bridge. It took all her self-control not to break in and share the similarities in their tales, but she didn't want to interrupt.

"Fortunately," Anna went on, "I didn't have to ask. The minute I stepped into The Ridiculous to The Sublime, a lovely woman with bright blond hair looked up from her seat behind the cash register and said, 'Rose, dear. I didn't expect you home until Sunday.' I started to tell her that my name wasn't Rose, but before I could utter one word, the woman came around the counter, took my hands, told me how tired I looked and said I should go upstairs and rest before I told her all about my trip."

Anna paused again to shrug. "Well, since upstairs was exactly where I wanted to be, I just let the woman take me there. Just as she opened the door to the apartment, a bell tinkled downstairs and the woman—Goldie—said she had to get back to the shop. She told me to rest till closing time, when we'd have supper together. Well, I didn't rest one minute. I looked…through…''

As Anna's words came to a hesitant stop, chagrin twisted her features. Rose grinned and finished the thought.

"You searched until you discovered the harp in the attic, then looked through everything in the apartment, including the photo albums, where you saw someone who looked *exactly* like you, then read my journals and discovered who Rose was."

Anna stared at Rose a moment, her eyes widening. "You did the same thing? Here?"

Rose nodded. "I'm afraid so."

"Well." Anna sighed. "I doubt you learned very much about the *inner me*. I stopped keeping a diary at the age of ten, when I discovered Mother reading it."

"That sounds like Elise."

Anna's face lost all animation for a moment. Then curiosity lit her dark eyes as she asked, "How did you pull it off? Pretending to be me, I mean, with all the family and the servants to fool, and the doctor—" Anna's eyes widened. "Ohmigod. Dr. Alcott. How did you escape being locked up in that clinic?"

Rose drew a deep breath. "It wasn't easy. I was able to convince Logan that I wasn't you, and…" She paused. "You know, it really is a very long story. Why don't we make ourselves comfortable."

They sat at the head of the bed with Rose's half of the quilt lying in a loose heap atop Anna's neatly folded section at the foot while they conversed in a rapid, disjointed, back-and-forth manner that flowed in an oddly seamless fashion and managed to cover a remarkable amount of information in a relatively short time.

Then, at exactly the same moment, both young women fel

silent. While Rose was trying to keep from pinching herself to make sure she wasn't dreaming, Anna spoke suddenly.

"Where's Logan?"

Rose frowned. "The last time I saw him, he was going into the house to speak with the Bene—your family—to cover for me while I snuck up here." She paused. "I heard Elise mention that you were locked in your room. Knowing Logan, I would say he's found a way to keep them from coming up here—to give us some time together."

Anna seemed to consider that a moment. "That sounds right," she said at last. "He's a good brother. Even if he really isn't…my brother, if you know what I mean."

Rose simply nodded, afraid speaking would reveal her relief at hearing Anna refer to Logan as her brother, without any deeper sort of affection.

"I sure wish Logan had been on hand when I got back here yesterday," Anna was saying. "I barely got in the front door before Elise was standing in front of me, saying, 'Well, I see you've recalled where you left your keys. Did your trip to Berkeley do anything for the rest of your memory?' I, of course, just stood there, like a statue. When she asked where Logan was, I said I didn't know, but hoped he'd be along soon, then ran upstairs and locked myself in my room. I know that Elise has a key, and I was afraid she would come in after me. But after standing on the other side of the door, trying to entice me out, she left me alone. She even sent Martina up with some meals."

"Well," Rose said. "Elise has had a bad couple of days. Logan and I have her convinced that I—I mean *you*—have amnesia. I guess she didn't want to tackle you without him."

A smile slowly stole over Anna's features. "Oh, I see." A second later she sobered. "Well, if Logan's covering for us now, then we'd better put the time to good use. Let me get those letters."

Rose sat in stunned silence, watching Anna cross the room to the closet, then emerge with the thick manila envelope Goldie had described. Anna opened it as she crossed to the bed, then upended it, sending two ribbon-tied packets and a single key falling onto the aqua coverlet.

Rose stared up at her sister and finally managed to ask, "You mean, you haven't read them yet?"

Anna shook her head. "Yours *or* mine. Though I was tempted." She reached down and lifted the one marked Rose and handed it to her sister as she went on. "I was hoping that somehow we could at least do *this* together."

Rose's eyes clouded, her chin trembled slightly, then firmed, and her eyes narrowed as she went on, "So, I guess we'd better start reading."

The papers in Rose's hand felt suddenly heavy as Anna sat next to her. Their eyes met and held for several moments before they looked down to read their names, written in Kathleen's neat calligraphic script. They turned the slender packets over at nearly the same moment, slid the ribbons off, then opened the folded pages.

Rose read slowly. Kathleen started with an apology for the lies she'd told and the truths she'd omitted, then proceeded to explain how she had come to raise only one of her sister's daughters. Much of this Rose had already learned from her conversations with Scott Miller and Nurse Reynolds. Even so, she was surprised to find tears filling her eyes as she read about Elizabeth Donnelly's request that her child be named Roseanna, only to die before Kathleen could tell her sister that she'd delivered *two* girls.

The decision to name one Rose and the other Anna had been the last decision Kathleen had been able to make without interference. Victor and Robert had arrived shortly after, and the battle for the twins began.

Kathleen hoped Rose understood the difficult choice she'd been forced into. If she'd kept both girls, without the money Victor offered in return for her cooperation and silence, she would never have been able to pay the twins' medical bills, let alone support them. While working on the Benedict campaign, she'd seen how much Robert loved the man who would have been Anna and Rose's father, and believed that Robert truly would give Anna the same love he would give to his very own child.

However, Kathleen hadn't trusted Victor Benedict at all. After Rose was healthy enough to leave the hospital, Kathleen had settled in a commune and changed their last name to Delancey because she was afraid that Victor might someday try to lay claim to her daughter, in spite of the vow of silence she'd taken.

As Rose read her mother's words, it was clear that this promise had haunted Kathleen all her life. She explained that upon learning of her illness, she became reluctant to take the secret of Rose and Anna's birth to the silence of her grave, leaving unanswered questions to plague them should the two girls ever learn of each other.

If Rose was reading this now, Kathleen wrote, then this must have come to pass. Along with the truth contained in these pages, she wanted the twins to know about some property in Maine that was being held in trust for them.

The letter ended with more words of apology, so very deeply heartfelt that Rose could almost sense her mother's arms around her, holding her, reminding her to be true to herself, and begging forgiveness for not having totally followed that rule herself.

Rose blinked away hot tears. Forgiveness went without saying, even for the lies she'd been told. Because the most important thing was true—Kathleen Donnelly *had* been her mother, in every sense but physically, and like a true mother had done what she thought best to protect her child.

After folding the letter and retying the ribbon, Rose looked up to find that Anna was just finishing tying the ribbon around her letter. When their eyes met, Rose saw that Anna's were also shimmering with tears. There was a moment of hesitation, then wordlessly the two women exchanged letters.

Kathleen's message to Anna contained the same basic information. She told Anna how very much she had wanted to keep both girls, but explained that she hadn't relinquished Anna only because of financial reasons. The twins *were* fathered by a Benedict, and the family did have a strong legal claim.

Anna was never out of her thoughts, Kathleen wrote. She had purchased the San Francisco Chronicle every day of her life, waiting until Rose had gone to bed each night to pore through the paper for any article that mentioned the Benedicts. She had kept a scrapbook, where she'd pasted pictures of Anna at five with her ballet troupe, one of a seven-year-old standing on a balance beam, another of Anna at fifteen accepting a ribbon at a high school track meet. The album was in a safe-deposit box, along with the information pertaining to the property in Maine.

Kathleen's last words were "I wanted very much to be your mother and raise you with your sister. I prayed every day that the people I gave you to have cherished you as much as I do. You have always been in my heart."

Rose dropped the letter and reached for Anna. Together they cried quietly for several minutes. Within seconds of each other they drew in deep, shuddering breaths, then broke apart. They looked at each other, found they'd both reached up to wipe the tears from the same eye, and ended up laughing, only to embrace each other and cry some more before they took another shuddering breath and parted.

As Rose leaned against the iron headboard and finished drying her eyes, she caught sight of a phrase written on the pages that had tumbled to her lap. She picked up the piece of paper and frowned as she read it out loud.

"'The man who would have been your father.'" She paused. "Mom used that same exact phrase—"

"In *your* letter," Anna finished. "I noticed that, too. Strange wording."

Rose shook her head. "Not if Mom was trying not to lie."

"You mean, Joe Benedict *wasn't* our father?"

"I don't know. But I have an idea who might." She paused, then together she and Anna said, "Grace."

Instantly both young women got off the bed. Neither bothered with the shoes resting on the floor, padding in barefoot unison to the door. Anna opened it, took one step forward, then stopped.

Rose stood behind her sister, staring at the collection of people in the hall. Logan towered over Grace, whose arm rested on his. Chas stood between his parents, supporting his mother in a similar manner. Not one of their faces registered any surprise at seeing two versions of Anna. However, Elise looked very pale.

"We need to talk to you." Chas broke the silence. His gaze took in both Rose and Anna. "May we come in?"

Anna glanced over her shoulder at Rose before nodding. The young women stepped back to allow the rest of the family to enter. No one spoke. Chas led his mother to the foot of the bed, where she collapsed onto the two halves of the quilt without giving any attention to where she was sitting. Robert remained standing next to her.

Logan brought the chair from the desk for Grace. Rose noticed that his face was set in grim lines, which only softened for a second when Grace thanked him. After the old woman was seated, Logan looked at Chas, who in turn shifted his attention to Rose and Anna, still standing by the open door.

"Well, while the two of you have been up here," Chas said with no hint of a smile, "the rest of us have been having quite a discussion downstairs. After Logan explained what has been going on the past few days, he convinced us that the two of you needed time to work some things out."

Chas paused. "First off, Rose, I want to tell you how impressed we are with your acting abilities." She fought a shiver as his dark eyes met hers. "Under normal circumstances, we would do something special, throw you a little welcome-to-the-family party where we could all get to know each other. However, at the moment the family is under siege. Scott Miller just called."

Rose and Anna simultaneously asked, "The reporter?"

Rose was getting so accustomed to having Anna's voice echo hers that she didn't even glance at her sister before demanding, "What does he want?"

"What do you *think* he wants?" Chas glanced from Anna to Rose and back again. "He wants a story. No—he thinks he *has* a story. He claims he wants to give us a chance to refute the information he has. But what he really wants is confirmation. And he refuses to wait. He's on his way here."

"Fine." Anna expressed the very thought running through Rose's mind. "It's about time the truth came out."

"Oh?" Chas took a step toward Anna. "And what truth would *that* be?"

Anna blinked, and took a step back. Recalling what Elise had said about Anna's habit of running from confrontation, Rose took her sister's hand.

"Well, actually, neither of us is sure," she replied. "Hardly surprising, I would say, since we've both been lied to all our lives. We *do* know that Elizabeth Donnelly was our mother. It *appears* that Joe Benedict was our father, but Mom's letters lead us to believe this is a lie, too."

"You're right."

It was Logan who said these words. Rose studied his face as he stepped away from Grace. Gone was the man she'd laughed with in her kitchen, danced with and made love to in her living room. In his place stood the unsmiling, narrow-eyed man she'd encountered on the balcony five days ago—the Benedicts' Mr. Fix-It. She felt a sudden chill as he began to speak.

"Did the letter say this was a lie?"

Rose shook her head. "No. It was an odd phrasing that made us question this." She drew in a quick breath. "But now that I think about it, I can't imagine Victor going to all the trouble to cover up the circumstances surrounding our births if Joe had fathered us. I suppose that would have made the news, but it wouldn't have caused a big enough scandal to cost his father the election. However, if Charles's other son, Robert, who was married with a small child, had been the one who—"

"No," Logan interrupted. "That's the story that Mr. Miller wants to print, but it's not the truth, either. What all these lies have been covering up all these years is the fact that the two of you were fathered by Charles Benedict."

Logan watched Rose's and Anna's expressions change from surprise to incomprehension. Rose recovered first.

Her eyes narrowed as she said, "How did you...?" She hesitated, then finished, "Did Grace tell you this?"

"No. She knew, of course. But it was Chas who told me."

These last words tasted bitter on Logan's tongue. But he didn't have time now to deal with the betrayal he'd felt upon learning that Victor hadn't seen fit to share this vital piece of family history with the man he'd trained to protect the family name.

"It seems some cracks had developed in Charles's marriage. Charles was dedicated to his work. His wife, Louise, had grown weary of politics and had turned to other interests. Lizzie Donnelly, with her fresh beauty and enthusiasm for the issues Charles was fighting for, arrived on the scene at just the right—or should I say, wrong—moment."

Logan paused and Robert broke in. "My father had the looks and energy of a man much younger than forty-eight. Lizzie Donnelly was a highly romantic soul, who justified her affair with a married man by inventing a fantasy that my parents' marriage would soon end."

"You're saying Lizzie just *made that up?*" Rose asked. "Gee, I don't suppose Charles had anything to do with that idea."

Logan saw Chas glare at her, but it was Robert who answered. "I'm sure he did. My parents *were* having problems. However, as the primary approached, my mother seemed to reconcile herself to the life she'd chosen. Lizzie informed my father of her pregnancy shortly after he won the primary that June, but by that time my mother was also expecting a child."

A frown formed over Robert's eyes as he went on. "Father won his seat in the U.S. Senate in November. Mother died from complications trying to give birth to that baby in late January. The baby died, too." He stopped speaking, cleared his throat, then continued with his story. "She never knew

about the affair, however. Father had begged his brother to
see to that. Joe and I didn't have any idea Father had been
involved with Lizzie Donnelly until Uncle Victor told us about
the baby Lizzie was expecting.''

Robert paused to take Elise's hand. "Victor decided that
since Joe and I had been in charge of the volunteers and spent
some time with Elizabeth and Kathleen, the other students
would accept the idea that one of us was responsible for
Lizzie's pregnancy. I already had a wife, so Victor called on
Joe to marry Elizabeth. He made all the arrangements for a
union that was to be dissolved at the end of two years, complete with a prenuptial agreement and arrangements for future
payments to be—''

"Why?"

Rose's sudden interruption drew Logan's gaze, along with
the attention of everyone else in the room.

"Why have Joe do that?" she asked. "Why not just send
Lizzie away to some home for unwed mothers, bribe the staff
to keep the identity of the father a secret, then pay her off,
like Victor did my moth—Kathleen?"

"Because," Robert replied firmly. "The child was going to
be a Benedict."

Silence fell over the room. Logan realized that each person
knew, to varying degrees, just what that meant, even Rose,
who had been among them for such a short time.

"Chas." This time it was Anna who broke the tense hush.
"If you knew this, why did you tell me, when I was very
little...that I was a changeling—adopted? And then when I
believed it, why did you tease me about that?"

Chas stared at her several minutes before he shook his head.
"I didn't know about all this when I fed you the changeling
story. I was feeling left out at the time. Not only was Dad
spending a lot more time with you, but you had that invisible
friend of yours."

His lips gave a chagrined twist. "But Victor overheard me
and told me the real story. He made me promise never to say
those things to you again and to never tell anyone else the

truth. I couldn't think of any way to stop you believing what I'd said, except to try and tease you out of it. I'm sorry."

Regret softened his expression, but a moment later his eyes hardened as he turned to Logan.

"However, I'm not sorry for having kept my word to Victor. He went to a great deal of trouble to make it appear that Joe was the one who'd had an affair with a young volunteer so that Grandfather could get into a position to do some real good for this country."

"That's right." Elise spoke as she stood. Rose turned to see her scowling at Logan. "And now, as Victor's protégé, it's your job to convince Scott Miller that this is exactly what happened."

"It shouldn't be difficult, Logan." Robert stepped forward as he spoke. "You can explain that Joe and Lizzie died only days after I learned that my wife had miscarried the child she'd conceived in Switzerland. That we decided to raise Joe's orphaned girl as our own. You can tell the reporter that it was a difficult, emotional time, and a family matter that had nothing to do with campaign issues or public policy, which is why Victor went to such lengths to cover this up."

Rose drew a deep breath. The implications in each of these speeches were clear. Logan owed his education, his more-than-comfortable lifestyle, his career to the Benedicts. It was payback time.

Anna broke the silence. "But what about Rose? Are you suggesting that the family continue to deny her existence? She's a Benedict, too."

Chas replied, "Yes, she is." His dark eyes shifted from Anna to Rose as he went on, "That's why Victor saw to it that she was financially taken care of. Apparently not as comfortably as Victor had intended, but then, he could hardly dictate how Kathleen would handle the money he gave her. I'm sure we can make up for that oversight now."

Rose bristled at the barely veiled hint that her frugal, hardworking mother had frittered that money away, but before she could respond, Chas had turned back to Anna, saying, "However, our immediate concern is Father."

Anna lifted her chin. "You mean *your* father."

"Oh?" Chas's eyes narrowed. "Who was the man at your ballet recitals? At your track meets? Who spoke to your teachers, who helped you with your math? And just who was the man who encouraged your dozens of impossible dreams?"

Chas paused, then went on more calmly. "That man didn't do anything wrong, except carry out Victor's plan to help his own father at a time when it was needed. Well, Robert Benedict needs *our* help now. Despite the fantasy life you like to retire to, I know that you're aware how much good he does for *many* people. He'll be able to do much more once he gets to Washington. I want you to think about that, before you place the sister you've only recently learned about before the man who raised you like his own daughter."

In the silence that followed these words, Rose found herself thinking that when it came time for Chas Benedict to run for office, his eloquence would stand him in very good stead. A glance at Anna revealed that her twin was torn between two loyalties, gazing at Robert before she turned to Rose.

"But some people already know about both of us," Anna said quietly. "That professor, the nurse at the hospital and Rose's friend Goldie. The truth will have to come out eventually."

Chas shook his head, but it was Logan who bit out, "No, it doesn't."

A fist gripped Rose's heart as she turned to him. His features were set, his lips a tight line. A deep frown darkened his eyes as he spoke again.

"First off, the fact that Professor Wilkins refused to talk to the reporter indicates that Victor paid him enough to ensure the man will keep silent regarding any suspicions he might have. Or perhaps Wilkins just doesn't want to be implicated in a cover-up. As to Dottie Reynolds, I called her at the hospital when I learned Miller was on the way. She assured me she has no intention of telling anyone else what happened all those years ago. She regrets having been a part of the lies that ripped Rose's and Anna's lives apart, but she feels that making the truth public now would only bring about more devastation, unless that's what Rose wants.''

Logan turned to Rose. His warm eyes held hers. "It's up to you. If you want, I can come up with some story that explains your connection to Anna. But you'd then be subjected to swarms of media, scrutinizing every second of your life, possibly criticizing Kathleen for having deprived you of the advantages of growing up a Benedict.''

His gaze shifted to Anna. "And if the whole truth comes out, Robert would get heat for preaching the importance of family while keeping his daughter in the dark about her own twin. This would undoubtedly cost him this and maybe any future election.''

Rose saw guilt creep into Anna's eyes and found herself frowning. She saw the logic in Logan's words, understood that the Benedicts could only acknowledge her existence at the cost of the family "destiny.''

She had no burning desire to be connected, publicly *or* privately, to this branch of her gene pool, other than to Anna. And the picture Logan had painted of the resulting media attention was beyond frightening. Yet something was bothering her, tightening that fist in the center of her chest, making it hard to breathe, impossible to speak, even though Logan had turned to her, and it was obvious he was waiting for her to say something.

After several seconds of silence he placed a hand on her shoulder. "Rose, I hope you understand that for the good of all concerned, the best thing for me to do is convince Scott Miller that the deep dark *scandal* the family has been hiding is the lie Victor set in place over twenty-five years ago—that Joe fathered Anna. If the man decides to print that story, some voters will certainly react negatively to the deception Robert's participated in, but I suspect that many more will admire his desire to raise Anna as his. But if the truth comes out, that it was Charles Benedict who had an affair with a volunteer, then not only would his legacy be tarnished, but Robert—''

Rose was vaguely aware that he'd stopped speaking. Halfway through his speech she'd stepped away from him, causing his hand to slide from her shoulder as she headed for the bed. Having reached her goal, she slipped her feet into the flats on the floor, then, reaching toward the center of the aqua coverlet, she retrieved her purse, floppy hat and the letter from Kathleen.

Oblivious of everything but the sharp, throbbing pain exploding repeatedly in her chest, Rose walked toward the sliding glass door. Although she'd heard every word Logan said, her mind echoed with the one phrase *for the good of everyone concerned*—the exact words that Josh had used when urging her to abandon Kathleen to the care of others.

Outside, the ocean breeze teased the bangs back from her forehead as Rose paused at the top of the circular staircase. She shoved the letter into her large purse, then piled her hair atop her head and trapped it there with the large hat. Just as she opened the gate and prepared to descend, strong fingers closed over her shoulder and spun her around.

Logan towered over her. Rose was aware that Anna stood at his elbow, but her attention was captured by the frown above Logan's mossy eyes as he demanded, ''Just where do you think you are going?''

Rose met his gaze. ''To Seattle, where I belong.''

He shook his head. ''Wait up here, in Anna's room. It'll be dark by the time I'm done with Miller. I'll fly you back. We need to talk.''

''No. I've heard enough talk. I need to go. Now.'' Seeing his frown deepen, Rose stiffened. ''Don't worry, no one will see me and mistake me for Anna. I'll walk along the sand to the public beach, then hike up to the main road and catch a cab. I still have my unused return ticket and enough money to pay the fine for changing my original flight.''

Logan opened his mouth, but before he could speak Anna stepped in front of him, saying, ''I want to go with you.''

Rose smiled at her sister. "Robert needs your support. From what I've seen, the man truly has tried to be a loving father to you. I could tell, in there, that you want to help him get through this. And you should, *but...*"

Her voice deepened as she took Anna into her arms. "You have a second home now, in Seattle. I expect you to visit whenever you can...and to stay as long as you like. We still have a *lot* of catching up to do."

Ending the embrace, Rose stepped back to gaze into her sister's teary eyes. Anna started to say something, but Chas whispered urgently from the open door, "Martina says that the reporter has arrived. We need to get downstairs."

Logan gently turned Anna toward the house. "Go with Chas and your—and Robert," he said softly, looking at Chas. "I'll be right down."

Rose watched the two men stare each other down as Anna crossed the deck. Once she was inside, Chas remained frowning at Logan one second longer, before he turned and stepped back into the room.

Aware that Logan had turned to her, Rose looked up. His green-brown eyes were dark beneath a frown.

"I get the feeling you're upset with me," he said. "Is it possible that you think I should tell the world that you are a Bene—"

Rose cut him off with a quick shake of her head. "No. That's an old lie. Telling the truth wouldn't change my past— and I wouldn't want to change anything about how I was raised. What's bothering me is that you're so willing to make this *your* lie. Look—" she paused to take a deep breath "—I don't want to ruin Robert. But you must see how these lies have affected everyone. You know firsthand what it cost you to lock away all those lovely memories of your parents. Why continue?"

Logan stared at her a moment, his face expressionless before he said, "I thought you understood. It's my job to protect the Benedicts."

"It's your *job* to protect a pack of liars?"

Rose knew her voice had risen. Fear had taken over. She watched Logan carefully, concentrating on his eyes. Doubt, anger, confusion all seemed to be reflected there.

Something died in her heart when she saw his frown deepen and realized that anger had won.

"What is this?" he asked, his voice low, controlled. "You came into my life a mere five days ago, completely turned it upside down, and now you tell me that my job doesn't meet with your approval? Now you want me to change it—you want to change *me?* That takes a hell of a lot of nerve."

Rose felt as if the very center of her being had been flash frozen.

"*Your* life has been turned upside down?" She paused as her throat tightened at the thought of never again seeing this man's face, laughing *or* scowling. "Look," she said finally. "It's not my intention to change anyone or anything. I learned a long time ago that manipulation is the quickest way to kill love."

As she paused, Rose saw Logan's frown lift slightly and caught a glimmer of hope and the old familiar warmth in his dark-hazel eyes. She wished she could see those eyes crinkle into a smile one more time, but the ache in her heart forced her to shake her head and say the words she knew would extinguish that glimmer, and any hope she might have, forever.

"You once told me you'd learned from the best," she said. "Twenty-five years ago Victor Benedict orchestrated what he thought was a necessary lie. Now you feel you need to back that lie up. Well, I'm afraid that I can't live with any more lies, no matter how much I may want—"

Rose stopped speaking to swallow past the tightness in her throat. Or maybe it was to give Logan a chance to say perhaps he could think of a way to repay Robert Benedict that didn't involve deception.

When Logan remained frowning behind a wall of silence, Rose forced herself to go on. "Look, you need to do what you need to do. So do I. Take care of yourself."

With that, Rose turned. Again warm, strong fingers closed over her shoulder. There was no attempt to urge her to stay, just a gentle holding her in place as Logan said, ''I'll make sure a cab is waiting for you when you get to the parking lot at Baker's Beach.''

Rose stared at the Golden Gate Bridge. As her eyes filled with tears, the long orange span seemed to buckle and twist. Logan's hand lifted from her shoulder, and his footsteps began to retreat. Blinking away her tears, Rose started down the stairs, away from the place of her dreams. *And* her nightmares.

Chapter 17

"Well, Rosie girl. Can Goldie Landers throw a yard sale or what? I even managed to get three sunny days in a row. Not necessarily *warm*, but sunny."

Rose glanced at the ivory fisherman sweater she wore over her jeans, then looked up from the cash register she'd been manning on the front porch for the past three days, to watch the older woman button her patchwork-quilt jacket against the late-afternoon wind.

"Well, I would hope you could organize one of these things, considering the thousand or so that you've attended over the years."

Goldie grinned. "Well, maybe after I've toured the world, that's what I shall do—hire myself as a professional yard-sale organizer. I'd still get to deal in junk, but wouldn't be tied down to a shop."

"I don't know, Goldie, what's the going commission on other people's junk these days? Enough to feed your canary?"

"I don't have a canary, as you well know. Besides, it was

only a thought. A girl needs to prepare for the future, you know.''

Rose knew that all too well. It was a subject she'd given great attention to since returning to Seattle six days ago—the only way she knew to keep from dwelling on her recent past, and second-guessing the decisive action she'd taken to make it impossible for Logan Maguire to play any part in *her* future.

So, she'd kept herself busy, helping Goldie price her merchandise. She hadn't watched television, and the only time she'd touched a newspaper was to unwrap a dusty mirror to wash for the sale. However, the fact that hordes of reporters had not shown up at her doorstep, clamoring for an interview with one of Charles Benedict's twin daughters, told her that Logan had done what he needed to do—kept the family skeleton locked firmly in the closet.

"I think it's time to give up the ghost," Goldie said as she started down the steps. "Time to bring the dredges inside and box them up for donation to the thrift store."

"I'll help you." Rose snapped a rubber band around twenty-five one-dollar bills, shoved them in the drawer and shut the register. "Starting with this."

She lugged the heavy item through the front door to the old oak desk in the center of the bare hardwood floor. It was the only piece of furniture left in what had been a shop crammed to the rafters with all those ridiculous and sublime things she'd grown up surrounded by.

The room felt incredibly empty. So did Rose. And it didn't make sense that an empty heart could ache so very much.

"Okay if I store this junk in the corner here?" Rose jumped at the sound of Goldie's voice, forced a smile and turned as the object-laden woman said, "Or is that massage therapist coming to see about renting this space today?"

"She's not coming until tomorrow," Rose replied. "Put those things down, and I'll get a box to store them in."

Rose stepped toward the smaller room to the left, the area that had been a dining room when the building was still a residence. Even before she reached the newly re-installed

French doors that closed this area off from the rest of the house, she caught sight of her harp, sitting in its new home in front of the window. It would be the perfect room to teach in, convenient for her students.

She grabbed several of the empty boxes she'd used to transport her music books down from the attic. As she returned to the area that had once been a living room, she decided that the second set of French doors, solid ones, scheduled to be set into the archway leading into the large space, would give the new tenant privacy and provide a reasonable buffer from the sounds of the harp lessons.

Rose was just beginning to box up the collection of old jewelry, candlesticks and handmade stationery, when Goldie came along to place more things on the floor. She glanced at the stuff with a smile as the woman turned and headed toward the door again.

"Wouldn't you know it," Rose heard the woman say. "I've brought in half my stuff and here comes another customer. Nice-looking Mustang, too."

Rose's heart thudded to a stop. It began to pound slowly and painfully as she carefully placed a rosebud-encrusted picture frame in the box and told herself not to be silly. Lots of people drove Mustangs.

"Rosie."

Goldie's voice sounded strange. Surprised that the woman was still in the house when prospective customers had just pulled up, Rose straightened and turned.

This time her heart took a painful leap. Through the open door she saw that not only was the red Mustang with the top down parked at the curb, but its oh-so-familiar owner was pulling a piece of luggage out of its open trunk.

Another figure, familiar yet oddly different, was rushing up the walkway. Rose's heart raced as she crossed the room. Just before she reached the door, a gust of wind blew it shut. Rose stared through the oval glass in the center of the door as Anna ran up the porch steps and stopped on the other side. The features Rose gazed at matched her own, but they were framed in a dark cap of curly, and very short, hair.

Jerking the door open, Rose pulled Anna into an embrace. "You cut it!" She released her hold on her sister to lean back and say, "You look great!"

Anna beamed. "I look like *me*. I've been wanting to do this for *ages!*"

Suddenly her smile faded as she stared past her sister. "Rose," Anna said. "Are you moving?"

Rose shook her head. "Just the harp." Seeing her sister's puzzled look, she explained. "I had it brought down from the attic. Goldie *is* moving, though. She's selling out and going traveling."

"Wow." Anna blinked. "Things are happening fast all over the place. I'm glad we got up here before she left. I'd like to get to know her, or have her get to know me, because when I was here before she thought I was—"

"Me," Rose finished. "I know. And speaking of things happening fast, I hardly expected a visit so soon. Not—"

Rose was suddenly aware of the tall figure in a leather jacket who had stepped onto the porch. She forced herself to keep her attention on her sister as she went on, "Not that I object to seeing you so quickly. I just thought that you'd have to..."

She wasn't sure *what* she'd thought. She was barely capable of thinking at all, what with her every sense tuned in to the man standing wordlessly at the top of the porch steps five feet away.

"Oh, we would have been here sooner," Anna was saying. "But the Mustang broke down in Coos Bay, Oregon, and we had to wait two days for a garage to get the part. I thought you might be missing this."

Anna took a step back as she spoke. For the first time Rose noticed that her sister had a large canvas tote slung over one shoulder. She watched as Anna reached in and pulled out a thick roll of purple-and-turquoise fabric. Rose stared for several minutes at the quilt she'd left on the foot of Anna's bed before reaching for it.

"Thank you," she said softly.

Anna laughed. "Oh, we didn't drive up all this way just to bring that. I need a place to hide out." She sobered then. Her eyes seemed to grow darker, whether with fear or sadness or both before she asked, "Is it okay for me to stay here awhile?"

Rose grabbed Anna's hand. "Of course. What happened?"

"You don't know?"

"Know what?"

Rose saw Anna glance over her shoulder. She forced her own eyes to stare straight ahead, meeting Anna's gaze when it returned to hers. "Scott Miller had the decency to warn us that his story about the 'Benedict scandal' would break to-day—Sunday—so it would get the most coverage. I decided now was not the time to break myself of running away from confrontation. I told Chas he could explain my absence by saying that I was so devastated to learn that I'm not the daughter of Robert and Elise Benedict that I ran off to Borneo, or joined a convent, or even that I've gone to Sweden, where I 'vant to be alone.'"

Rose was silent a moment, trying to digest this information and wondering how it connected to Logan's presence on her porch.

"Well," she said at last, "the attic is all yours. There's even a day bed up there that I used to use as a couch for clients awaiting their lessons."

"Thank you." Anna smiled weakly, then shrugged. "The truth of the matter is that I need a place to hide out for a while to decide what to do next. *After*—" she paused to glance over her shoulder again "—a certain someone decides it's safe to get a birth certificate under the name Anna *Donnelly* with my correct date of birth."

She looked at Rose again. "Do you realize that I have spent my entire life reading the horoscope for a Scorpio, when I'm really a *Libra*. And Elise had the nerve to wonder why I couldn't get my act together!"

Anna gave Rose a wide grin, then turned to Logan. "Let

me have my bags, please. I want to go up and get settled. Goldie, can you give me a hand?''

A moment of panic gripped Rose as both women grabbed one of the suitcases Logan had been holding all this time, then pushed past her toward the stairs at the back of the house. As she watched them disappear, she heard Logan's footsteps on the wooden porch.

Unable to keep from feasting her eyes on the face she'd once dreamed of so often and hadn't seen awake or asleep for almost a week now, Rose swiveled around to find Logan standing just outside the entrance, not two feet away. She studied his face. When she couldn't read his impassive features, she focused on his green-brown eyes and found no clues to his emotions there, either.

The growing silence urged her to say the first thing that came to her mind. "Can you do that?"

"Do what?" he asked.

"Get Anna a new, corrected birth certificate?"

He shrugged. "It depends on whether I take the Washington State Bar or not."

Rose drew a shaky breath, then she repeated, "The Washington State Bar?"

"Yeah, maybe. For the moment, though, I'm going to work for a fellow who once managed the private airport in San Francisco. He's in charge of a small municipal airport up here now and offered me a position as a mechanic. The job comes with a studio apartment in the rear of one of the hangars."

Rose's heart began to race as the implications of this information began to sink in. "Then you're no longer working for—"

"The Benedicts?" Logan finished. "No. Chas did such a good job handling Scott Miller that—"

"*Chas* spoke to the reporter?"

Logan held her gaze as he nodded. "Yep. When I joined the family and Miller after our little talk on the balcony, I pulled Chas aside and told him the honor of lying to Miller was all his."

"So he fired you?"

Logan shook his head. "I quit." He paused, aware of his muscles tensing. "As I walked down the stairs, I kept reminding myself of all the opportunities the Benedicts had provided me with—the education, the flight training, the important job. But I found myself remembering all the lies I've told in the name of negotiation, of protecting the family business. Nothing big, nothing actually illegal—but lies all the same."

He paused to draw a deep breath. He continued to gaze down at Rose as he went on. "It suddenly struck me that in my attempts to prove my gratitude and loyalty to the Benedicts, I've done things that my real family—my parents—would be less than proud of. I have you to thank for—"

"No," Rose interrupted in a harsh whisper. "I didn't do anything. That's why I left, so I wouldn't try to manipulate you, attempt to turn you into 'the man of my dreams.' You saw past the smoke screen of deception all by yourself."

"Not without your help." Logan's lips quirked into a tiny smile. "From the moment we met, you not only forced me to look at parts of myself that I didn't want to see, you made me feel emotions I buried for years. You helped me reclaim my past, then forced me to take charge of my future, to ask what it is that *I* want out of life. I have to admit, it's scary. And I'm only sure of one thing at the moment." Logan paused, a determined look on his face as he went on, "And that is that I love you."

These last three words vibrated through Rose's body to release the fear gripping her heart and replace it with the tenderest of aches.

"I don't expect you to feel the same way," Logan was saying. "But I'm willing to hang around, court you, whatever it takes to convince you that we belong—"

Rose halted his words by placing her fingers gently on his mouth. An excited tingle rushed down her arm to settle in her stomach. She drew in a slow breath as her lips quivered into a smile.

"Logan," she said. "When I finally found Anna, the missing *something* that I'd been aware of all my life fell immediately into place. But that same day, after I left you on that balcony, I realized that something new was missing—the piece of my heart that I'd given to you.''

Her throat grew tight with the memory of walking away from him, from all the dreams she'd built around him. Her voice grew more husky as she went on, ''You don't have to court me. I already—''

Rose choked as tears filled her eyes. She blinked in an attempt to clear her vision, then opened her mouth to finish speaking. Before one word could escape her throat, Logan bent toward her and silenced any further speech with a kiss.

It was an incredibly tender kiss. His lips trembled on hers. His arms held her in a tight embrace, one that promised warmth and comfort and so much more. Rose twined her arms around Logan's neck, holding on to him as she deepened the kiss, along with the bond that had already been forged within their souls. As she basked in a sense of wholeness, her heart swelled with the knowledge that even the strangest of dreams can, indeed, come true.

* * * * *

SILHOUETTE®
SENSATION™

AVAILABLE FROM 15TH FEBRUARY 2002

OUT OF NOWHERE Beverly Bird

A beautiful socialite wasn't the kind of murder suspect Fox Whittington was u
to. He didn't know whether to haul her off to jail—or take her in his arms and
kiss her senseless…

NAVAJO'S WOMAN Beverly Barton

The Protectors

She was the only woman he'd ever loved, and duty had torn their tender unio
apart. Now Andi needed him and this time Joe wouldn't walk away without h
honour—or his woman!

THE ENEMY'S DAUGHTER Linda Turner

A Year of Loving Dangerously

Undercover agent Russell Devane needed to get close to the enemy's daughte
He got close—too close—and found himself fighting a forbidden attraction to
beautiful Lise Meldrum.

THE AWAKENING OF DR BROWN Kathleen Creighto

Dr Ethan Brown was finding 'phoenix' Joanna Dunn just too hard to resist. D
he indulge his dreams of a future together—even if she had a nightmare of a
past?

EVERY WAKING MOMENT Doreen Roberts

US Marshall Blake Foster had fallen into the oldest trap in history—he'd let
suspect Gail Stevens get under his skin. He wished he didn't have to go throu
with this job, because no matter what happened, he was going to get burned.

THE MAN FOR MAGGIE Frances Housden

A no-nonsense, sceptical lawman like Max was the last person Maggie would
have imagined turning to for support, let alone romance. But perhaps he coul
save her from what she saw in her dreams?

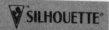

NORA ROBERTS

NIGHT MOVES

TWO ROMANTIC THRILLERS IN ONE BOOK

From dusk till dawn,
the hours of darkness are
filled with mystery, danger
...and desire.

Available from 18th January

*Available at most branches of WH Smith,
Tesco, Martins, Borders, Eason, Sainsbury's
and most good paperback bookshops.*

0102/121/SH26

SILHOUETTE®
INTRIGUE™
is proud to present

1201/SH/LC27

TOP SECRET BABIES

These babies need a protector!

THE BODYGUARD'S BABY
Debra Webb - January

SAVING HIS SON
Rita Herron - February

THE HUNT FOR HAWKE'S DAUGHTER
Jean Barrett - March

UNDERCOVER BABY
Adrianne Lee - April

CONCEPTION COVER-UP
Karen Lawton Barrett - May

HIS CHILD
Delores Fossen - June

Unwrap the mystery